Other books by the author:

The Hummingbird Kiss, a memoir (2021)
My Mother's Requiem, a memoir (Spring, 2024)
The Lullaby Motel, stories (2021)
The Pink House, a novel (2016)

Historical fiction:
The Whispering Women (2022)
The Burning Bride (2022)
Secrets and Spies (2023)
The Butterfly Cage (August 2023)

Cinnamon Girl

Trish MacEnulty

Livingston Press
University of West Alabama

Library of Congress Control Number: 2023939054
Printed on acid-free paper
Printed in the United States of America by
Publishers Graphics

Typesetting and page layout: Joe Taylor
Proofreading: Annsley Johnsey, Angela Brooke Barger, Savannah Beams,
Kaitlyn Clark, Tricia Taylor

Cover design: Jenny Q @ Historical Fiction Book Covers

6 5 4 3 2 1

Cinnamon Girl

In memory of my Godmother,
Elise Hallowes,
who exemplified grace, kindness, and elegance
in everything she did

and
for Celina and Jack

"Nothing behind me, everything ahead of me,
as is ever so on the road."
— Jack Kerouac, *On the Road*

1

*7*hanks to Mattie, my grandfather's second wife, I spent my childhood as a small adult.

Mattie spirited me away from my alcoholic mother before I was two years old. The story Miz Johnny told me was that Carmella (my mother) was living in a two-bedroom trailer on the outskirts of town when Mattie stopped by one day to check up on me after my dad and my mom had split up. Mattie found my mother sprawled on the couch wearing high heels and a black slip with an empty Jack Daniels bottle tucked in the crook of her arm, and me trapped and crying in a playpen, wearing nothing but a dirty diaper. Mattie took me away that day, and then sometime after that – the details get fuzzy – my mother got on a Greyhound bus and never came back. My dad lit out for the West Coast shortly after she left. Granddaddy died of a stroke when I was four, and I hardly remember him anyway. That left me and Mattie and Miz Johnny, a maid whose family had been interlinked with mine since the days of slavery – not one of us related by blood but bound together nonetheless – in a big brick house on a hill in Augusta, Georgia, a few blocks from the Savannah River.

My dad, Billy Burnes, never made it as far as the West Coast. He spent a couple of years at Southern Illinois University before dropping out to become a D.J. at a Top-40 radio station in St. Louis. He visited us every Christmas and usually for a week or so during the summers. The summer after I turned ten years old, he brought a pregnant girl named Cleo with him and said she was his wife. We never saw or heard from my mother. Mattie never mentioned her. And who was I to miss a person I couldn't remember? Especially when I had Mattie and Miz Johnny. Mattie spoiled me, and Miz Johnny disciplined me when she could catch me.

Before marrying my wealthy grandfather, Mattie had been a world-class opera singer. In order to entice her in to marrying him, he bought the old theater in downtown Augusta so she could turn it into her very own opera house. She was getting older anyway so she took the offer. While other kids stayed home at night watching "Bonanza," I was at the Southern Opera Guild. For hours I played dress up in elaborate costumes or had swordfights with imaginary enemies in the rehearsal room. During performances I would turn pages for the pianist or sit in the lighting booth and read cues for the spotlight man. When rehearsals ran late, I slept backstage on the piles of black curtains while the sound of arias shrouded me like a dream. Sometimes I spied furtive kissing in the rehearsal room. Sometimes men kissed other men, sometimes they kissed women whose husbands were at home, drinking scotch.

I didn't have friends my own age, but it felt as though Mattie's friends were my friends. Since I considered myself a small adult, and they considered themselves large children, we met somewhere in between. Our house was the central location for evening parties where they sang showtunes around the Steinway that Carl played, hunched over the keys, a cigarette in his mouth, a highball glass on a stack of sheet music. I usually stretched out underneath the piano with my marbles or plastic horses and created stories till I fell asleep.

When I was twelve, a girl named Gretchen moved from half-way across the world with her German father and American mother. She was an outsider, like me, and for the first time I had a friend my own age. I liked Gretchen a lot, but the real attraction was her older brother, Wolfgang, an aloof philosophical boy with shaggy hair and bushy eyebrows, a boy who made my teeth sweat the first time I saw him.

Beyond the borders of our small town, all kinds of things were going on. Rock music had conquered the world, men in puffy white suits were jumping on the moon, a crazy man shot down Martin Luther King, Jr. and another one gunned down Bobby Kennedy. After both killings the house on the hill went into mourning though I didn't understand why we cried over the deaths of men we had never met. There were riots and revolutions and hippies and Woodstock and all kinds of things the good citizens of Augusta, Georgia, tried to ignore, but the world would not be ignored. It was slouching toward us inexorably and arrived in a rain of smoke and ash in May, 1970. But it was not the brutal race riot that ended my perfect childhood. My perfect childhood dissolved a few months earlier when something growing inside Mattie suddenly emerged and stole the life out of her. I was fourteen years old.

2

As I stood shrouded in the darkness backstage, watching Mattie sink to her knees in the bright spotlight and collapse in a pile of pink silk, I was not thinking of death or even of opera. Around her the singers mourned and the tenor bellowed "Mimi" in a crescendo of notes. But my mind transposed the scene. Instead of Mimi and her Bohemian friends, I was the one sinking to the ground, gazing into the hazel eyes of Wolfgang, who had finally realized how much he loved me. He was bending down ever so slowly to kiss me.

At that moment the curtain closed for the final time, and the performers came rushing off stage. Fallene, the contralto, said to Mattie, "No one dies as brilliantly as you do, Mathilda."

Then Mattie stood in front of me, her eyes sparkling full of spotlights, her hands clasping mine.

"How did you like the performance, precious?" As if the applause wasn't enough. She always needed my approval. I always gave it. I may have become a teenager without either of us expecting it, but I still adored her.

"Brillant," I said, stealing Fallene's word because I hadn't fully collected myself back out of Wolfgang's arms. Then as reality came into focus, I added my favorite word of the moment, "Phenomenal."

Mattie smiled with relief as if she'd feared I might suddenly say that she was awful and she should never show her face on a stage again. She kissed the air beside my ear as her cheek brushed against mine. "Come help me out of this straightjacket."

Just like that I was once again Mattie's little helper. I followed her back to the dressing room where the other women were already stripping out of their long dresses and holding the hair off the backs of their necks, standing in front of a large revolving fan. "Jesus, it's hot out there," one of them said.

We weaved through the women to Mattie's dressing table in the back. Lightbulbs shone from the sides and top of the mirror, and Mattie sat down to wipe off her pancake make-up with a tissue smeared with cold cream. I helped her take off the blond cascading wig and then placed it on the Styrofoam head with its crayoned blue eyes.

The women's voices in the dressing room climbed over each other in that after-show mix of hilarity, exhaustion and yearning for it not to end quite yet. The thing they felt was almost palpable. And I knew they'd all head somewhere to unwind. Usually, the unwinding happened at our house where Miz Johnny would have left plates full of little sandwiches and the bar would be stocked, the Steinway tuned, its ivory keys waiting for Carl to sit down and dance his fingers over them.

"You know I could never play Mimi in New York at my age," Mattie said to no one in particular, "and yet I don't think I've ever done her better."

"It just goes to show you," Fallene called from her vanity nearby. "Age gives us the experience to bring depth to a role."

"You're right," Mattie said, wiping the tissue across her eyelids. "But I don't need to grow another second older, thank you."

Fallene laughed. When they were together, they obsessed about their ages. Mattie swore she'd go home and jump off the

London Bridge if she had to grow old and feeble with her hips breaking and her skin sagging to the ground the way her grand-mother had. Mattie had left England at the age of nineteen, but it was still "home" to her and she made a point of keeping her fancy-sounding accent intact.

Louise came trundling over. She and her husband Max, a postman, were in all of Mattie's operas. Louise usually played some minor role, and Max, an enormously fat man, always played the lead tenor in spite of his bulk because he had as good a voice as you could find on the entire continent, Mattie always said, perpetually astounded that Max was just a postman in Augusta, Georgia. *Who would have dreamed?*

"Are we heading to your place, Mathilda?" Louise asked.

"Of course," Mattie said.

She clumsily tried to unzip herself. I took the zipper from her fingers and tugged it down.

"Thank you, precious," she said. She pulled the dress from her shoulders. I turned away to go buy a bottle of coke from the machine in the hallway with the nickel in my pocket. Even then a drink for a nickel was a novelty. But as I was turning, Mattie bent forward sharply and gasped.

"Mattie?" I asked, wheeling back toward her. "Are you all right?"

Our eyes met in the mirror. Sweat beaded against her hairline. Her gray eyes looked startled.

"What is it?" I asked.

She held onto the chair in front of her and grimaced.

"I just had the worst pain."

"Is it gas?" Fallene asked.

Mattie straightened up slowly and let the dress fall to the

floor.

"Look how fat I am," she muttered. "I couldn't even put on a girdle earlier."

Fallene stood up. We both stared at the bulge in Mattie's abdomen beneath her white nylon slip.

"You need to see a doctor," Fallene said.

*M*attie went to the doctor on Monday while I was at school. Usually, I would bike over to the park after school with Gretchen and we would go to our favorite hideout—a bridge over the canal that we could hide under and try French inhaling Winston cigarettes stolen from Gretchen's mother. Later we would go to the corner store to buy a grape Nehi and some bubble gum. We'd run the younger kids off the jungle gym so we could climb on top of the bars and watch the boys doing whatever stupid things they had thought of doing that day.

But on that Monday I went straight home to the two-story brick house with dormer windows and a large porch. The lawn was wild and weedy because Mattie didn't care about such things. She said what happened inside a house was more important than how it looked outside. The screen door needed painting. One of the shutters on the living room window hung by one hinge. Miz Johnny did all she could to keep the spider webs off the porch, but otherwise the exterior of our house was left to its own devices.

I leapt up the steps and went inside. I'd been worried all day. During lunch I had gone off to the restroom by myself. As I sat in the stall taking a small moment of privacy, I heard a voice inside my head. A voice in your head should be an angel's voice telling you that everything is going to be fine, but this voice was not angelic. It said simply, "Curtain call."

Mattie sat in the sun room with a cup of tea, reading the newspaper when I walked in. She looked up at me. Her pale eyebrows rose and fell. She seemed to be mustering up a comforting lie, but then she didn't have the heart to tell it. Instead she let her eyes fall; her shoulders hunched forward as if she were hiding something. I pulled a wicker chair up next to her, took her hand, and nestled my face against her shoulder.

We stayed like that until Miz Johnny called us for dinner.

Spring came. The azaleas had a brawl of color in our yard. The dogwood turned snowy white, and forsythia wands of gold waved their spells. While the earth obliviously burst forth in a fountain of color, the news in the papers was mostly bad: Anti-war protesters blew themselves to pieces in New York City. Four college students were killed in Ohio by National Guardsmen. The Beatles broke up. Each of these events occasioned a call from my father, who wanted to know if I was aware of what was going on. He was weirdly concerned about my education in that way. But how could I care about these things when my world was disintegrating?

We never said a word about Mattie's sickness, which turned out to be ovarian cancer, or how long she had to live, which turned out to be not much. I kept going to school, and Mattie planned next year's opera season as if she expected to be around for it while Miz Johnny cleaned and cooked and tried her damndest not to show undue tenderness to Mattie.

3

As I lay in my bed night after night, I wondered what would happen to me when Mattie died. Since my dad now had two boys with Cleo, I wasn't sure he wanted me. Whenever he came to visit us, he was always affectionate but I felt as if he were playing a role that he didn't quite fit like happened sometimes in Mattie's operas when Max, the fat postman with the amazing voice, had to play a handsome young lover.

The Christmas of 1969 Billy and Cleo had not come to visit us for Christmas because one of the kids was sick. Instead he had sent me a transistor radio and a letter explaining that late at night, radio waves bounced off the ionosphere, and I'd be able to hear radio stations from other parts of the country, including his in St. Louis. On those nights when I couldn't sleep I would carefully move the dial up and down. Suddenly my dad's deep voice would cut through the air, and it would sound as if he were sitting right there in the room with me.

"This is Bad Billy Burnes on KXOK, playing Top-40 hits and your requests," he would growl. Then he'd play something by the Beatles, the Carpenters, or Diana Ross— not the kind of music that was ever played in the house on the hill. One night he played "Cinnamon Girl" by a band called Crazy Horse. He said, "I want to dedicate this song to a very special someone in my life. She owns my heart." I thought it was sweet that he had dedicated a song to Cleo.

In my room on my antique dresser, I kept a "treasure box,"

an old cigar box that I decorated in the fourth grade with rhinestones and paint. This box had things I thought I should keep forever: some silver spoons with a great-grandmother's initials, a little gold cross Miz Johnny had given me, a pencil once owned by Wolfgang, an old daguerreotype of some ancestor from before the Civil War, a few of my favorite marbles from childhood and the only picture I had of my mother, Carmella. The photo was a black and white picture of her and my dad, standing by a long sleek car. I was not born when this picture was taken. My mother was not smiling. Her hair was dark and thick. I could not, of course, see the color of her eyes. I imagined they must be brown because I had brown eyes, and Billy's were the greenest of greens. She was staring at the camera, a defiant look on her face, while my dad, still a teenager, stared at her. I always thought she was looking at the future, looking at me.

No one ever spoke about my mother. I knew that she wasn't from Augusta and she had no family here. Her mother, I think, was Cuban or Puerto Rican, which is how she wound up with a Spanish name and how I wound up with dark eyes. She'd been working at the National Golf Club as a waitress where my dad was a caddy. That's how they met, and that's all the information I could ever pry out of Miz Johnny.

The only other mention of my mother I could remember happened when I was around nine or ten at one of Mattie's parties. I had fallen asleep under the piano but I woke up and heard the adults talking. They were asking Mattie why I had a black eye.

"She got in a fight with a boy at school who said her mother was a you-know-what-loving whore." I heard a gasp. The boy, Marvin, came from a KKK family and the word he had said was one I was never allowed to say. I wasn't sure what the other word, "whore," meant, but I beat his ass anyway. He got in one good lick before I creamed him. Fighting is childish, I know, but I allowed myself the satisfaction of seeing tears dribbling down his face. When I'd come home and told them what had happened, Miz Johnny got really quiet, and Mattie sent me upstairs to take a bath.

"Where is her mother anyway?" Carl, the piano player, asked. Carl had come to teach music at the university around 1960 and immediately gotten swept up in Mattie's orbit. He was at least twenty years younger than she, but I'm pretty sure he was in love with her from the moment they met. She fawned over him, but she fawned over everyone, which is why she was so loved.

All Mattie said was, "She's gone. Probably dead."

Probably dead, Mattie had said. Not definitely dead. Maybe alive. Somewhere.

To our surprise, one day in late April we received a call from Billy. He was coming through Augusta on his way to Washington for a protest against the Vietnam War.

He was dropped off at the house by a couple of guys who drove away in a black Chevy. His hair had gotten even longer than it was the last time I saw him, and now he had a thick copper-colored mustache that framed his mouth so he looked like Fu Manchu.

"Aren't you all grown up?" he said, gaping at me. It had been almost a year since we'd seen each other.

"I'll be fifteen next month," I said.

"I know, but it's surprising, that's all," he answered. I was taller but still as flat-chested as ever so I don't know why he gawked at me.

When we went inside, Mattie hugged him and kissed his

cheek leaving a red smear of lipstick.

"You do look like one of those young people in *Life Magazine* who are always marching on Washington for one reason or another," Mattie said.

Billy nodded. "That would be me. We'll keep it peaceful though. Not like Chicago. This war has got to stop, Mattie."

"I quite agree," she said. Mattie and my dad were always oddly formal with each other. "But don't march in Augusta, please, Billy. They aren't very open minded around here."

"Don't worry. I'm just here to visit with you and Eli for the night," Billy said.

"And how are Cleo and the boys?"

"They're just fine," he said.

Miz Johnny cooked a steak and baked potatoes in Billy's honor, and we ate in the dining room with her hovering over him.

"Mattie, have you lost weight?" Billy asked.

Mattie had been to the beauty parlor that day. Her hair was perfectly coiffed, her make up perfect, her clothes perfect. That was Mattie. Perfect. So perfect that her stepson had no idea that behind the perfection she was dying. For some unknowable reason, Mattie guarded her secret. Outside of me, Miz Johnny, Fallene and Carl, no one knew. I followed her lead.

"I might have lost a few pounds," she said and smiled her perfect smile.

"Well, you're as beautiful as ever," Billy said. He turned to me. "How about we go bowling tonight?"

When I was little, bowling was a ritual part of each visit, and I had loved it. It didn't seem to matter so much anymore. But an hour later we were at the bowling alley with the sound of the heavy balls rolling along the smooth floor and clattering against pins a constant background noise. A group of high school guys kept looking at us. I could tell they were trying to think of something to say about Billy's long hair and the "Make Love Not War" t-shirt he was wearing. We had a few "freaks" in Augusta, but you didn't seem them in bowling alleys. Then the guy who owned the bowling alley came over and gave Billy a bear hug.

"Billy! You look like a damn hippie!" he said with a laugh. The high school boys lost interest in my dad.

I was a terrible bowler, and my balls gravitated to the gutter as soon as they left my fingers. I lost both games.

After we left the bowling alley, we drove along the river. Billy pulled into a little park and we got out of the car. On nearly every visit, we woiuld take a walk by the river. This time we found a spot on the concrete bank and let our feet dangle over the water. I looked up at the stars twinkling above like so many cheap rhinestones.

"Why are you protesting the war, Billy?" I asked. I had always called him Billy instead of Daddy because that's what I heard everyone else calling him. "My history teacher says we're there because we have to stop the communists. He says it's like a domino effect. If they take over Vietnam, then they'll take over other countries. Pretty soon the whole world will be communist."

"That's bullshit," Billy said. "I'm sorry you have to grow up in this backwater."

"But why is it bullshit?"

"Look, Europeans have been interfering in Indonesian politics for years. Why? Because they want the resources those countries have. Resources like rubber. The Vietnamese chose Ho Chi Min as their leader. He's like Lincoln or Washington was for us. If we would let them have elections, he would win by a landslide, but we don't want democracy for anyone in the world but us. Our soldiers are dying — and killing people — for nothing."

"Yeah, but…" I said, not entirely convinced.

"Think about it," he said. "That little country is halfway around the world. Why would we have the right to tell them how to govern their own country? How would you feel if someone who didn't even speak your language came over here and started dropping bombs on your houses and your fields and told you what kind of government you could have?"

I had no answer for him. Before our TV broke, I had seen the coffins on the news. I had seen Mattie's tears as she watched. Maybe my history teacher was wrong. He'd also said the War Between the States was not over slavery but over states' rights and one of the Black kids had gotten up and walked out of the classroom.

"Hey, Eli, has Mattie talked to you about sex?" Billy asked, as if just realizing some parental duty he had neglected in his annual visits. I wasn't about to tell him I hadn't even started having periods yet.

"I grew up on opera, Billy. And it's all about sex. Whatever they left out, Gretchen's older sister explained in gory detail two years ago," I told him.

"I just don't want you to make a mistake," he said. The water rustled around restlessly below us, and the sky felt like heavy wool.

"Like you did? I was a mistake, wasn't I?"

He cleared his throat and said, "We didn't expect you, no. But I'm not sorry you were born, baby. Some mistakes are good." He had turned to face me, his head tilted as if maybe he could slide his words sideways into my brain, and I would believe them.

"Then why did you leave?" I asked.

"I was only 18 when you were born and only 20 when Carmella left. I couldn't take care of a kid. I figured you were better off here. I didn't even have a job. And I couldn't stay here. My heart was broken."

He put his hand over mine on the cracked concrete. It felt warm and big.

"Where is my mother?" I asked. "Is she dead?"

He tugged at a piece of grass behind him.

"I don't know where she is, Eli," he said. "I don't want to know."

The next morning I found Billy in the kitchen boiling some water.

"What are you doing?"

"We're gonna pierce your ears," he said.

I immediately clapped my hands to my ear lobes.

"Does it hurt?" I asked.

"Not much," he said. He took a metal ice cube tray from the freezer, pulled up the handle, cracking the cubes free, and dumped them into the sink. Taking one of the cubes, he told me to hold it to my ear.

"But it's cold," I said, placing it to my ear. I sat down on the wooden stool by the green linoleum counter. The sunlight was searching the room like it always did in the morning. I smelled coffee and the pine cleaner that Miz Johnny used on the counters and the floor. "Have you ever done this before?"

"No, but I watched Cleo do it at a festival," he said. "It's easy."

After my earlobe was frozen, he poked a hole through it

with a needle he had sterilized in the boiling water. He was right, it didn't hurt. The freezing hurt much worse. Then we did the other ear.

"Better put these earrings in now, and you've got to get some hydrogen peroxide to keep them clean." He pulled a little box out of his pocket and opened it. Inside was a pair of little gold hoop earrings. "It's your birthday present. Better early than never, right?"

A car horn honked outside. Billy kissed my forehead and said "I'll see you later."

"Billy," I said. I was about to tell him about Mattie. Then the horn honked again.

"What?"

"Nothing. I'll see you later," I said.

The house had felt different with my dad in it. Now he was gone again. I kept touching my earlobes with the earrings in them. I couldn't wait to show Gretchen. I wondered if Wolfgang would notice. Did they make me look older?

Miz Johnny sucked her teeth when she saw my ears and then asked if I'd told Billy about Mattie as she fixed up a tray with some tea and biscuits.

"No," I said. "Seems like she doesn't want him to know."

Our eyes met. Miz Johnny was a small, dark-skinned woman with a fierce presence. It felt like she was pouring her strength into me. She reached over and squeezed my arm. That was about as much affection as I would ever get from Miz Johnny, but it meant as much as a bear hug from anyone else.

Then she grabbed the tray and hurried out of the kitchen.

4

*G*retchen's older sister, Lana, struck a match against the brick wall, lit the papery end of the joint, and took a long deep hit before passing it on to me. Lana had a sharp face and scornful dark eyes. Her brown hair was short and greasy, but she was pretty in a frightening kind of way. At school, boys got quiet and furtive when they saw her. Generally, she ignored them, but if she laughed at one of their jokes, they would turn into monkeys vying for her attention. Her laughter was like a drug. It made sense that she would be the one to introduce Gretchen and me to the "terrible maryjane" that our teachers warned us about.

When that paper burning smell hit my nostrils, I forgot the woolly feeling of sadness that had been wrapped around my neck ever since Mattie's diagnosis. I inhaled the smoke and tried not to cough before passing the joint to Gretchen's waiting fingers. We sat on the balcony of their third-floor apartment with our legs dangling through the iron bars. Looking down you could see the big gravel parking lot and trees and old beat up cars. The summer evening felt dreamy and endless.

Wolfgang came out on the balcony with us.

"You shouldn't be smoking that shit with them," he said to Lana.

"I'm not forcing them," she said in a flat voice. "It's a free fucking country."

Wolfgang was lanky like a scarecrow with thick, dark brown hair. He was seventeen years old but he seemed older. He burned with a quiet fire that drew me. He went back into the apartment.

After we smoked the joint, Gretchen and I got giggly. We had never smoked pot before and we weren't sure what to expect so probably we were acting crazier than we felt. Lana stood up and warned us not to fall off the balcony before she slid open the glass door to the apartment and disappeared.

Gretchen's mom pulled up in her old Buick. Gretchen and I realized our throats were parched and our tongues thick and dusty, so we went inside where Lana sat on the couch watching TV.

"It's your day to clean the kitchen. Better get your fat ass in there," she said to Gretchen without moving her eyes from the screen. Even high Lana had the temperament of a scorpion.

While Gretchen washed the dishes, I wandered down the narrow hall and peeked into Wolfgang's room. He sat on the floor in a patch of sunlight, reading a book.

On the wall he had taped a poster of a man in a beret above the word Che. I had no idea who it was or what that meant. A bookcase made of boards and glass bricks covered one wall. The top shelves were all books, and the bottom held records. An American flag hung upside down over his bed.

"What are you reading?" I asked.

"Schlachthof Fünf," he said.

"What does that mean?"

He held out the book, and I read the cover, *Slaughterhouse-Five*.

"Sounds gruesome," I said. "What's it about?"

"World War Two," he answered.

"So it's a history book?" I asked.

He looked at me as if I were too stupid to breathe.

"You should read *The Adventures of Huckleberry Finn*," I said. "That's a really good book."

"It's a kid's book," he said.

"No, it isn't," I said, feeling miffed. "I read lots of books, by the way."

It was true. When you don't have a lot of friends, you can find plenty of companionship in the pages of a book. And when our television stopped working, Mattie never bothered to get it fixed.

He lowered his book and looked at me. His lips were full, and his hooded eyes made me squirm inside.

"Like what?"

"Like…" I thought about it. Most of the books I read were ones that Mattie had lying around, books about haunted castles on the moors or spy books. Mattie loved James Bond, and therefore, so did I. But I didn't mention those books. "Like *Jane Eyre* and *Wuthering Heights*. Like *Moby Dick*." I had not read *Moby Dick* but it was on a shelf at home so I thought that counted.

He smirked and went back to his book.

"Well, what do you read?" I asked.

"Books that matter," he said and turned the page.

I walked over to his bookcase and perused the titles. One whole shelf was German books, but on the next one I found some titles in English: *Soul on Ice, Native Son, Trout Fishing in America, The Lord of the Rings, Dune, Man and Superman.*

I had read *Superman* comics but didn't know there was a whole book about him.

"You have eclectic tastes," I said. I loved to show off the big words I knew.

"Eclectic?" he said with a roll of his eyes.

"Yeah, it means you like all different types of books," I said.

"I know what eclectic means, smarty pants," he said.

He went back to reading his book, absently rubbing his lower lip with his thumb. I wondered what his lips tasted like.

"What the hell are you doing in here with the boring book-worm?" Gretchen asked, barging in. "Come on. Let's go to the park and smoke a cigarette."

She pulled a bent Winston from her pocket and waved it at me. I shrugged at Wolfgang, not wanting to leave, and followed her out. I didn't even like to smoke.

I started spending more time with Gretchen's family. Mattie was getting worse. She lived on pain pills now and her pretty, plump face had cratered. The house on the hill suffocated me. Fallene, her friend who I had always thought was kind of flaky, stayed with Mattie most nights till she went to bed. I no longer thought she was flaky.

One Sunday night I stayed at Gretchen's for dinner. They ate heavy German food, bratwurst and stuff like that. I liked these family dinners — Gretchen's mom and her sister arguing, and Wolfgang and his father talking in German, and Gretchen always with something to laugh about. Afterwards, the family piled into the living room to watch *The Ed Sullivan Show*. This was a real treat since we no longer had a working television on the hill. That night a group called the Jackson Five played. The main singer was a kid younger than me. He wore a purple hat and a fringed vest and moved like he was made of silk. Both Gretchen and I were mesmerized by the handsome little man-boy. Lana sneered and made fun of him. This made Gretchen so furious she stormed off to her room. I stayed a while longer. A guy in a black beret with a pink pompom on top came on and did a bit about being the "Hippy Dippy Weatherman." Forecast for tonight: "Dark." Wolfgang cracked up and I laughed, too, because if Wolfgang thought it was funny, it must be.

When the show ended, I went to Gretchen's room. We sat and talked about boys she liked at school. I pretended to like a kid named Freddy, but really I could not have cared less. After a while, Gretchen's father came in and said it was time for me to go home.

"Mrs. Burnes will be worried," he said. "Wolfgang will walk you home." Gretchen's dad had deep downward slanting eyes that always seemed on the verge of tears even though he was, in general, a cheerful man. He was a mechanic. Mattie took her Bonneville to him whenever it needed an oil change or a tune up.

I left the apartment with Wolfgang. Someone had spray painted the word "pussy" on the stairwell wall, and it embarrassed me to walk past it with Wolfgang. Gretchen waved to me from the balcony as I walked a few paces behind his lanky frame.

"Don't let the boogie man get you!" she yelled down at us. I waved my middle finger at her and she waved hers at me. We wanted to be bad kids, but it was hard. Her parents didn't know enough to care what she did, and Mattie always said you can't rebel against a rebel. I didn't want to think about Mattie, and in fact, I was in no hurry to get home. The night before, the pain killers had stopped working, and Mattie had stayed up all night whimpering.

Wolfgang and I walked down past the elementary school. I thought we would take the streets because it was night but Wolfgang cut across the street toward the playground. I would never have ventured into the playground at night by myself. I raced to catch up with him. I didn't know what to say to him but he didn't seem to need me to say anything. We cut across the big field of grass. There were plenty of streetlights but when we passed under the trees it was dark. I took a deep breath.

"Isn't this exhilarating?" I asked, trying out this new word that felt like marshmallow cream in my mouth.

Wolfgang grunted a short quick laugh.

When we got to the swing set, Wolfgang sat on one of the swings and lit a cigarette. He was way too tall for the swing and his skinny legs stuck out, his big shoes scraping across the dirt. He didn't offer me a cigarette, and I didn't question why we had stopped. Maybe he had forgotten what we were supposed to be doing. I lay down on one of the rubbery swings on my belly and held my arms out like I was flying. My shadow sailed back and forth underneath me.

I looked over at Wolfgang, and for a moment his glance fell into mine. Then he looked away. Wolfgang was not like any other boy I knew. Most older boys were mean, but Wolfgang tolerated Gretchen and me. It wasn't that he liked us much, but he didn't hate us either. I sat up in the swing and placed my legs on either side swinging sideways instead of back and forth.

"Wolfgang," I said, "Gretchen's already been kissed."

He looked over at me with his bushy eyebrows slightly arched.

"So?"

"I've never kissed anyone, and I'm almost fifteen. Do you think I'm ugly?"

Wolfgang looked away, which confused me until I realized he was trying to hold in his laughter. Then he cocked his head sideways and said, "Do you want me to kiss you, Eli Burnes? Is that what you want?"

I nodded my head. I did want him to kiss me.

"You're too short," Wolfgang answered.

I shrugged my shoulders and made circles in the dirt with my sneakers. Wolfgang smoked his cigarette.

"Come on," he said, standing up from the swing. "You need to get home."

I looked up at him.

"I could stand on something," I said.

Wolfgang placed his hands on his hips and rolled his eyes. I got off the swing and walked over to a railroad tie that bordered the jungle gym. It raised me about four inches off the ground. Wolfgang came over and stood before me.

"Boys don't kiss you because you're weird," Wolfgang said.

"You're weird, too," I said.

"I agree," he said.

Then he put his hands gently on my waist and closed his eyes as his face lowered toward mine. I placed my hands on his arms and rubbed the smooth cotton of his t-shirt under my fingers. I decided I'd better close my own eyes. His lips landed on mine like a cloud descending on a mountain. It was that soft. I could taste his mouth and smell the fresh smoke on his skin. Then his tongue glided over my lips and I thought I would fall off the railroad tie. My bones were vibrating into tiny molecules in my body. If this was what a kiss was supposed to feel like, then what happened when they touched you somewhere else, somewhere underneath your clothes. I wanted to scream in joy. I wanted him to keep kissing me. I wanted my lips to catch fire. Then the kiss ended, evaporated, my lips steaming. Wolfgang strolled away towards my house.

I ran to catch up to him. In a few blocks we were there. I had managed not to think about Mattie all night long but I would have to think about her as soon as I got inside and saw her lying sick and spidery in her bed.

"See you later, Eli," Wolfgang said.

"Wait a minute. Am I good? A good kisser, I mean?"

Wolfgang chuckled and said, "Go inside, Eli Burnes. You are jail bait."

I was pretty sure that a seventeen-year-old boy would not go to jail for kissing a fourteen-year-old girl. I figured that jail bait was an insult and some sort of compliment at the same time. And I thought I knew something else—that I was a damn good kisser. Because it didn't really take much except that you like it. And I did. I loved it.

"Good night," I said. "Danke for taking me home."

"Guten nacht."

He walked away. I looked up at the doorway to the big house where Mattie was lying upstairs in her four-poster bed, engaged in the dark business of dying.

5

The next morning Miz Johnny knocked on my bedroom door. I was already up, getting dressed for school.

"Come in," I said. Ninth grade was coming to an end, and I was looking forward to sleeping late in the mornings. On the other hand, no school meant more time to sit at the house and do nothing but watch as Mattie got sicker.

"Come with me," Miz Johnny said. "I need to talk to you and Miz Mattie."

When we entered Mattie's room, Mattie sat up in bed and smiled.

"How you feeling, Miz Mattie?" Miz Johnny asked.

"I'm actually feeling quite well today," Mattie said. "It's amazing what a good night's sleep will do for you." She glanced at the bottle of pills on her bedside table.

"I'm glad," Miz Johnny said and plunked herself into the armchair by the window. A few weeks ago, I'd climbed up the oak tree outside and hung a birdfeeder so that Mattie could watch the birds. A cardinal perched on the edge, tossing seeds everywhere.

"Miz Johnny, is everything all right?" Mattie asked.

"No," Miz Johnny said. "It's not."

I scooted onto the end of the Mattie's bed. We waited for Miz Johnny to say what was on her mind, and a feeling of dread mixed with curiosity sat heavy in my chest.

"You know that boy who died in jail last week? That Charles Oatman boy?"

"Yes," Mattie said. "It was in the paper."

Miz Johnny nodded. "His grandma is a good friend of mine. We been knowing each other since we were little girls."

Then she sighed and looked out the window.

"What about him, Miz Johnny?" Mattie asked softly.

"They took the body to Cary's funeral home to fix him for the viewing."

Miz Johnny stopped talking again. She seemed to be trying to collect herself. We waited silently. Mattie's hands were clasped and her forehead furrowed. Outside the window a mockingbird and a blue jay squabbled over the bird feeder.

"Somebody beat that boy to death," she said in a low voice. "Somebody burned him with cigarettes on his buttocks. Somebody burned him with cigarettes on his arms and legs and his back. They stabbed him with forks and lashed him across his back. Charles was slow. He wasn't quite right in the head. And he was a little thing, not more than a hundred pounds soaking wet. Don't know what he was doing in that jail with grown men." Miz Johnny shook her head. Then she looked at us and her eyes were dark as the bottom of the river. "First, the sheriff said he fell out the bunk and hit his head. Then they say that the other men in the jailhouse killed him over a card game."

"Oh, how awful," Mattie said. "How awful."

My heart beat like a tin drum. A boy, a Black boy, had been tortured in our town and beaten to death. I thought of that handsome kid on *The Ed Sullivan Show*, the way he twirled in a tight circle, and I let out a little cry.

Miz Johnny looked at me.

"There's going to be a demonstration today so you can't go to school. Matter fact, I don't want you leaving this house till I say so, you understand me?"

I nodded. She rose from the chair where she had been sitting. Her mouth was set in a tight grimace, and the gray hairs in the neat braids that circled her head gleamed like a silver crown.

"I made those biscuits you like and tea. There's vegetable soup in the fridge," Miz Johnny said.

"Thank you," Mattie said.

Miz Johnny gave me one of her looks that said, you better do what I tell you if you know what's good for you, and patted Mattie on the hand before she left the room.

I caught up with her in the kitchen as she was getting her purse. In spite of all the bad things in the news, it was impossible for me to imagine our little town in danger.

"Miz Johnny, what's going to happen today?" I asked.

"People're going downtown to try to find out what happened to that boy," she said. "They're mad as hornets. These young people today want to be treated better. They want to be treated like white people."

"But," I said, confused. "Colored kids have been coming to white schools since I was in fourth grade. Augusta is integrated, Miz Johnny. I don't understand why they're mad."

She turned to face me. "When my boys were growing up, they went to Mrs. Lucy Laney's school, Haines Academy. They got a good education there. Not just book learning. She taught them to be young men. They learned about respect and dignity. Mrs. Laney cared about them children. And they are both successful men." She shook her head angrily. "But now with this so-called integration, Negroes aren't separate, but we're not equal either."

I did know what she meant about the schools. I saw how the Black kids in my classes sat to themselves and the teachers hardly ever called on them. And no one crossed those invisible lines that said who could live where in our town. Everyone knew their place and kept to it.

"Folks are tired of keeping to their places," she said, as if reading my mind. "Some of our neighborhoods don't even have running water or sewage."

I looked around our big kitchen and tried to imagine what it would be like not to have water whenever I wanted it. And not to have a bathroom?

After Miz Johnny left, Mattie came downstairs and had breakfast with me.

"I'm feeling much better today," she said. She did look better, and the fact she had eaten something gave me some hope. Maybe she would go into remission. I'd heard of such a thing.

Mattie settled down with a John Le Carré novel in the sun room at the back of the house. I, on the other hand, felt restless. I wondered if I was the only kid who didn't go to school that day. I wandered around the big quiet house. When I came by the sun room, I saw that Mattie had fallen asleep, her book resting on her lap.

I tried reading, too, but boredom crept up and curled in my lap like an old cat. Finally, the phone rang, and I grabbed it quickly.

"Eli, want to go see what's happening?" Gretchen asked.

"I can't leave," I said, dismally.

"You can. Just say you're coming over here to my house," she said. "Wolfgang has the keys to my mom's car. We can go see what's going on. We won't be long." She had said the magic word: Wolfgang.

*F*ifteen minutes later I was waiting on the corner of our deserted street when Wolfgang and Gretchen appeared in their mom's Falcon. I dove into the back seat and Wolfgang headed toward Broad Street.

"Wolfie knows a guy who lives down there by Green's."

Green's was the department store on Broad Street. It was where Black people had staged a sit-in a few years back. That was when there were still restrooms and water fountains that were marked "colored only" but I could barely remember that time. As we drove down those ordinary streets, I noticed the white-flowered dogwoods waving their spindly branches. We didn't see much in the way of human activity until we got near the municipal building and looked down a side street. Then we saw what looked like thousands of Black folks converging on Greene Street. None of us said a word.

Wolfgang parked the car, and the three of us got out and cautiously walked toward the crowd. It was like a magnet pulling us. We were three white kids. Maybe they wouldn't want us at their demonstration, but that didn't stop us from wandering along the side street to where the demonstrators had gathered.

"Holy shit," Gretchen whispered when we got to the back of the crowd. A thin young woman looked at us suspiciously but most folks directed their attention toward the building where a tall man stood on the steps and talked to the crowd through a bullhorn. I couldn't hear what he was saying.

"They better get out here and tell us something real," a guy with a thick 'fro said in a disgusted voice.

I glanced above the crowd. Policemen stood at the windows of the building pointing guns down at the speaker and at people in the crowd. Why did they need guns? Couldn't they just let the people talk? Then the state flag started to flop in the air. People at the bottom of the flagpole were ripping it down. I couldn't see what happened to it, but smoke trailed above the spot so I figured they were burning it. Wolfgang tapped me on the shoulder. His thick eyebrows were clenched tight over his eyes.

"We got to get out of here," he said quietly.

I followed him and Gretchen back down the side street. Behind us people shouted, and something large hit a wall. I turned around to see a garbage can rolling into the street, spilling its contents of papers, cans, and chicken bones onto the black pavement.

The guy Wolfgang knew lived just a block away right on Broad Street in an upstairs apartment. We walked fast and scared.

"Did you see those cops with guns?" Gretchen asked as we stepped into the hallway behind Wolfgang. "They want to shoot those people."

"They're just trying to scare them," I said. "You can't shoot unarmed people."

Gretchen looked at me like I was stupid, and I knew it was a stupid thing to say. Four college kids had just been killed. But still, it couldn't happen here. This was Augusta, city of gentility, famous for Woodrow Wilson and golf courses.

We climbed up the narrow steps to Wolfgang's friend's apartment. I had never been in one of the apartments over the businesses downtown. It belonged to a guy named Pete, who had already graduated from high school. The apartment smelled like fresh paint. The only furniture in the living room was a big unfinished spool table, a couple of bean bag chairs and an RCA color console television squatting on four legs in the corner of the room.

Pete had three beers in his refrigerator. I didn't care for the taste of beer, but today seemed like a good day for beer if I were ever going to drink it, so Gretchen and I said we'd split one.

I had just taken a sip of the harsh yellow brew when we heard a loud crash and yelling outside in the street. We crowded around the window. Down below people were throwing rocks at plate glass windows and at cars. Garbage cans flew like drunk pigeons and careened off the tops of cars. I felt like I was watching one of Mattie's operas on a very big stage. I expected someone to stop and sing an aria at any moment.

Wolfgang's body next to mine was warm and smelled like cigarettes. Gretchen giggled nervously and turned to me with her eyes bugged.

"Do you believe this shit?" she asked.

I shook my head and turned my gaze back to the throngs of people running in all directions, zigzagging along Broad Street. Some of them carried bricks. Others just picked up whatever happened to be available. I watched a boy in blue jeans and a black t-shirt. He looked to be about twelve or thirteen. His arms were wiry, and he buzzed around crazily. He had a piece of charred red cloth draped over his chest like a Miss America banner.

"There's the flag," Wolfgang said.

"What?" I asked.

"He's wearing a piece of the flag," he said.

"I thought they burned it," Gretchen said.

The Georgia flag didn't mean a whole lot to me. Mattie and her friends said that Governor Lester Maddox was a bonafide bigot.

"The mayor got on the TV last week and said we didn't have no race problems," Pete said with a laugh. "I guess he's eating some roast crow about now."

The boy with the piece of flag looked up, and for a second I glimpsed his face. His eyes were lit with an inward fire. There was something joyous in it.

"Oh shit," Pete said and pointed down the street.

A swarm of people had surrounded a car and began to shake it.

"Is someone inside?" Gretchen asked. We couldn't tell.

"Dang, man, they're going to tump it over," Pete said.

And they did. They tumped that car on its top so it looked like a rolled over bug. The excitement of the crowd gripped us, and I felt a nervous thrill. I took a swig of the nasty-tasting beer to try to steady my sizzling nerves. Gretchen pried the can from my hand and drank also.

"Don't get drunk," Wolfgang warned us.

"On one can?" Gretchen scoffed.

I felt a shower of emotions, each one rushing after the other. I was scared, happy, appalled, worried and ashamed. In the corner Pete's television was on with no sound. I occasionally glanced over at it and the effect was surreal as I watched the images of a smiling woman holding a bottle of Ivory dishwashing soap, showing off her young-looking hands, and then turned to see the chaos in the street below. Cars blazed, people ran through the streets carrying clothes, toasters, food and whatever they could get out of the stores. Shards of glass gleamed on the sidewalks.

"We could go get some records, Eli," Gretchen said. "I want the Led Zeppelin album."

"Shut up," Wolfgang said.

"I was just kidding," she answered, chagrined.

In all the excitement I had forgotten about Mattie, but suddenly I felt a tightening in my chest as if my heart were a clenched fist. What if they got to our house? Would she be okay?

"Can we go back home soon?" I asked.

Wolfgang shook his head. "Not for a while. It's not safe out there."

And so we waited. By late afternoon the rioters had moved to other parts of town, but we were still afraid to leave. We sat at Pete's spool table and watched the news when it came on. Augusta got a brief mention. The governor, they said, would be calling in the National Guardsmen—the same guys who killed those college kids. I didn't know how you were supposed to handle riots and demonstrations, but shooting people didn't seem to be the way to do it. Surely they would not do that again.

I looked over at Gretchen. Her hands were trembling. Wolfgang reached over and placed his own hands on top of hers. He had small hands for a guy but they were beautiful. Mixed into this crazy day was my dumbfounded admiration for everything about him.

"Well, frauleins, now you've seen a real riot," he said.

"I need to get home," I said. "Mattie's going to be worried. And I'm worried about her."

Wolfgang agreed. We stood up. Wolfgang thanked Pete for letting us hang out.

"No problem, man. Anytime the niggers go crazy you can come up here and watch," he said.

Wolfgang's expression darkened, and he pushed a shank of hair out of his eyes to glare at Pete.

"Don't use that word, dude. Why do you think those people out there are so pissed off? You Americans forced them to build your country for you and then oppress the living shit out of them," he said. Wolfgang had learned to expertly curse in English.

"I didn't mean nothing by it," Pete said. "That's just the

way we talk, man."

"Not around me, okay?" Wolfgang said.

"Okay."

When we came outside, the smell of gasoline and smoke hung in the air. The windows of the department store were shattered. A mannequin tilted to her side like a petrified woman, still smiling though the clothes had been ripped off her. I could see a few shadowy figures slowly wandering through the debris inside. I suddenly had a terrified thought. The Opera House! It was only a block away.

I started running down the street. The trees in the park looked steadfastly on.

"Wait, Eli!" Gretchen shouted.

"The Opera House," I said over my shoulder. She and Wolfgang trotted after me.

Panting, I stopped short across the street from the old building. Beside it, the ladies' clothing store was nothing but naked mannequins amid piles of clothes and shattered glass. But the Southern Opera Guild stood untouched. In a chair in front sat Curtis, the janitor, wearing his old hat and holding a shotgun across his lap. He lifted a pint bottle to his lips and drank. When he saw me, he raised the bottle as if to say, "Cheers."

"Come on, Eli," Wolfgang said. "We must go."

We walked quickly, glass crunching beneath our feet, toward where we had left the car. We all breathed with relief when we saw the old dented Falcon had not been torched.

Wolfgang took a side street to Greene Street. We turned north, and headed back up to the hill. As the light bled from the sky, we passed random groups of people roaming the street. Wolfgang didn't stop for stop signs. At one intersection we found a barricade of debris—old couches, pieces of wood and boxes piled up with some teenaged kids tossing gasoline on it and getting ready to light a bonfire.

"I don't like the look of this," I said.

"Turn around, Wolfie," Gretchen said in a pleading voice. Just then the kids noticed us. They turned as one and grabbed sticks, bats, anything they could find and started running toward us. Wolfgang threw the car in reverse and turned his head around to look out the back window. He drove backwards fast. A brick flew toward the car and busted out one of the headlights. Wolfgang didn't stop. He backed onto the sidewalk, wheeled the car in the other direction, and hauled ass. Something hit the trunk, but we kept going.

"Oh, God, Mom is going to kill us," Gretchen said.

A car in front of us was on fire. Bright yellow like the sun as if Apollo's chariot were an old Chevrolet, the flames swarmed underneath the car and wrapped orange arms around its sides, filling the interior. The smoke that billowed from the flames was thick and black like rubber and seemed too heavy to float into the sky.

The once quiet streets of Augusta were filled with sound. Screams, laughter, shouts, glass breaking and then suddenly an explosion about a block away. A building, a gas station, lit up the black sky. I was terrified. All of us were. Even Wolfgang's unflappable exterior was showing cracks.

"What do we do?" Gretchen whimpered. We were stranded down in that part of town that belonged to Augusta's Black folks, filled with restaurants offering hamburgers for a quarter, fried chicken, sweet potato pie and other things to eat. There was a bank, a theater, a billiards parlor, some nightclubs and a shoe repair shop where Miz Johnny always took our shoes when they needed mending, and outside there was a little stand for shoe shines, where a teenage boy shamed men into getting their shoes shined. I had walked these streets carelessly my whole life, feeling a kinship with the people who worked in the businesses, the lady at the bakery who always gave me a sugar cookie for a cent, the man at the Penny Savings bank who smiled at me and asked if I wanted to open an account when I came in with Miz Johnny to do her errands. This part of town was originally settled by free Blacks back in slave days, and Miz Johnny said it was the heart of the city. Now it looked and sounded like a war zone, as if the havoc we were creating in a small country on the other side of the planet had traveled the molten layers of the earth's core and erupted here in the midst of our tranquility.

We'd lost the marauding kids who had chased us with bats and pipes, but we had no idea how to get out of the area. Ahead of us was the burning car, and behind us the crowds ready to set their torches to us. The smoke of burning tires lacquered my throat.

Wolfgang looked down the side streets, confused, not knowing which way to go. Gretchen and I sat squeezed in next to him. I chewed my lip, looking for help when suddenly I saw the red brick towers of the Tabernacle Baptist church.

"Turn down here," I said as Wolfgang had edged the car forward. He didn't ask me why, just cut the wheel sharply to the right.

"Park in the lot of that church. Miz Johnny lives about two streets down. We can cut through the yards and get there. The car'll be safe in the church lot."

Wolfgang obviously didn't have a plan of his own, so he crept along the street to the big church. He pulled to the very back of the lot and shut off the car.

"Maybe we should just stay here," Gretchen said.

"Someone will see us if we stay here," Wolfgang said. Gretchen's family had been in America for two years now, and the kids spoke perfect English, but fear had resurrected Wolfgang's German accent, so his "w"s sounded like "v"s.

In the distance flames tore down the walls of a building. I couldn't even remember what used to be there.

"Okay, then. We go," Wolfgang said. "I hope you know where you're going, smarty pants."

I hoped so, too. I couldn't stop shaking from fear and, yes, from excitement, too. An electric current ran through the city and if you got close to it, it leapt inside your skin and jittered your bones. We dashed around the back of the church through the bushes and into a backyard. The house in front of us was dark. A dog in the yard next door started barking at us, but dogs everywhere were barking, so we paid it no mind.

"Which way?" Wolfgang whispered.

I wasn't really sure. Miz Johnny's house was either on this street or the next one. We slid along the side of the house and came to the front. Then I saw it. The azalea bushes on either side of her porch were still in bloom.

"There," I whispered and pointed. A car filled with men hanging out of the windows, yelling and throwing bottles, passed by, and we shrank back. A siren shrieked. Crossing the street seemed perilous. Then we heard them, the crowd running along Gwinnet Street. There were curses and yelling and things banging. We hid in the shadows of the house.

"What do we do?" I asked.

"Wait," Wolfgang muttered.

In a few moments, a throng of maybe thirty or forty people

came running along the street. Some of them carried things they had taken from stores. Others stared at the chaos with wide eyes. Then a scream: "Police coming!" A moment later, a police car squealed down the side street and pulled up to the stop sign. An officer got out of the passenger side of the car. The crowd yelled at him from a distance. He lifted a shotgun to his shoulder. Most of the people turned and ran when they saw the gun. Then a flash erupted from the gun. The explosion echoed against the houses, and people ran helter skelter, screaming. The sound was terrible. I closed my eyes and felt Gretchen's fingernails digging into my arms and hot tears of fright swelling against my eyelids. When I opened my eyes again, the police car was speeding down the street.

"Ach du sheisse," Wolfgang whispered, which I was pretty sure meant 'oh, shit.'

"No, God, no," a man wailed as he stood over a body lying in the street. "They killed my brother! God, please, no."

My lungs felt as if they'd been singed. My legs were like noodles as I sank to the ground, unable to breathe, the shock of what had just happened like nails in my heart. The anguish in that man's voice as he cried for his brother accused us all.

We had to move. We had to forget the man lying in the street, and we had to get to safety.

"Come on," I said. I jumped up and ran across the street with Wolfgang and Gretchen following. Instinct took me to Miz Johnny's dark porch. I flew up the porch steps and banged on the door.

"Who's that?" Miz Johnny asked from the other side of the door.

"It's me, Miz Johnny, Eli. Please let us in."

The door swung open. Miz Johnny wrapped her fingers around my arm, pulling me inside. Wolfgang and Gretchen stumbled in after me. She slammed the door shut behind us and locked it with a deadbolt.

"What in the name of Jesus are you all doing out in this mess?" she asked. She was close to screaming. I had never before heard her say Jesus' name except after the word "praise." "Eli Burnes, you have pulled some stunts in your time, but this is . . ." She was at a loss for words. She jammed her hands on her hips, her eyes full of jet fuel. "I oughta slap you upside your head."

"I'm sorry, Miz Johnny," I said. "I didn't think we'd get caught in it."

"It's my fault," Wolfgang said. "We should not have been out there."

"Who are you?"

"This is Wolfgang, Gretchen's brother, Miz Johnny. We didn't mean to do anything bad," I said.

"You're lucky you ain't dead," she said. "Who's looking after Miz Mattie?"

I looked down at the rag rug on her pristine floor.

"And she sick?" Miz Johnny waited for me to say something. When I didn't, she turned around and went to the kitchen where she had a phone on the wall. She picked it up and started dialing.

"Miz Mattie? You okay?" she asked. "Good. I'm glad you got someone there with you. Eli is over here. Yep. Don't worry. She's okay. I'll take care of her tonight. Yes'm, I heard the governor has called in the National Guard."

After Miz Johnny hung up, she pointed at Wolfgang and said, "You'll sleep on the couch. These two girls can sleep in my boys' old room."

"Is Mattie okay?" I asked guiltily.

"Carl's over there with her. She's all right. No thanks to you."

Next Wolfgang called his father and offered some sort of explanation in German. Gretchen shrugged her shoulders. She might get grounded for a week, but then it would blow over. I could tell she thought it was worth it.

Miz Johnny fed us chocolate cake and milk, which was so much better than that nasty beer. Wolfgang's polite demeanor seemed to disarm her and she stopped scowling after a while.

Wolfgang took off his shoes and stretched out on the couch under an afghan. Gretchen and I got the twin beds where Miz Johnny's sons used to sleep. It took a long time for us to fall asleep but eventually we did, our dreams punctuated by the sound of sirens.

*W*hen morning arrived, state troopers and National Guardsmen were stationed at every corner. They stood by their cars, holding shotguns, gazing at the passersby with alligator eyes. The street where the man had been shot the night before was empty. We stopped and looked at the road. A dark spot like a giant amoeba was all that was left. The air smelled sour with smoke and wet ruins. A firetruck was parked down the street, and we came upon some firemen standing on the broken walls of a still burning building. Their hoses sprayed over the black bricks in rainbow arches. We drove home silently. A police car passed us, its single red light on top pulsing for no reason. A shotgun hung out the window. It made me feel sick.

We felt a stupefied grief for our scarred world.

Wolfgang pulled in front of my house. My neighborhood

didn't look much different than usual. Some trash scattered around the yards, but nothing like what Miz Johnny's neighborhood looked like.

I walked in the house. On the living room couch, I found Mattie sleeping underneath a quilt. Carl came in from the kitchen, with a silver tea pot and two china cups on a tray.

"How are you feeling?" I asked Mattie.

"Eli, darling! Are you all right? You shouldn't have been out in that," she said. "If I'd realized where you were I would have been worried to death. I thought you were at Gretchen's until Miz Johnny called."

"I'm sorry," I said. I wanted to talk to her about the man who was killed, but it was so good to see her up and dressed. I didn't want to say anything that might upset her. She seemed unaware of what I had seen and heard.

The news came later that day. Six Black men had been killed by police in the riot. Two of the dead had been looting. Three were bystanders. No one knew why the sixth one was killed.

6

*M*attie's cancer was not in remission. The pain returned with a vengeance. The air in the house felt like it was seeping in from another dimension.

About a week after the riot, I was invited to have dinner at Gretchen's house. It was Wolfgang's 18th birthday, and his mom had made a pineapple upside down cake. No one in the family seemed happy about him turning 18. Even Lana kept her tongue in check.

After the somber 'celebration,' I walked home by myself. Wolfgang pretended the kiss in the park had never happened. To be honest, I didn't even care anymore. The only thing that mattered now was Mattie.

As I looked up at the ramshackle old house, a sense of dread filled me. I slowly plodded up the stairs and entered Mattie's room. Miz Johnny was lying on the divan, sleeping. Lately she'd taken to staying all night, tending to the fading Mattie. I shook her awake; she struggled to a sitting position, placing her hands on her knees.

"Was the doctor here?" I asked.

Miz Johnny nodded. "He give her something for the pain."

"What did he say?"

"Not much longer. That's all. Not much longer. I think she's ready."

I looked over at the bed. Mattie's hair was still lustrous and thick, splayed against the white pillowcase. A thick purple quilt covered her body, and the room air conditioner hummed.

I took her hand. Mattie's eyes fluttered open, and she smiled. I crawled into the bed and wrapped my arms around her. She struggled for each breath. Tears melted along my cheeks, and if her life wasn't flashing before her eyes, it was certainly playing out before mine.

I remembered once when I was about ten after her performance of *Madame Butterfly*. Even the big newspaper in Atlanta had written about it—the stunning performance by Mrs. Mathilda Burnes, the former Metropolitan Opera star who founded the Southern Opera Guild in Augusta, Georgia. "Who would have thought that a world-class soprano could be heard in an outpost such as Augusta. Not since Jessye Norman has a voice so sublime been heard in our state," the reviewer had written. "Brava, Mrs. Burnes, Brava."

That morning after we read the review, I asked her if she ever missed New York.

"Darling, I had my moment. To hang around New York or London or Rome would have simply meant fading away into obscurity. Here I get to do it on my own terms. Here I am a queen not a courtier."

She shook her auburn hair from her face and gazed at me with her gray eyes and smiled. "Besides," she said, "if I'd stayed there I wouldn't have met you, would I?"

I got up from my chair and slipped onto her lap where she fussed over me as if I were an oversized cat.

Lying next to her now, I fell into the moment's spell, gazing at the roses in a large green vase on the table and the delicate tea cup with flowers painted on the white china and a gilt handle, and feeling the breeze traipsing through the sheer curtains. I was losing her, and it wasn't fair. I wanted to scream, but I held it in the way people will hold back a snarling dog when a stranger comes to the front door. I muzzled the anguish in my heart.

"I love you," I whispered. I don't think she could hear me. Something seemed to be pulling up from her chest. Her back tensed. I thought the moment had come, but then she settled back into herself. Eventually I fell asleep. I never knew when the end came. I only knew that when Miz Johnny shook me, Mattie was cold and her face was not one I recognized.

"Eli, Eli, girl, wake up. Miz Mattie has passed. You need to get up. The doctor's coming to write up the death certificate."

I looked at Mattie's motionless form. There was no trace of her there. It was as if a costume, a wig, and a mask were lying in her place. Where did *she* go? That was the first time I realized how you not only see and hear a life but you can feel it against your skin even if they're nowhere near you. In Mattie's room with her mirrors, her make up, her perfumes, and her closets and bureaus overflowing with clothes, her absence was like a hole in reality. And it followed me as I went into the hall and down the stairs.

I wandered blindly into the living room, that absence lagging behind me like a recalcitrant shadow. Standing in the middle of the room on the Persian rug, I gazed up at the enormous portrait of her. She wore her crimson gown, her hair swept away from her face into some sort of French twist, and her pearls resting on her collarbones just below her long slender neck. Was it possible that someone this glamorous had come into this sleepy southern town and lit it up like a bright jewel? And that she had loved me?

I glanced at the coffee table littered with programs from years of her operas. Everyone said they were extraordinary. All I knew was that Mattie spared no expense. "Break the blooming bank," she used to say. "Do it right or don't do it at all."

I stopped at the Steinway where Mattie sang while Carl accompanied her. I plunked a few notes. Then I knelt down and crawled under the piano. I looked up at its underbelly the way I had when I was little. Like a sudden rainstorm, sobs erupted from my chest and shook my whole body. It seemed that I would never stop crying, but eventually the sobs subsided. My nose was full of snot so I got up and found a tissue box on a shelf and blew. My heart was drained empty as an old bucket with a hole in the bottom. I felt something wet in my underpants as if I had peed on myself and I stuck my hand inside. My fingers came out red. Damn, I thought. I had finally started my period. I jammed some of the tissues down there between my legs.

Miz Johnny shuffled into the room.

"I called your daddy last night. He should be getting in sometime today. He's gonna take you back to St. Louis to live with him," she said.

"Why can't you and I stay here in the house?" I asked.

"They're gonna sell the house, Eli. And I am retiring. I'll miss Miz Mattie, but I'm old, child. I want to stay home and take care of my grandbabies and fiddle with my garden."

Miz Johnny had her own life. I should have realized that before now, but I hadn't. I mean, I knew she had two sons that she loved and she had grandchildren who were growing up, but she didn't seem to care that she was leaving me. Miz Johnny had never been one to coddle me. Mattie spoiled me and Miz Johnny administered the discipline. But to me the two of them together had been my world, and now my world was being dismantled like the set after a show was over, flats taken down, furniture returned to wherever it had come from, props stored back in the prop room, the musical instruments packed in their black cases and taken home.

Miz Johnny absently pulled a rag from her pocket and began to wipe down the shelves of the bookcase.

"I don't know what's going to happen to all this stuff," she said.

I looked around. What would happen to it all? Someone comes along and creates such beauty in the world. Then they go away, and the beautiful things are suddenly just stuff. I wished I could create a museum like they do when really famous people die and you go to visit their houses. I could put velvet ropes at the doorways so people could look in and I would be the guide who explained, "Yes this is where she had her parties. She stood here by the piano and sang. It wasn't always opera that she sang. Sometimes it was showtunes like 'June Is Busting Out All Over' or 'My Funny Valentine.'"

'Stay, funny valentine, stay.' Those are the words. Mattie's eyes would find me when she sang, her voice like a lace ribbon leading you wherever she wanted to take you. I was getting sentimental. But I had just lost the one person who loved me totally and completely.

The doorbell rang. It was probably the doctor come to do whatever it is they do with dead bodies. Miz Johnny went to answer it, and I gazed out the window. Dawn was already creeping in among the houses and the garages, stealing over the dogwoods, jostling the birds awake as if were just another day.

Then I went upstairs to the bathroom and found the Kotex pads and the little belt that Mattie had bought for me a year ago. I put it on and washed out my underwear. I wished I could tell Mattie that I was all grown up now. She wouldn't have to worry about me.

7

*M*attie's body was taken to the funeral home. Fallene and Louise and Max had shown up and were sitting on the claw-footed sofa. Carl moped around, nursing a whiskey and soda on ice that I had fixed for him. Other people began dropping by, all of them surprised by Mattie's "sudden" death. Even Louisa and Max had not known how serious her illness was.

Miz Johnny puttered around, trying to make sure that everyone had plenty to eat. Other people began arriving, bringing ham and potato casseroles. Who was going to eat all that food? More friends arrived, ashen-faced and sad.

"Lemme get you something to eat," Miz Johnny said and hustled off to the kitchen. All my life I had seen Miz Johnny work. That's what she did. But today she should be allowed to grieve.

"Miz Johnny, I need you. Please come here," I called to her from the dining room.

After a few minutes, she came in, grumbling.

"What is it that a grown girl like you can't do for yourself?" she asked, standing in the dining room doorway.

"Miz Johnny," I said. "Mattie wouldn't want you to wear yourself out. You should rest. Let them take care of themselves for once."

"I can't do that."

"Why not? Slavery has been over and done for about a hundred years. Go up to my room and take a nap."

I had never ordered Miz Johnny to do anything before, but

she didn't get mad. She just shook her head.

"I'm scared to lie down, baby. I'd rather be busy," she said.

The same was true for me. The last thing I wanted was to be alone, trying to go to sleep. So we both began serving the stream of people who trailed into the house with their sad, curious looks.

All day I walked around, feeling as if I was wearing a diaper and wondering if people could tell I was on my period. Gretchen had warned me that the flow would be heaviest the first couple of days. I wondered if I would have to get up in the middle of the funeral and go change the damn pad. I'd been waiting forever for this to happen, and now I wished I would could go back in time to when Mattie was alive and my body wasn't a stranger. Don't be stupid, I thought. I was grown now and I'd have to act like it.

By that evening, the only ones left were Mattie's closest friends—Carl, Fallene, Max and Louise. None of them could tear themselves away from the room where they had spent so many hours drinking and singing with Mattie. I realized that even as I had lost Mattie, I would be losing her friends, too.

Miz Johnny sat down with us, pretending to dust something once in a while as if that way it would be okay. Carl put a hand on her shoulder and asked if he could get her anything. I knew that there was no other living room in Augusta where a Black maid could sit among the guests. But this was as much Miz Johnny's house as it was anyone else's. She had been here for fifty years at least, working since she was just a little older than me.

A loud bang in the driveway startled us all, and I went to the front porch to see what the noise was. A rusted, falling apart blue pickup truck that looked like it was older than me sat in the driveway, chugging. It backfired once more before finally shutting off. Billy got out of the truck and came toward the front porch. His hair was so long now he wore it in a ponytail.

"Hey, kid," he said.

"Hey, Billy."

I hadn't ever thought it bothered me that he wasn't a real dad to me, but that day I couldn't help but feel he was an imposter, someone who had pretended to care about me when it wasn't inconvenient.

He looked down at me as if he didn't know what to do next.

"Rough night?"

"Yep."

"Sorry. Very sorry. Why didn't anyone tell me how sick she was?" he asked.

"She didn't want anyone to know. We just respected her wishes," I said.

"Well, I wish you would have told me."

He gave me a stiff hug.

"You know my mom died when I was ten," he said. "It's not easy."

Here we were – a couple of orphans. Now we would have to live together, pretending to be father and daughter.

I led him inside.

"Oh, William," Fallene said, rushing over and falling on him, weeping. Max strode over to my dad with his hand outstretched. Carl slunk over by the piano as if that gave him a reason for being there. Louise sat on the sofa and wept. They mourned Mattie deeply, but the fact that they were all performers in one way or another meant they couldn't help but create a poignant scene.

Gretchen's father came to the house and got the keys to the

Bonneville. He was going to sell the car for us. He stood in the foyer of the house on the shiny hardwood floor and gave me a sad smile.

"You vant to come to the house? You eat mit us, I think," he said, nodding his head.

Billy was busy making arrangements for the funeral so I said okay. It would be good to get out of the gloom-ridden house for a while.

I got in the passenger seat of the Bonneville.

"Do you think we'll get much money for it?" I asked.

"It's pretty old," he said. "But someone vill take it."

He started humming. The car smelled like Mattie. He cranked up the air conditioner, and luke-cold air came rushing out of the metal slots. I rolled up the window and it felt as if I were in a glass casket.

We pulled up to the old hotel that had been turned into apartments; Gretchen's dad parked the car. We climbed the three flights of stairs to their apartment. The smell of cooked cabbage and meat seeped into the hallway.

"Gretchen!" her dad called. "I brought your friend home for supper!"

Gretchen's mother called back from the kitchen, "I just sent her to the store. Who is it?"

She came to the kitchen doorway and saw me. She was a tall woman with a red face which managed to get even redder when she saw me.

"Oh, it's you, Eli. I'm so sorry about Mrs. Burnes. What a horrible thing for you to have go through."

I shrugged and couldn't answer.

"Gretchen's not here right now. You can wait in her room."

I peeked into Gretchen's room. Lana was in there painting her fingernails a dark purple. I didn't want to see Lana. Lana would not be able to spare an ounce of sympathy. Not that I wanted any, but I didn't want her to torture me either. If Lana had been born thirty years earlier, she would have been held in high esteem by the Gestapo. Gretchen's father was already making for the bathroom and her mother had disappeared back into the kitchen.

I walked down the hallway and stood at Wolfgang's door. I knocked.

"*Ja?*"

"It's me. Eli," I said and held my breath. I could hear the TV voices murmuring from the living room, and Steppenwolf playing behind Wolfgang's door which finally opened just as I was about to walk away. He stood there, his wire-framed glasses slightly askew, his dark hair sticking out of his head like deranged blades of grass.

"Mattie died," I said.

His face softened, and he stepped aside. I walked into his room. He sat down on his bed and propped some pillows behind his back. I sat on an old chest by the window. "That's sad about your grandmother," he said. I didn't correct him. Everyone thought of Mattie as my grandmother though technically she was my step-grandmother.

"I know." I felt somehow comfortable around him as if we'd known each other a long time though in fact we hardly ever spoke to each other. Still we had been through a riot together and we had kissed. He knew what my lips tasted like. But death numbs you in a way.

His closet door was open and inside was a green duffel bag with clothes and books jammed inside of it.

"Are you going somewhere?" I asked.

Wolfgang didn't answer me. Instead he scratched his ear and ran a hand through his hair.

Just then Gretchen burst into the room.

"Here you are," she said. "Mom told me you were here. Poor, sad girl."

She hugged me and I wished she hadn't because the tears that had been down hiding deep in my chest spilled upwards again and caught in my eyelashes. I wiped them away quickly.

We ate dinner. Gretchen's family dinner was a feast of noise. Lana cursing under her breath. Gretchen laughing. Her father talking about the old country. Her lean mother trying to persuade everyone to eat more. Only Wolfgang was silent. But no one seemed to notice. After dinner, Gretchen helped her mom with the dishes while Lana took over the bathroom.

I stood for a minute without anything to do. They wouldn't let me help with the dishes. Then I saw Wolfgang go out onto the balcony for a cigarette, and I followed him.

"Where are you going, Wolfgang?" I asked, leaning into the night air. "I saw your duffel bag packed and ready to go."

He paused and then said, "Canada. My draft number is 37." He stuck his hands in his pockets as he gazed over the railing into the parking lot below.

"I don't understand," I said.

"My number is low. I'll be one of the first ones called up in the draft next month."

"Ach du scheisse," I said. The balcony suddenly felt shaky or else it was my legs.

"Vietnam," he said as if it were the name of a flower.

Then he turned to face me, his lips screwed up, his eyes

wide. I stared back at him, at the uncomprehending look on his face, and in that moment my destiny was clear. I would go to Canada with him.

8

*C*hurches in Augusta were usually Black or White, but for Mattie's funeral service the rules were forgotten. Curtis, the Opera Guild janitor, was there dressed up in a suit and his battered fedora along with Mort and Randolph, two jazz musicians from Atlanta who had played at our house with Carl in the wee hours of the morning on their visits to Augusta. Gospel singers from the Black churches attended. They had loved to hear Mattie sing. And there was a wreath of flowers from a young Black opera singer from Augusta who had already gained fame around the world.

Gretchen was there with her parents and Wolfgang had come as well. I sat with my dad in the front row. Miz Johnny was in the second row with a tall handsome man I realized must be one of her sons. She wore a pretty navy blue dress and a little hat with a veil hanging over the top half of her face.

As sad as I was, I couldn't help feeling that this was one of Mattie's parties done big. I hadn't really thought much about death before. There was, of course, the likelihood that my mother was dead, but that was more or less an abstract notion to me. This, on the other hand, was real. Sitting in the hard pew I sensed something. Earlier I had thought that Mattie had left a gaping hole in the fabric of the universe, but now I had the feeling that Mattie knew everything that was going on. I had never considered the whole life-after-death phenomenon before, but it seemed as if a part of Mattie was now attached to me, an extra appendage that I would always have.

As we stood outside the church, people filed past us. Mattie had been adamant that there would be no additional graveside service. So Billy and I had to stand there and shake hands with people. At the end of the line, Miz Johnny came by with the tall man. When they stood before us, I realized he was the son who had moved away to Atlanta a long time ago. His unreadable gaze fell on me.

"Hello, Randolph," Billy said. They shook hands. I wasn't really paying attention. I was trying to see where Wolfgang and Gretchen were, but something about Billy's voice made me turn and watch the two men. "I was sorry to hear about Martin."

The man frowned and nodded. "I was sorry to hear about Bobby," he said in a deep voice.

I knew they must have been talking about Martin Luther King Jr. and Bobby Kennedy. Billy had worked on Bobby's campaign, and Miz Johnny's son must have known Martin Luther King, Jr. I put together that the two of them were on the same side, politically speaking, but I also felt a tension between them.

Randolph turned and looked at me. "This is Carmella's girl?"

"Yes," Billy said stiffly. A strangled silence descended. That's when I remembered the fight I'd had with that kid in fifth grade and what he said about my mother.

Miz Johnny's son said, "She's got her eyes."

I shifted uncomfortably.

"Come on, Randolph," Miz Johnny said. "I need to get over to the house. People will be coming by."

They left, and I looked at Billy's face. It might as well have been made of plaster for all the emotion I could find there. He turned to shake hands with someone else, and I noticed Wolfgang standing beside a no-parking sign in front of the church.

"I'm sorry about Mrs. Burnes, Eli," Wolfgang said when I wandered over.

"Yeah, you told me that. Have you thought about it?" I asked.

"Why do you want to leave your dad? He seems like a good guy," Wolfgang answered, looking over his shoulder at Billy. An opera patron stopped by and squeezed my arm.

"So sorry for your loss. She was a wonderful, wonderful woman," the woman said.

"Thank you," I said. I turned away before she could continue.

Wolfgang shucked the jacket he was wearing. He looked odd dressed in anything other than jeans and a t-shirt.

"He's got a family," I said. "A wife and two little boys. I just . . . I just don't want to live with them. That's all. I want to be free."

"Free from what?"

"Everything," I admitted.

Wolfgang looked down at the ground.

"I can't go on the road with a fourteen-year-old girl," he said.

"You won't be," I answered. "Today is my birthday. I'm fifteen."

His mouth dropped open.

"Everyone kind of forgot about it," I said.

"Well, you're still jailbait," he said.

I looked at him without saying anything. I could see the wheels turning in his head. Finally, he sighed.

Cinnamon Girl

"You'll have to bring your own money. I can't feed both of us. And you'll have to get a job. And we're not going as boyfriend and girlfriend, okay? That kiss in the park. That never happened."

Rules, of course. There were even rules to freedom.

"That's okay. I have money." I had almost fifty dollars saved up.

Wolfgang looked at me, his eyes full of trepidation. They matched my own fear, a fear I didn't want to feel. I shivered in the heat.

*A*fter the service our house filled with people. I savored a ball of melon. It melted in my mouth, breaking, dissolving into sugary juice and soft pulp. The pain of Mattie's death came to me in waves: a clutching sensation right above my breast bone like a fist trying to pull my body in upon itself, and then it would release and I would feel almost normal.

Carl took his seat at the piano while Mattie's other friends sang and drank and told stories.

"Remember when Maxwell's cummerbund burst open on the stage. I'll never forget the tears streaming down Mattie's face as she tried not to laugh," Fallene said. Max blushed.

"But she kept on singing. A true professional."

"What about the time the orchestra conductor was drunk, and she fired him on the spot. She went down in the pit and conducted the show herself. Thank God she wasn't in that one. She would have had to sing from the orchestra pit." Followed by peals of laughter.

"And the union blackballed her. Remember? That was a doozy. She didn't care."

I listened to the stories and eventually realized my father

was not in the room. I slipped out to try to find him. As I wandered through the house, I heard some low voices coming from the breakfast nook. I quietly sidled up to the wall next to the doorway.

"You've gotta be kidding me. There's nothing left?"

"It cost a lot of money to put on the productions your step-mother put on. And the investments your father made before his death were not good ones. Not to mention that his bookkeeper made off with about fifty thousand dollars several years ago."

"The old capitalist. He was always threatening to disinherit me. It never would have mattered." My father's voice.

"There is a small trust fund for the girl."

"For Eli?"

"Basically it's enough to get her through college. She'll get a portion when she's 18 and then a sum each year till she turns 21."

"What about the house? The furnishings."

"Better take what you can get now because the creditors will be here tomorrow."

Silence.

"I guess that settles that."

"I'll handle the sale for you, William."

"To tell you the truth, I never wanted any of it anyway. It's tainted. I'm glad Mattie did something good with the old man's money."

Silence.

"When will you leave?"

"Tomorrow."

"So soon?"

"Yeah. You'll send Eli's stuff to my place?"

"Certainly."

I stole away from my listening post. Everything would be gone? I stood in the dining room, looking at the silver service set, the china, the linens that had been in our family since the Revolutionary War. Billy came in the room.

"The family money originally came from the blood and sweat of slaves, Eli," he said. "We're better off without it."

I didn't know if he knew I had been listening, but I nodded.

The guests left. Carl was the last one. He looked up at Mattie's portrait. He had a beakish nose and thin hunched shoulders. I knew he was wishing the painting would come to life and step down off the wall into his arms. He turned to me.

"I want to give you something," he said. He handed me a small square box just a half-inch thick. I opened it and saw a plastic reel of recording tape inside.

"What's on it?" I asked.

"Some of her best arias. I thought you would want to have them," he said. Then he dashed out the door. Poor Carl! I put the reel into my treasure box along with the picture of Billy and Carmella, a bottle of Mattie's Estée Lauder Youth Dew perfume, and all my other treasures.

9

I woke up at 4:30 the morning after the funeral. Wolfgang had said to be ready to leave at 5:30 or he would go without me. That gave me forty-five minutes to decide if I was really going to do this. Could I? Could I leave my dad sleeping in the next room, thinking I was going to go live with him and his kids and Cleo in goddamned St. Louis? Cleo had seemed okay the few times I'd met her and Billy was easy enough. Would he even care if I didn't go back with him? He would probably be relieved. I knew he had money problems. Look at that piece of shit truck he was driving. No, it wasn't so much Billy that I had to get away from.

I had to get away from anything that reminded me of Mattie. It was such an awful feeling like a vat of boiling acid, like I'd eaten my weight in tar, like I wanted to rip my hair out and strangle myself with it. I didn't want to be around Billy and Cleo and their kids and pretend like we were one happy family. No! I needed to erase my life.

And there was something else. There was the idea of adventure. I wanted an adventure. Somehow it felt that Mattie had been instilling this desire in me my whole life with her stories and operas. Now I felt a new me coming to life, pricking its way out of the shell. And that adventure looked to me like Wolfgang, a suitcase, and a bus ticket north.

Yet still I lay there, listening to the ticking of the clock by my bed and the hum of the air conditioner in my window. When I glanced at the clock again, it was 4:55. I slowly extracted myself from the warm nest of my bedcovers. Night had blindfolded the windows. I got up and turned off the air conditioner, shivering in my cotton nightshirt. I slipped on some blue jeans and a Santana Abraxis t-shirt that Gretchen had given me. Then I stepped into my sandals.

I saw my big trunk full of everything I owned, including my treasure box with Mattie's tape, ready to go into the back of Billy's pickup truck. I could never drag that around the country with me. And what did I need with all that stuff anyway? Maybe he would take it back with him and keep it until I came to claim it.

I picked up the smaller navy blue duffel bag. My hands moved automatically, putting a few necessities into the bag – my toothbrush and toothpaste, deodorant, some extra underwear, t-shirts, a pair of shorts and another pair of jeans. I put in a couple of sanitary pads. I could buy more if I needed them. At the last minute, I grabbed my transistor radio and stuffed it into the bag.

Carrying my little duffel bag, I stole out of my room out into the hallway. The door to the guest room was cracked just a sliver. Billy snored in his childhood bed. My feet padded across the wood floor as I stepped along the hallway. I froze for a moment as Billy shifted in his bed. Then I hurried forward. Without knowing why, I went into Mattie's room. The emptiness was appalling. There was the high four-poster where Mattie and I had curled up together at night while she told me stories. There the vanity where she sat to put on her "face" and gaze critically at her work, pretending she didn't notice how beautiful she was. Now the bed where she had died was empty, bed clothes stripped off. What would happen to her stuff? Her closet full of dresses? Her creams, her scarves, her little knick-knacks from all over the world? I looked for her pearls, the ones that adorned her neck in her portrait. They were gone. I wondered if she'd given them away.

I shook the sadness off me. The boy I worshipped was taking me away to Canada with him and who knew what grand things awaited me. My invisible and unknowable life stretched a hand before me. I glanced around at Mattie's empty room once more. I understood that things change and they change irrevocably. Mattie was gone, and my perfect childhood was over.

I picked up the duffel bag that I'd left in the hallway and tip-toed down the steps. It would be nice to have a cup of coffee and one of Miz Johnny's carrot muffins before I left. But there was no time for coffee, so I grabbed a napkin full of muffins from the top of the bread box and crammed them into my purse. Then I waded through the early morning stillness toward the front door. I could hardly believe what my feet were doing. My new life was out there, bigger and stranger than I could possibly imagine.

10

I had left a note on my bed that said: "Dear Billy, I don't want to be a burden to you and Cleo. You've already got two kids you have to take care of. Don't worry about me. I'll be fine. I call you in a week or so. Love, Eli."

At the bus station after I made a stop in the smelly bathroom, Wolfgang handed me my ticket. The bus grunted and belched. The smell of diesel fuel weirdly soothed me. I only hoped that Billy hadn't somehow woken up early and found my note and was even now on his way here to stop me. Another part of me sort of hoped he was. Then Wolfgang turned to me.

"You shouldn't come," he said.

That was the deciding factor.

"You can't stop me. I paid for this ticket with my money."

"I'll probably get busted for kidnapping," he said.

"You're a draft dodger anyway, so what difference does it make?"

He shrugged. As smart and worldly as Wolfgang was, I think he wanted to have some company. We climbed onto the bus. The sun was blooming like a rose on the horizon as the bus doors closed; with a grudging squeal the bus pulled away from the curb, and we rode through the outskirts of Augusta on our way north.

I felt like I had never been anywhere before. Suddenly it was easy to forget about Billy and Miz Johnny and the house on the hill. As we rode through the day, watching America build and unbuild itself, Wolfgang played with the dial of my transistor radio trying to catch radio stations along the way. I propped my knees on the back of the seat in front of us and stared out the window. For the first time in a long while, it occurred to me that perhaps my mother wasn't dead. Hadn't she done this same thing? Gotten on a Greyhound bus and just disappeared? Maybe she was in New York, and I'd be walking beside the Statue of Liberty, which was the only New York thing I could picture, and she'd see me and somehow we'd know each other. I couldn't get very far with this scenario, however. I couldn't picture her. And besides, did I really want a mother who was a drunk?

"Why are we going to New York?" I asked.

"There's a lot of people underground there. We can get some ID. Somebody will put us up. I got the number of a guy from my friend in Washington."

"Wolfgang, how do you know people like that? I mean, no one in Augusta is against the war," I said. "No one goes to marches or anything."

"It's not hard to find out if you really want to. I thumbed over to Washington a couple of times. The SDS had offices there. You just go in and start talking to people. They give you names, people to talk to. And there's magazines."

"SDS?"

"Students for a Democratic Society. You know all those protests and riots at the colleges? SDS organized those. They have chapters all over the country. Or they used to."

"Used to? What happened?"

"I don't know. Some had to go underground."

"Oh," I said. I stopped asking so many questions because it made me feel stupid that I knew so little. I had no idea what he meant by underground. Did they live in tunnels?

There were only two ways I knew the world: opera and books. My favorite opera was *Carmen* because Carmen was a gypsy and men adored her and she didn't care much about anyone except herself. I admired that. My favorite book was *The Adventures of Huckleberry Finn* because who wouldn't want to fake their death and take off on a raft down the Mississippi.

Another book I liked was *Jane Eyre* which I had read again after Mattie got sick. No matter how shitty your life is, Jane's is worse. I thought of Mattie with her laughter and her voice that exploded like the sun from her throat. Jane's guardian, on the other hand, hated Jane and locked her in a room with a terrifying ghost. Compared to Jane, I'd had it good. Not only had I had Mattie, I'd had Miz Johnny with her blackberry preserves that we would always make from blackberries we picked ourselves. But not having had a deprived childhood might have made things worse. Jane had nothing to grieve for, nothing to miss. Things could only get better for her. For me, the best part of my life might already be over. And here was my own brooding Rochester. I glanced at Wolfgang, his pale skin, the wire-rimmed glasses, the sturdy cheekbones and the jawline with its little bit of hair. At least he didn't have a crazy wife hidden in the attic because he sure didn't have an attic.

Wolfgang caught me looking at him, and my face turned hot.

"What are you reading?" I asked.

He showed me the book. It was called *Twilight of the Idols* by someone named Nietzsche, a name I didn't dare try to pronounce.

"Is that the only book you brought?" I asked.

He reached into his bag and pulled out a thick dog-eared book, the spine held together with duct tape. He dropped it in my lap.

"*The Lord of the Rings?*" I said, reading the title page. "What's it about?"

"Read it if you want to find out," he said.

So I started to read it, but I was tired and dozed off, my head against the window. When I woke up, we were in the Port Authority in New York City, Wolfgang shaking me awake.

I'd never imagined a place like this. It's one thing to see New York in movies, but there's nothing like the actual feel of it. People everywhere. Throngs of them. Men in their suits, young straight guys with their short hair and goofy smiles, old ladies clutching bags, Black guys in flare pants with 'fros, freaks and hippies, smelling like patchouli oil, bums that smelled like something rotten, and strange men with long black beards, black suits and black eyes. I was agog, and we hadn't even left the Port Authority.

Wolfgang took my wrist and tugged me through the masses. He found a payphone and dropped a dime into the slot. Then he looked closely at a scrap of paper he held between his thumb and his pointer finger and dialed. My stomach growled. I hadn't eaten anything since we'd transferred buses in Richmond. All in all, the trip had taken a little over 24 hours. A hotdog cart stood outside the door.

"Food," I said, nudging Wolfgang.

"Forget it. We need to save our money. Someone will feed us."

"Who?" I asked.

"There's a whole network of people up here helping draft resistors," he said and then he turned to the phone. "Hello?"

I continued to stare at the people, sitting on benches or

begging or walking by with their eyes pinned in front of them. It was so different from the south. In the south, you had to say hi to everyone you passed, but that would be impossible here.

Wolfgang hung up the phone.

"Okay," he said. "We're near Times Square, and there's a coffee shop a few blocks to the south where Frank wants us to meet him."

"Frank?" I asked.

"Yeah. The people in Washington told me to contact him. He's gonna help us. Did you see a cigarette machine anywhere?"

I pointed out a cigarette machine not far from where we were standing and watched as he went over and spent 35 cents on a pack of Camels. So as soon as we walked out the door, I went up to the hotdog stand and got a hotdog with mustard and onions, not caring if my breath smelled bad. I ate it, standing on the street with people walking around me, and Wolfgang smoking his cigarette, shaking his head. I'd never eaten a hotdog while standing on a sidewalk. I had a feeling I was going to be doing a lot of things I'd never done before.

As we walked to the coffee shop, I gazed at the buildings slapped up against the sky. The sky was a different entity altogether—white and distant. We had to walk through Times Square, and every few feet there seemed to be a scraggly guy yelling at us to come look at the exotic dancers. Or some other guy who wanted to sell us Jesus. Wolfgang held onto my arm tight and kept me near him, which I was glad of. Finally, we found the coffee shop where we were supposed to meet this guy Frank.

"What do we do now?" I asked, playing with the salt and pepper shakers.

"Wait for Frank," he said.

A waitress came by and asked what we wanted.

"Two waters," Wolfgang said.

She stood by the table, looking down on us with her arms crossed.

"Sorry, Charlie. You have to buy something," she said.

Wolfgang looked away from her. I knew he was afraid of not getting to Canada, but he was going to have to loosen up a little.

"Two coffees," I said.

The waitress wrote that down on a pad as if she couldn't remember such an enormous order.

"Anything else?"

I shook my head.

We were finishing the coffees which we had sipped as slowly as possible when finally a guy in black bellbottoms and a T-shirt with a picture of a leaf on the front of it showed up. He sat down at the table with us.

"Wolfgang?" he asked.

Wolfgang nodded.

"Frank Zappa," the guy said.

"Zappa?" Wolfgang echoed.

Frank laughed. "Not really. But I sure as fuck don't use my real name anymore. Look, I got bad news for you. Our group has been disbanded for the moment. The FBI is crazy, man. Ever since the townhouse explosion last March, they've got their noses so far up our asses they can smell our Twinkies before we eat them."

"What happened to the SDS?" Wolfgang asked.

"They're history, man. It's Weatherman now. Or Weather Underground. Depending on whether you're wanted or not. The Movement is in total disarray."

Wolfgang looked discouraged.

"Hey, it's not so bad. There's plenty of us still helping guys like you elude the long arm of Uncle Sam."

Then he seemed to see me for the first time.

"Who's this?" he asked.

Wolfgang hesitated and then said, "My girlfriend."

I smirked at Wolfgang. How else to explain me?

"How old are you?" Frank asked me.

"Sixteen," I lied.

"Runaway?"

"Orphan."

For some reason that made him laugh. Then his face grew serious and he wiped his hand over his mustache.

"Okay, Wolfgang and Orphan, I know a place you can stay for a few days. We'll get you some ID and you," he looked at me with his eyebrows raised, "you need to start wearing makeup or something. You should look eighteen and not twelve."

I wanted to hit him. I didn't look twelve.

"Make up?" Wolfgang asked.

"Steal some. You've got to learn how to live on the streets now, kids. Live by your wits. You can't go out and get a job for *the man*. Besides, stealing is a form of social protest. It's a way to weaken the capitalist system. Never pay for anything if you don't have to, man."

He gave Wolfgang an address and a code phrase to use. Then we aided and abetted the capitalist pigs by paying for our coffee. And we left.

As we stood outside on the sidewalk, Frank leaned his lanky body close to us and said, "The people you'll be staying with are Black militants. They're armed. They have to be. If we're ever gonna have justice in this country, the pigs aren't simply going to hand it over to us. But that means you need to be really careful. If they think you're pigs, they'll kill you."

"Do we look like pigs?" Wolfgang asked and lit a cigarette.

"Well, pigs don't usually travel with underage girls. I'm just saying, be cool, man. These guys owe me a couple favors. I got the pigs off their asses a while back, so I don't think you'll have any problems. You cool?"

We nodded. I wasn't sure whether I adored this guy or despised him. I figured it didn't matter because he wouldn't be in our lives for long.

"All right. The place is in Spanish Harlem, so you should be safe. Know any Spanish?"

"Not much," Wolfgang said.

"You?"

I shook my head.

"Well, just fake it. If anyone messes with you, tell 'em you're friends with Bobby Seale. All right. Sayonara, kids."

He turned his back on us and walked away, disappearing into a throng of people.

"Wow," I said. "Who is Bobby Seale?"

"One of the founders of the Black Panthers," Wolfgang said, looking down at the address. "We got to figure out how to get to this place."

"Should we ask a policeman?" I said.

"Don't be a smartass." He tossed a cigarette to the sidewalk where it smoldered before a shoe obliterated it.

11

*W*e were in Spanish Harlem. I'd never seen or smelled or heard anything like this. Voices calling from everywhere, cars honking and buses rumbling by, and under the ground a rumbling from subway trains. Steam swept out of grates in the sidewalks, food smells wafted from open doorways. People walked past us as if we were patches of thickened air. Wolfgang had been to New York when his family first came over from Germany, but he didn't know the city. We walked for miles along the sidewalks. No one bothered us. We were just a couple of hippies like all the other thousands of hippies.

We finally found the address, and Wolfgang opened the front door, which wasn't locked. Inside the hall was dimly lit; the floor was made of small tiles. Spanish words leaked under a door. We climbed six flights to the top floor and then walked along a narrow hallway to 6F. Wolfgang knocked on the door. After a few minutes, we heard a series of locks opening, and then the door swung wide. There stood an imposing girl about 20 years old with light brown skin, a short afro and a tiny gold ring hanging from her right nostril. I stared at her, fascinated. She stared back at us.

"What do you want?" she asked.

"Mother Jones invited us," Wolfgang managed to croak out. She stared at us for another minute, then turned her back and walked inside, throwing a "come in and lock the door behind you" over her shoulder as we followed her inside.

Since I was last, I turned and stood bewildered at the array of locks on the door. I fumbled with the deadbolt and then Wolfgang came back and took over, deftly turning knobs and sliding chains and bolts into place. Then the two of us walked hesitantly down the hallway to a living room with tall windows overlooking the street. The girl sat on a stool, intently watching the street below. I figured she must have seen us searching for the place. A dark-skinned guy in a suit sat in one chair reading a paper with his legs crossed. He barely glanced up at us, but another guy – a light-skinned guy with a halo of soft-looking hair – stood up and smiled.

"I'm David," he said, holding out his hand. Wolfgang took it in a hippie handshake. "That's James sitting down reading some commie newspaper, and our lookout is Val."

Val continued to stare out the window.

"I'm Wolfgang, and this is Eli," Wolfgang said.

"Shit, what kind of accent is that?" David asked.

"German."

"And you're running from Uncle Sam? How can they draft you?"

"My family are American citizens, unfortunately," Wolfgang said, looking for a place to sit.

"Here ya go," David said, and began clearing off magazines and newspapers that were piled up on the couch.

James stood up and dropped his newspaper on the floor. He wasn't tall, but he was the most commanding person I'd ever seen. His eyes burned, and I felt immediately intimidated.

"We don't bring any drugs in here," he said. "We don't keep weapons or build bombs in here. And we don't eat pork here. Is that clear?"

Wolfgang and I silently nodded our heads. I wondered

about Frank telling us these guys were armed. Maybe he'd just been trying to scare us.

As I stared at James, I understood what was so wrong with the south, and I understood the fuel behind those fires that had raged during Augusta's riot. No Black man spoke like that in Augusta unless he was James Brown. This James obviously didn't "know his place." He was the most fearless man I'd ever met. I'd been so accustomed to a world where fear was the coin of the realm that I hadn't even been able to see it.

"Are you Muslim?" Wolfgang asked.

"Black Muslim," James answered. "We're doing you Yippie Weather people a favor. Don't abuse it."

"We won't," I spoke up. James cocked his head at me.

"Was that a cracker accent?"

Panic filled my throat. I never had an accent in Augusta, or so I thought. But I guess all Mattie's elocution lessons had fallen by the wayside if two words were enough to give me away.

"I'm from Georgia," I said.

Val turned from her window.

"You shuwa ah," she said, laughing. "Say something else."

I sank into myself mutely.

David chuckled and said, "Don't worry about it. Hey, there's a bathroom down that hall if you want to get cleaned up. I'm going out to do some business. Coming, James?" The two of them left. David swaggered when he walked. James walked in a crisp manner – a man on a mission.

Wolfgang took a shower while I sat on the couch and read an old copy of "New Left Notes." The main story was about a Black cafeteria worker at Columbia University who got fired for no reason so the SDS led a boycott and demanded to speak to the supervisor. The supervisor was a white woman who wouldn't answer their questions. The students boycotted the cafeteria and the man got his job back. So it wasn't just the south that was racist, I thought.

That night at dinnertime, we ate red beans and rice and a salad that Val made.

"So tell me something, Georgia. Were you raised by your mammy?" James asked, squinting one eye at me from across the table. I was nibbling on my rice and beans. Wolfgang had found a chair by the window and had his head deep into a book about Marxism.

I didn't understand what James meant by "mammy." Maybe it was a strange pronunciation of "mommy," or maybe he thought I lived on a plantation like Scarlet O'Hara.

"My mom ran off when I was little. I was raised by my step-grandmother and Miz Johnny, our maid," I said.

It only took a second or two of silence for me to realize I had said something wrong.

"Was Miz Johnny a Black woman?" James asked.

I nodded, wishing I could extricate myself from this interrogation.

Val cleared her throat and said, "She's just a kid, James."

"And I'm about to educate this kid," James said. "So why don't you stay out of it." Then he turned to me, "Now why was this Black woman cleaning your house and wiping your backside when she probably had her own house to keep clean and her own children to take care of? Have you ever wondered about that?"

I shook my head. Then I ventured, "I think she loved me."

James threw back his head, and his perfect white teeth flashed in laughter.

"She didn't love you, White girl," he said.

I brought my hand to my face as if he had slapped me. I felt my own cheek under my fingertips, my skin that angered James. Was he right? Had Miz Johnny never really loved me? She never said that she loved me. I simply assumed she did because she fed me and scolded me and taught me manners.

"I guess she needed a job," I said.

"That's right," James said, "but she couldn't get a good-paying job. She couldn't be a secretary or a teacher or a nurse because the only work fit for a Black woman is cleaning up behind White folks, right?"

Val slapped her thighs and groaned.

"James, why is it that you only mention certain jobs like nurse or teacher? Is that because those things are women's work? You're just as bad."

James glared at her. "I'm just being realistic."

"Well, so is this kid. She's from Georgia for God's sake. She didn't make the rules."

"But if no one points them out to her, how is she going to know they're wrong?"

"My point exactly," Val said, shoving herself away from the table and opening the refrigerator door. "You want a Coke, kid? What's your name again?"

"Eli," I said. "Eli Burnes. But I do know it's wrong. Mattie, the woman who raised me, she wasn't from the south. And she got a lot of people in Augusta mad at her because when she married my granddaddy, she raised Miz Johnny's weekly salary by five dollars. And she wouldn't just call her 'Johnny' like my granddaddy did. She always called her Miz Johnny. So did I. But we couldn't just take her job away from her."

James leaned forward and said, "I'm trying to make you see that the system is rotten. Racism and bigotry is pervasive. You white hippies think you can call us brother and sister and just wipe out hundreds of years of beatings, lynchings, raping our women and starving our babies. Isn't that what you think?"

"No," I said, but my voice was weak because I did think that we were making a difference. "I hate racism."

Of course, I hadn't hated it. Not really. I didn't think about it much. Even during the riot, I hadn't really thought about what made the people rioting so angry. I looked up and saw Wolfgang staring at me from the other room. Maybe he was thinking the same thing.

That night Wolfgang and I slept on the pullout couch. I'd never slept with a boy before. Wolfgang pretty much turned his back on me, but in the morning when I woke up, his arm was across my belly. The weight of his arm made me feel warm and calm. But I had to pee so I slipped out from under it and padded into the bathroom—a narrow room with a barred open window over the toilet. I had slept in my clothes so I showered and put on a fresh shirt and underwear. I wondered what we would do about laundry.

After I dressed, I stood up on the toilet and looked out the window at a brick wall about ten feet away with windows into a thousand lives. Everything was so different here. And I was different because I had been here. One night and I was not the same girl.

I wanted to get out into the city, but Wolfgang seemed to think we should stay in the apartment. James and David were busy writing some kind of "manifesto" and they spent most of their time at the kitchen table. Val had Smokey Robinson on the stereo as she looked down at the street below her perch by the window.

Wolfgang might as well have been in heaven. He was immersed in the books that were stacked in piles around the living room. I tried to read as well, but none of the books had stories in them. They were about capitalism and socialism and colonialism and imperialism; my eyes got crossed in all those isms.

Then Wolfgang and Val started talking about someone named Angela Davis, whoever the hell she was, and I could have screamed from the boringness of it all. Eventually I went in the bedroom where there was at least a fan blowing and lay there under the whooshing air until I remembered I still had that book Wolfgang had given me. Lord of the something. I found it and soon became immersed in a place called Middle Earth full of Hobbits and Elves. That world was nothing like this one and yet somehow felt familiar.

We stayed in the apartment all day, eating baloney sandwiches. While Wolfgang and the others talked about what was going on in the world, I read that book all afternoon and late into the night. In my mind, Wolfgang and Gandalf somehow merged, and I was little Bilbo Baggins.

When I woke up the next morning, I stumbled groggily into the living room.

"Where's Wolfgang?" I asked.

"He and James went out to mimeograph some leaflets. You all might as well be useful while you're here," Val said.

"Oh."

David scratched his head and looked at me in his friendly way. He had small even teeth and curly eyelashes.

"Val was thinking of a way you might be useful," David said.

I wasn't sure I'd ever been useful before. Well, I had helped around the Opera Guild, but I had a feeling that Val's idea of being useful would be something quite different.

"I'm gonna teach you how to boost," she said.

"Oh." As if I knew what that meant.

"Have you ever boosted anything before?" David asked me.

I sat down on the floor and stared at the Olivetti typewriter on the coffee table. I had no idea if I'd ever boosted anything before.

Val laughed.

"She doesn't know what the hell you are talking about, boy."

"I got your boy," David responded and grabbed his crotch.

I laughed in surprise, and then stopped as Val rolled her eyes at me.

"Shoplifted, girl. Have you ever stolen anything before is what he's trying to find out," she said, exaggerating each word as if I were deaf in addition to being an idiot.

"Oh," I said for the third time. I sat for a moment, gazing at the letter "h" on the typewriter and thinking that was the first letter of the word "home." Then I said, "I stole a Three Musketeers bar once from The Hill Drugstore." I didn't add that I felt so guilty I couldn't eat it and in fact never ate a Three Musketeers bar again.

Val smiled. "Well, see there, you've even got experience."

"I don't know," I said, as we hustled down the street. "How is stealing useful to the cause?"

"First of all, it disrupts the capitalist system. The people should not be denied the right to live, hell, to eat like anybody else," Val answered. She was wearing a little beret and sunglasses.

Her hips were wide and she walked fast with a forward tilt. "In our case, the people are being so harassed by the police that the people can't get a job. So if we don't boost, we starve. There's a higher law: the law of survival."

I had to practically run to keep up with her, but then she stopped and pulled me down on a bench. Her mood earlier had seemed somewhat playful, but now she frowned bitterly.

"The Black Panthers set up free breakfasts for children in California. We empowered neighborhoods all across this country. We're trying to give Black folks a fighting chance to have lives of dignity and *they* want to kill us for that."

I took a deep breath. I hadn't understood those books and magazines back at the apartment, but I did understand this. I was from the south, after all. I had heard the White boys at school tell "nigger jokes" – jokes that were short on funny and long on meanness – and now I realized there was something insidious underneath those jokes. If it hurt me, if it bothered me, how much more must it bother the people who were the targets of the ridicule.

Val continued, "The White power structure would rather see Black folks in the ghetto fighting each other for a scrap of bread, hooked on drugs, stealing welfare checks from their grandmas than to be contributing, you know, making a better world. They somehow think they'll lose something if we, if our children, have anything more than crumbs and shit."

Val's face looked like a portrait of history, a thousand years of pain etched into the tiny lines around her eyes.

"You oughta be a speaker, Val," I said. "I think people would listen to you."

"Not me. I'm not gonna stand up in front of people. That's for James."

We were silent for a moment. An old man came by and said to Val, "Sister, can you spare a quarter?" She reached into her pocket and gave him all the change she had. "Bless you," he said. "Bless you, Sister."

We watched him limp down the sidewalk.

"Well, I'll do it," I said. "Show me how to do it."

"Boost?"

"Yeah, boost."

We took the train to Brooklyn, and lo and behold there was a McCrory's. Val told me not to walk with her, told me to look at stuff, pick things up and then put them back. So that's exactly what I did. I handled various items – wallets, pots, flip flops, sewing kits, hair brushes, hand mirrors, sunglasses, magazines, tubes of Brylcreem, cans of VO5 hairspray, and packets of bobby pins. A lady with beehive hair and glasses asked if I needed any help.

"No, thank you," I said as politely as I could. She lingered near me as I continued to inspect various items. After about ten minutes of this inspection, I noticed Val at the end of the aisle. With a nearly imperceptible nod of her head, she exited the store. I gave her a minute and then put down the picture frame I was holding and followed. Val stood across the street. I dodged through traffic. As soon as I caught up with her, we strode away. She found a diner and the two of us went into the bathroom. She washed her face in the sink and looked at my reflection in the mirror.

"I got you some make up, but all the make up in the world is not going to put titties on your chest," she said and laughed.

I glanced down. She was right about that.

"Maybe we'll get you a padded bra."

"No way," I said, imagining Wolfgang pressing against

two hard boulders on my chest. It was better to be flat.

"Suit yourself," she said and we walked back out. Soon we found our way to a park by the river. I instantly felt at home with the water rushing by. On the other side, Manhattan was beautiful. Val began to show me her haul: a couple lipsticks, some mascara and eyeliner, bracelets.

"My mother tried to get a job at a McCrory's," Val said. "Of course, they wouldn't hire a Negro."

"When was that?"

"Not all that long ago. Five years maybe. Right after my daddy died. That man worked two jobs to put me and my three brothers through school. He worked all the time. It finally killed him. He had a heart attack when he was only 47."

"Shit," I said.

"Yeah, it was fucked up. Okay, now we're going to the grocery store. This time it's your turn. We need some steaks for dinner."

It was easier than I thought, my heart thudding like a hammer on the bone, the feel of the cold package of meat against my belly, under the loose shirt that Val insisted I wear. It was quite a trick to walk naturally with three steaks wedged between my body and my clothes. But I remained calm as we stood in the checkout line with a can of green beans. Maybe all those years of watching operas had taught me something about being someone else. And it wasn't such a hard part to play. An innocent girl. I'd been one all my life so it came naturally to me.

12

*T*he next day Wolfgang and I finally decided to head out for a while. We had no idea how to use the subway so we walked all the way down to the Village and wandered around for hours. We each had a hot pretzel with mustard for lunch. Then Wolfgang wanted to go to Washington Square Park. That's where everyone hung out, he had heard, and he wanted to see what he could find out about getting to Canada. So we found ourselves sitting on a low concrete wall across from an enormous stone arch. The wall formed a circle, rather than a square, and inside it were hippies and a few old street bums just hanging out, enjoying the day. A guy on a unicycle rode around in circles and nearly ran into a girl with a dozen bangle bracelets on her arm and a thick head of glossy black hair that floated to her waist.

"Hey," the girl said, plopping down on the ground in front of us. "I'm Sassy. Where are you guys from?"

Wolfgang laughed in surprise at this audacious, black-haired girl. I stared in wonder. If you took her features separately she would seem to be one ugly duck – buck teeth, deep sunken eyes, eyebrows almost as thick as Wolfgang's – but combined together in one face she was astonishingly pretty, especially with that humongous smile beaming.

"We're from Georgia," I said. Wolfgang gave me a scathing look. The girl intercepted his glance.

"Don't be so uptight, man. I'm with the movement. Frank told me about you. I just wanted to make sure you're okay. Where are you staying?"

"Spanish Harlem," Wolfgang answered.

"With James and Val?" she asked.

"You know them?" I asked.

"They're good people, so is David. But you can't stay there long. You'll draw down the heat on them." Her eyes were wide now and she seemed to me to be vastly wise.

"You know the FBI infiltrated nearly every organization. That's why it's all had to go underground. They stir up violence, man, whenever they can. They even pretend to be construction workers and then incite the hardhats to come and beat the shit out of hippies."

"The hardhats?" Wolfgang asked.

"The what?" I said.

"Working class guys who don't get that we're not out to hurt them," Sassy said. "It's easy to whip up fear and hatred. And we're an easy target."

I shuddered. Why had the world gotten so mean? I couldn't imagine anyone wanting to hurt the hippies. They looked pretty harmless.

"Hey, are you hungry?" Sassy asked. Out of a big cloth bag hanging from her shoulder she pulled out a couple of apples and a plastic bag of pistachio nuts. "Eat up, children."

We had already absorbed the rule to never turn down food.

"What's your role?" Wolfgang asked, dropping pistachio shells onto the ground.

"I'm kind of a messenger. I mean, no one talks on the phone anymore. They're all tapped. So I look out for people, and deliver messages."

"How about telling someone we need some IDs to get into

Canada with," Wolfgang said.

"It's already taken care of," she smiled again. "Meet me here tomorrow at noon and I'll bring you some ID's."

"Cool," Wolfgang said. It suddenly struck me what we were doing, leaving our country. It wasn't really Wolfgang's country, but it was mine. Love it or leave it, the people back home liked to say. So we were leaving it, but I realized that didn't mean I didn't love it. What it meant to love a country, I wasn't sure. The one thing I knew I did love was the Savannah River, that iridescent serpent that pilfered from our banks and took what it could out to sea. But Georgia was far away, and Canada would have rivers.

The air was warm as twilight transformed the hot day into something else. A couple of guys began beating on conga drums, the sound taking over the big round concrete plaza. Sassy jumped up in her long indian-print skirt and swayed her hips. All around us people moved to the beat.

"Get up!" Sassy laughed. "Dance."

My legs obeyed. I got off my butt and moved my legs and my arms. The drums were a hundred beating hearts; my pulse echoed the rhythm. I whirled. My bare feet pitter-pattered on the concrete. Beside me Sassy shimmied and shook. Wolfgang watched with an amused look on his face while Sassy and I danced with a small throbbing tribe. I felt like a creature of the wild, I was a leopard, I was wind. Laughter whirled inside me like a tornado.

When I stopped twirling around, I noticed Wolfgang sitting on the wall, talking to Frank.

"Hey," I said, walking over to them. "When did you get here?"

"A few minutes ago, Isadora," Frank said, chewing a piece of gum which smelled like Juicy Fruit.

"Isadora? You mean like Isadora Duncan?" I asked.

"Yeah, you're smarter than you look, Orphan." Sassy danced up to us and plopped down on Frank's lap.

"Frankie," she said in a deep voice. "What's happening, Frankie?"

"Pigs are happening. Hard hats are happening. Death is happening."

Sassy stood up.

"Okay, I get it. You don't need a weatherman to know which way the wind blows," she sang and held up a finger as if testing the wind.

"Let's go. We've got business to take care of," Frank said. I saw a serious look cross Sassy's face and I wondered if her free-spirited hippie act was just a cover. Sassy was an enigma.

"Okay. Meet me tomorrow like I said." Sassy was already gathering her stuff from the ground where she had dropped it.

They walked off together. I didn't think they were boyfriend and girlfriend, more like business partners. What a new and intriguing world this was.

The warm city air engulfed us as we walked down the street: exhaust, subway steam, the human sweat smell of summer. Wolfgang pushed his thick hair from his forehead and glanced around with wide eyes behind his wire-rimmed glasses. I could not see him carrying a gun through the jungles of Vietnam. Suddenly I felt sad. I was missing Mattie, missing our living room, and the singers gathered around the piano.

"I'm homesick," I said.

"I never should have brought you. It was a mistake," he said.

"But it'll be good in Canada, won't it?" I asked.

"Yes," he said. "And not so goddamn hot." He wiped at the sweat that was trickling along his thin face.

"And better than Vietnam, too," I said, remembering what this was all about. It seemed quite simple at that moment. There were people who wanted guys like Wolfgang to give up everything and go kill people they didn't even know, people who had done nothing to them personally. And then there were guys like Wolfgang who wanted to do something else with their lives. At that moment it seemed pretty cut and dried. Wolfgang was running for his life. And because I cared about him and because I was young and lost, I was running, too.

We found a subway station. Wolfgang bought some tokens. We looked at a map on the wall and figured out that we needed to go uptown. It wasn't so hard, after all. The train arrived in a clatter of steam and noise. After the doors slid open, we pushed through the crowd to get a seat. It took a couple of stops for the subway train to empty enough for both of us to sit down. When we did, we were silent, rocking back and forth, each lost in our own thoughts.

I wondered if Billy was worrying about me. Then Miz Johnny crossed my mind and the things James had said. I never thought of her as being able to do anything besides maid work, but surely if she'd the opportunity she could have done almost anything. No one worked harder. I wondered, did she think about the changes happening outside Augusta. It hurt me to think of anyone ever disrespecting her, and yet she must have seen awful things in her lifetime. She would not have talked to me about those things, but I did remember once when she snapped, "Those white-sheet-wearing cowards ever come in my yard again, I'll take a shotgun to them, I swear before God!" I couldn't imagine why or when the KKK had ever messed with Miz Johnny, and she wouldn't say.

Mattie finally told me that Miz Johnny's youngest son had been seen with a white woman a long time ago and the KKK didn't like that. At the time I hadn't thought anything of it, but now after hearing Billy and Randolph's awkward conversation at Mattie's funeral, I had a feeling I knew who the white woman was.

We got off the train at 115th Street. It was nearly dark when we got to street level; we had a couple of blocks to walk to get to the apartment. Spanish music flowed through open windows, and people sat out on the stoops with their babies, trying to keep cool. The music moved me. It was somehow sad and happy at the same time. I couldn't understand the words, and yet it felt as if I couldn't understand anything anyway. Why was there so much hatred? And was it all because of skin color and the length of someone's hair? Or was there more to it?

We passed some young guys on one of the stoops. They were laughing, and the distinctly sweet smell of a burning joint wafted past us.

"Que pasa?" one of the guys asked.

"Nada," Wolfgang answered. At least he knew that much Spanish.

As we approached the apartment building, a cop car was parked at the corner and a dark car with its engine running sat in front of the building. A burly White man stood by the door of the building with his arms crossed. Wolfgang's pace slowed.

"Something's wrong," he whispered.

I felt it, too. All my muscles suddenly tightened.

Wolfgang draped an arm over my shoulder and pulled me close to him. I put an arm around his waist.

At that moment, David came toward us from the other direction. I saw him stop and look at the car. His face became a mask. He lowered his head and walked past us without looking at us.

"Keep going, keep going," David muttered. His eyes never met ours, and we didn't look back at him. We walked past the apartment building at a leisurely pace. Wolfgang leaned toward me and pretended to be laughing about something. As scared as I was, I loved the feeling of his body so close to mine.

We were two buildings down when I heard shots and then a woman screaming. Wolfgang and I shrank into a doorway and watched. A crowd quickly gathered. People milled about, trying to see what was happening. There was a strange moment of silent anticipation. Minutes later sirens were wailing and the small street was a kaleidoscope of light.

"It's happening again, Wolfgang," I whimpered, reliving the riot, smelling the smoke and hearing that man screaming in the street. Wolfgang glanced out from the doorway.

"They're putting somebody in the back of the ambulance," he said.

I stuck my head out in time to see the back doors of the ambulance close and to see Val shoved in the backseat of the police car. I could hear her raging. It must have been James who had been shot. But was he dead? I clutched Wolfgang's arm. We stood petrified in the brick hollow as the dark car zipped away with the cop car right behind it.

We stepped onto the sidewalk.

"Don't look back," he said.

We walked a few blocks and then turned the corner. I leaned against a wall. Tears fell down my cheeks. I kept thinking of the man in Augusta, the man the police had shot down for no reason, his body on the road, his brother standing there, wailing in

Cinnamon Girl

grief.

"Eli, there's no time for this. We have to get out of here," Wolfgang said.

My breath caught hard in my chest, but he was right. For the first time, I realized what a stupid thing I had done.

13

The road unraveled behind us like a spinning skein of black yarn. Wolfgang and I were squashed in the back seat of a red Corvair with patches of rust dotting it like leprosy. Sassy sat in the front seat, her thick hair whipping in the wind while Frank drove. An enormous St. Bernard was wedged on the other side of the backseat. He gazed down at me placidly, his big pink towel of a tongue hanging from between his drooping furry cheeks.

Wolfgang and I had spent the previous night dozing on subway trains and in The Port Authority. Other than what we were wearing, our clothes had been left behind. Wolfgang still had his Nietzsche, whose name I had learned how to pronounce: Neechee. The only thing I knew about him was that he had once said God is dead. Judging from the looks of things, he might have been right.

A thick coat of silence lay over us except for the dog who whined occasionally and grunted as he tried to turn around and stick his head out the window into the onslaught of hot air. Wolfgang and I clung to each other, not as lovers but more like terrified children on a life raft. James, it turned out, was still alive, but the cops had said he resisted arrest. Then they had planted weapons on him. Val's word would be meaningless. James was going down for a long time.

Frank banged the steering wheel.

"I shouldn't have sent you two over there."

We understood that the color of our skin had drawn attention to the three Black activists hiding in Spanish Harlem. In

New York, even in this short time, I had seen Black and White and Spanish people mixing together like you never saw in the South, but I guess we were somehow conspicuous.

Sassy turned to us and said, "Look, when they became activists they knew it was dangerous. The Feds probably had them pegged for weeks."

"Maybe," Frank said.

Sassy reached back and ran a finger over my knee. She wore turquoise and silver rings on all her fingers.

"You'll be okay," she said over the wind.

We were on our way not to Canada but to a town called Canandaigua to stay with Sassy's sister, who was also taking the dog, which had apparently been left behind by a couple of Weatherman bombers who had to go underground. In the confusion of getting out of town, Sassy had not gotten us the passports. And now we were pretty close to broke.

"Do we need passports?" Wolfgang asked. "It's only Canada."

"You need some kind of ID if you want to work there," Frank said.

Sassy rubbed her hand in the dog's fur, and his big feet danced on the seat next to me.

Sassy's sister was nearly six feet tall with long, wavy blond hair. From a distance it would be hard to tell they were sisters, but up close they both had the same deep-set dark eyes and the same overbite behind large lips. Her apartment just off Main Street had a bay window with pretty white lace curtains, posters on the walls and, for some reason, a giant picture of Frank Sinatra above her bed.

Sassy's sister set up a cot for me in her room, and I lay down, thinking about death – Charles Oatman, the boy who had been killed in an Augusta jail; the six men during the riot; Mattie, maybe even my mother. If I hadn't grown up on opera I might not have been able to stand it, but tragedy was woven into the fabric of my world. I soon fell asleep and didn't wake up till the next morning.

The next day I wandered into the long living room with the cool light slanting in through the white curtains and found Wolfgang lying on the floor. Before I saw him, I'd had the fear that he might have left and gone on to Canada without me. We weren't boyfriend and girlfriend, according to him, and I wasn't much use to him. But there he was with his ear next to a stereo speaker listening to someone sing in a loud beautiful wail: "Sometimes I feel like a motherless child." The words pierced me and I sank down to the floor beside Wolfgang.

"Who is this singing?" I asked.

"Richie Havens," he answered.

"What are we going to do?" I asked.

Wolfgang shrugged.

"Guten Morgen." Sassy's sister stood in the kitchen doorway, holding a steaming mug.

Wolfgang sat up in surprise.

"Sprechen Sie Deutsch, Sonya?" he asked.

"Ja," she answered, coming in and sinking down onto the sofa. She set the cup down on a table beside the couch, turning her head so that her long neck stretched over a delicate set of collarbones, peeking out from a white peasant blouse.

Goddamn it, I thought. I knew just enough of Wolfgang's native tongue to understand that she had told him she could speak

"Deutsch" which was not Dutch, which anyone with any common sense would have thought, but German.

They began to converse like two people on top of a mountain and I was just some rock far below their feet. Sonya said something that sounded like "Glock In Shpeel Mafia" and Wolfgang – that traitor – smiled broadly. Wolfgang smiled! His two front teeth overlapped and they were more yellow than white but it was undeniably a great smile sending beams radiating from his eyes. Right then I knew I was doomed.

I went into the bedroom to sulk. I lay down on the cot, careful not to touch the horrible bedsheets where that beast of a girl would probably lure Wolfgang. I rolled over on my side and faced a wooden bookcase full of college-girl books. I missed the Gandalf book which was back in the Spanish Harlem apartment, never to be seen again. My eyes landed on a fat paperback called *Valley of the Dolls*. I imagined Ken, Barbie, Midge and Skipper living in a valley in a little trailer. But the cover had pills on it, not dolls. I put that book back and slowly slid out the others till one intrigued me. The title was *The Happy Hooker*. I vaguely knew that a hooker was something bad. The woman on the cover of this book seemed both happy and bad. I opened the book and read. It didn't take long to figure out what a hooker was. A hooker actually got paid to have sex. Just the word sex made me rub my thighs together. Sex to me was kissing and touching and maybe someday being naked with a boy. I knew there was more to it than that. Mattie had given me the basic facts and even in Augusta there were girls who were loathed and admired for things they were said to do with boys. Of course, Lana had been only too ready to answer any questions that Gretchen and I'd had.

"The man sticks his thing inside you and gets cum all over

you," she said.

Yet somehow even with all this knowledge, sex was a dark room that I could only peer inside. It was terrifying to me, and yet I had an ache inside that wanted me to plunge into that mystery.

Holding the book in my hands, I felt like a pirate who had discovered a treasure map. I couldn't put it down. The happy hooker informed me of many things, but the most useful piece of information, given my present circumstances, was that I should practice oral sex on an ice-cream cone, preferably in front of the man I wanted to seduce. Oral sex must be some serious tongue kissing, I decided. The next thing I decided was that I would seduce Wolfgang. I needed an ice cream cone if I wanted to out-seduce the blond Glockenshpeel Mafia, who was now standing in the doorway watching me read her book.

"Learn anything?" she asked.

What could I say to that? I sheepishly put the book back on the shelf, wishing I was a worm so I could slither out of the room. Then she said, with her hands on her hips, "You lost all your clothes back in the city, didn't you?"

I nodded.

She walked over to her closet and I thought she was going to give me some of her old clothes which would have been welcome but humiliating at the same time. Besides, I couldn't imagine what apparel belonging to that Amazon would fit me. Instead, though, she pulled out a baby blue Singer sewing machine. Then she rummaged through a basket beside her dresser and pulled out various pieces of fabric that she threw on the floor.

"I'm gonna show you how to make a halter top," she said, plopping down on the floor in front of the sewing machine. Hating her at this point seemed useless so I sat down on the floor beside her.

"You make a kind of triangle of the fabric, see. Fold the top over. . ." She glanced around and found a leather string on the floor. "Like this."

She folded the fabric over the leather strip and then zipped it under the whirring needle of the machine. "Now, you just tie the ends around your back and the top around your neck and voila, a fashionable halter top. Great for summer and very sexy looking." She gave me a little smirk.

"Put it on," she said. "You can wash out your t-shirt in the sink and let it dry on the towel rack. If you want you can use any of that fabric to make yourself a couple more."

She stood and walked out of the room. I realized maybe for the first time how spoiled I'd been all my life and how ill-equipped I was for survival. It hadn't even occurred to me to wash out my clothes in the sink. I would have just gone on stinking until they rotted off me, I guess. So I went in the bathroom and changed into the halter top, found some soap and washed out my t-shirt. It was with an amazing sense of maturity and accomplishment that I went back into the living room, expecting Wolfgang to notice me. He didn't. He barely looked up from where he was still sitting on the floor, studying the jacket of a record album.

Sassy was sitting on the couch, running her fingers through the dog's fur. She must have just arrived because she'd been gone earlier. Then I suddenly felt a finger run across my back.

"Nice top," Frank said and walked past me, carrying a bottle of apple juice. I shivered from his touch.

"Thanks," I muttered.

Frank sank into a beanbag chair, and I sat down on the floor by Wolfgang.

"Look at this beautiful dog," Sassy said. "He's such an old soul sent here by the gods to watch over us."

Frank pulled out a baggie of grass and proceeded to roll up a joint. He licked the edge of the paper and then put the whole thing in his mouth and pulled it out through puckered lips. He caught me staring and winked. I felt heat rise to my face. Then with a flourish he pulled out a Bic lighter and hit the striker with his thumb. A flame danced from the top of the lighter; the joint took the flame and extinguished it to a red ember. Frank took a deep toke, held his breath and then seemed to melt as he exhaled. I was in awe of this ritual though I had only smoked that one time and hadn't known what to expect.

"Yummy," Sonya said, taking the joint from his fingers and inhaling. Her eyes watered and she held a finger under her nose before she blew the smoke out into the room. She stretched her hand with the burning joint toward Wolfgang. He shook his head.

"That's unfriendly," she said.

It was weird that Wolfgang didn't smoke pot, but that didn't make him any less radical than anyone else. Wolfgang was never one to do something because every else did it. Sassy reached over and took the joint from her sister. The dog lifted his snout to sniff curiously at the smoke and then placed his big head back down on his front paws, grunted and closed his eyes.

Frank watched silently, his eyelids low, his full lips in a slight pout. He turned to Wolfgang and asked in a quiet voice, "Are you sure you're not a cop?"

"What?" Wolfgang asked, his face turning red. It was rare to see emotion on Wolfgang's face.

"Maybe Orphan here is some FBI pig's kid. Maybe you're the one who snitched out James, David and Val."

Wolfgang rose in rage.

"I don't smoke because I do not give control of my mind to anybody or anything else. Not to the U.S. Government. Not to some pseudo-Marxist revolutionary organization, and never to a drug." His nostrils flared as he glared at Frank. Everyone else was silent for a moment.

"Wow. Heavy," Sassy said.

Frank lowered his eyes and said, "Look, man, cool it. I believe you. It's just we have to be careful. The pigs would love to stop us from saving the likes of you and keep us from getting your asses into Canada."

Wolfgang sat down again. He'd used up more emotion in that outburst than he generally used in a year.

"I need to get some money," he said forlornly. "Most of my cash was in my bag at the apartment in Spanish Harlem."

"You could get some quick cash panhandling," Sassy suggested.

"He can't panhandle," Frank said. "He looks like a draft dodger. They'll bust him so fast his little peach fuzz mustache will burn off." Then he looked at me and deliberately smiled. Traitor that I was, I smiled back and took the joint from Sassy's fingers. I touched the paper end to my lips and sucked.

"Eli can do it," Sonya said.

I immediately gagged on the smoke and started coughing.

"Me?" I asked between gasps.

Frank appraised me.

"Perfect. She's got that waif-like look. Poor little orphan child. She could probably scare up thirty or forty bucks in an afternoon."

First boosting and now this. If Miz Johnny could see me

now, my spiny ass would be black and blue.

"Not in Canandaigua," Sonya said.

"Rochester," Sassy interjected.

"So we've got a plan," Frank said, standing up. He took a hit of the joint, squinting his blue eyes through the smoke. Frank was somehow strange looking and kind of cute at the same time. Suddenly I was all for panhandling. I would impress them all with how much money I could make. If Bilbo Baggins could be a hero, so could I.

14

From Canandaigua to Rochester was not a very long trip. It was hilly and pretty. Frank and Sassy stopped at an A&P to get a bag of Oreos because Frank had the munchies. Then they dropped us off in downtown Rochester. Rochester was bigger than Canandaigua, but much smaller than New York City. We passed a huge hotel that looked like a castle. Frank had told us that the city was the home of Eastman Kodak and that if we went a few miles farther north, we would hit one of the finger lakes. Rochester did have a river, a muddy cut down its middle. And it had plenty of big stone buildings.

I had never even thought of these places before. Never really wondered what lay past the confines of my little world. Now it was as if I were pulling open curtains upon curtains on new and curious worlds. Yet even though it was strange, nothing could diminish my sense of boldness. Maybe that was because I had so few rules as a child under Mattie's benign neglect. So while Wolfgang parked himself on a bench in Manhattan Square Park, I found Main Street and without a qualm, held out my empty palm to strangers and said in my most polite voice, "Excuse me, do you have any spare change?"

Many were startled. some simply ignored me; others stopped and stared, men especially. Then they would dig into their pockets for quarters, dimes and nickels. Occasionally someone would give me a dollar. It was a game to me like trick or treat. I soon collected six dollars and stopped in a soda shop to buy an ice cream cone. I found Wolfgang still sitting on a bench with his book.

I scooted down beside him and jingled the coins at him. I licked my ice cream cone suggestively and offered him a lick.

He shook his head, ignoring my skillful tongue work.

"I don't like this," he said. "When we get to Canada, we'll get jobs. It's disgusting to beg."

"It's not disgusting," I said. "It's fun. They can spare it."

Wolfgang shook his head. I wanted him to be glad he had brought me. I wanted him to see that I was helpful and good. The jealousy I'd felt that morning had been like a sour ball of wax in my belly. It had a bad aftertaste I wanted to wipe out. I also felt ashamed for taking a hit off the joint when I knew he thought it was a bad idea. At least I had only taken the one hit, so I hadn't felt much more than a temporary light-headedness.

I finished the ice cream cone. I forgot all about being seductive until I was almost finished and then it was too late. It didn't matter. To Wolfgang, I would always be his little sister's friend, the one he had mercy kissed in a playground. I looked up at the sky, which was blue and pretty here but a shade paler than back home. The trees looked naked without Spanish moss draping like old beards from their limbs.

"I'm gonna go get some more cash-ola," I said.

"Be back by six o'clock," Wolfgang said, looking at the pocket watch he kept in his jeans – a gift from his father.

"Yes, Miz Johnny," I said.

I strolled back to the busy streets. I wandered past banks with pillars in front, offices, stores, and restaurants. An Italian restaurant caught my eye and I wished I could go in and get something to eat. I'd never been in an Italian restaurant before. I caught the eye of a couple just coming out.

"Hi, may I trouble you for some spare change?" I asked. They were taken aback, but the man gave me fifty cents before they hurried away. I didn't feel like I was begging. I felt I was exchanging the gift of my smile for a few pieces of silver.

After being rebuffed by my next couple of targets, I approached a stout little woman with gray hair. She walked purposefully down the street. When I spoke to her, she stopped short and looked at me with wide eyes.

"What did you say?" she asked.

"I wondered if you had any spare change?"

"What on earth for?"

"So I can eat," I answered, somewhat truthfully. She stood on the sidewalk before me with her leather purse dangling from her forearm, looking at me through a pair of brown-framed glasses.

"Well then, come on," she said. "I'll feed you."

I would have preferred cash, but the idea of food appealed to me, and she took me by the elbow and led me into the Italian restaurant.

"You are a bit thin," she said as she ushered me to a table. I sat down and put the linen napkin in my lap as I had been taught. She noticed and approved. A waiter came by and I ordered spaghetti with meatballs. The lady ordered a salad.

"Now why are you out here on the street without any food? Where are your parents?" she asked.

I told her a story of half-truths: how my grandmother was dead and my father didn't want me. My meal came and I told her that the only Italian words I knew came from operas. She wanted to know all about that so I told her about the Southern Opera

Guild, about having the theater to myself during rehearsals and then I told her how Mattie came to be my grandmother.

"The night my grandfather met Mattie she was singing an aria from *Manon Lescaut*. Mattie played Manon Lescaut in Buenos Aires and she said it was one of her favorite roles," I explained in between bites of spaghetti. "When she sang that aria, it would sort of fly over your head and lift you in the air. I've heard it all my life and it always made me feel as if my heart were being taken away. In the song, Manon has left the man she loves for a wealthy man. She sings *'In quelle trine morbide.'* Which is French not Italian. It means that in those silk curtains she feels a chill. I can only imagine what Grandaddy felt as he stood there in that chandeliered room listening to the most beautiful voice he had ever heard. Granddaddy was a southern gentleman but somehow he had managed to go his whole life without ever hearing an opera before."

The lady's head tilted as she listened to me. I could tell she was impressed. You could always impress an older person by talking about opera and you could always make young people think you were a complete weirdo. After dinner she paid the bill. I asked if I could have a peppermint patty and she bought me two.

"Where will you go?" she asked when we got outside. "Do you have somewhere to stay?"

I nodded and suddenly remembered Wolfgang in the park with his father's pocket watch.

"What time is it?" I asked.

She looked at her wristwatch and answered, "Six fifteen."

"Oh, I have to go. Thank you for dinner," I said, turning and dashing down the street. I was like Cinderella and the clock had tolled midnight. I hurried along through the crowds of people until I got to the park. Then I went straight to Wolfgang's bench. He wasn't there. The slim volume of Nietzsche that fit in his back pocket, the only thing we hadn't lost in the raid, sat there all by itself.

I looked around in confusion. Where could he have gone? I walked every inch of the park and then ventured around some of the surrounding blocks, but Wolfgang was nowhere to be seen. Had he finally left me, after all? It felt as if I were sinking into the ground beneath my feet. Panic rose in my throat. A large black bird flew out of a tree in a flurry of wingbeats, cawing loudly. I walked back into the park and sat down on Wolfgang's empty bench and stuck his book in my purse. I had no idea what to do.

I kept waiting, kept looking, kept hoping. But Wolfgang did not come. Instead a drunk guy who smelled like piss sat down next to me and asked my name. I didn't answer. Then he reached out and put his hand around my arm. I jumped up and fled to the other end of the park. But I didn't dare leave. What if Wolfgang came back for me?

So I skulked around, trying to avoid other people. I found a bathroom where I hid for a while. When I came outside it was dark. I went back to the bench. The drunk guy was gone. Again I wondered what to do? I turned in a circle, wishing an answer would arrive, wishing someone would tell me what to do. I had no idea how to get back to Canandaigua. I realized I couldn't plan ahead, not even as far as tomorrow. The only thing I could take care of was that moment. I decided to find a hidden spot among the bushes and trees, lie down, and wait till morning. Which is what I did.

When I woke up, I was freezing. My clothes were damp. I still had on the halter top I'd made at Sonya's. My hair was full of leaves. I had bug bites on my arms. I was hungry and lonely and desolate. But it was morning. I had survived. I'd heard people in the park during the night but no one had seen me. I went back to the bench. It was still empty. I wondered what the nice lady who had bought me dinner was doing. Thinking of the spaghetti dinner only made me feel worse because as I'd eaten, I'd been feeling happy, unaware of how awful my night would turn out to be. I couldn't stop shaking from the cold. I still had a little money from my panhandling the night before. Suddenly panhandling didn't seem much fun. It certainly wasn't how I wanted to spend the rest of my life. Was Wolfgang in Canada already? Or had he gone back to be with Sonya in Canandaigua? The latter thought made me want to vomit.

I got up and decided I should get some coffee to warm up.

After a cup of coffee and a piece of toast with grape jelly, I wandered around the streets of Rochester for hours. I was not the same bold girl I had been the day before. People avoided looking at me. I smelled bad. I probably looked worse. I found the river and sat down, looking at the water. The surface glittered in the sunlight like tiny scales as if it were a living thing.

"Hello," a voice said.

I looked up. A dark-skinned man in an orange turban was looking down at me.

"Hello," I said.

"The river is nice to look at, isn't it?"

"I guess so," I said. I looked down at my dirty feet. I didn't feel like exchanging pleasantries with some freak in a turban.

"Have you ever read the book *Siddhartha*?"

"No," I said.

The man sat down beside me.

"In the book, Siddhartha tries to find himself in all kinds of pleasures. But nothing brings him happiness. He tries strong drink, wild women, gambling. Finally, he turns his back on the world and he becomes a bridge tender. He finds peace beside the river. It is a nice story."

I shrugged, but I understood what he meant. This river was soothing. The sun had warmed me. I was alone and friendless, but somehow my spirits had risen.

"You will be all right," the man said. He got up. As I watched him walk away, I saw a red Corvair driving down the street. I jumped up and yelled.

"Hey! Hey!"

The car stopped. I ran toward it and reached the driver's window.

"Your boyfriend got arrested yesterday," Frank said.

I dropped to my knees. No, I thought. No. No. No.

I showered for a long time, but when I got out I still felt cold inside. My t-shirt was clean now, and I borrowed an Indian-print skirt that Sonya had made. The skirt reached to my toes and felt somehow comforting.

Sassy hugged me when I came into the living room.

"Poor orphan," she said.

"What's going to happen to Wolfgang?" I asked.

Frank sat on the couch.

"He'll be inducted into the U.S. Army," Frank said. "He's absolutely fucked. He'll be pissing in rice paddies before long."

"There's nothing you can do, Eli," Sassy said.

I wandered over to the bay window and stared out.

Frank came and stood behind me.

"Sorry, kid," he said, putting a hand on my shoulder.

I looked up at him.

"What about me?" I asked.

Sassy spoke up.

"You can come with me down to Georgia. There's a rock festival in some place called Byron. And since I never did get to Woodstock I am not missing this."

"Oh," I said. How ironic, I thought, that I would be heading back home. "Are you driving, Frank?"

Frank shook his head.

"I've got work to do. I'm going to Chicago to help out there."

I didn't ask what kind of help he was giving.

"Some guys I know are driving down," Sassy said. "If you want we can drop you off wherever it is you came from."

"I can't go back there," I said.

"Then come to the festival. You'll get to hear Jimi Hendrix."

"But what about Wolfgang?" I asked once again.

"Nothing you can do about it, kid." Frank shrugged.

"I guess I'll go to the festival then," I said. It wasn't like I had much choice. It seemed I would be open to suggestions for a while.

I found a quiet spot in the apartment and thumbed through Wolfgang's book, *Twilight of the Idols, Or How to Philosophize with a Hammer*. It had no story, just lots of sayings and ruminations on Socrates and other stuff, but one sentence leapt out at me: "What does not kill me makes me stronger."

15

*W*e drove away from Canandaigua in the back of a Ford van. There were curtains on the back window which I pushed aside to stare forlornly at the receding town. We passed an amusement park by the lake that Sassy and Frank and I had gone to the night before. Maybe they were trying to cheer me up. I'd ridden on the wooden roller coaster and screamed and laughed, but inside my chest was hollow. It only felt worse as we left.

I didn't know the people in the van. They were friends of Sassy's. She had grown up in Canandaigua. They didn't seem to be part of the movement. They were just a bunch of people who liked to smoke dope and who wanted to hear rock'n'roll. I nestled down on the floor of the van and tried to sleep through the trip. They had a tape deck and so there was a constant soundtrack. I didn't know a lot of the bands they played, but then I recognized a song. *I wanna live with a Cinnamon Girl.* I thought of Billy dedicating that song to Cleo on his radio show. I may have been stuck on the road with a bunch of strangers, but it was better than living with a family that didn't want me.

We stopped in North Carolina and went swimming in a quarry until the cops arrived and ran us off. Someone bought a loaf of Merita bread, some bologna, and a box of Vanilla Wafers from a 7-11. I boosted a pack of Juicy Fruit gum. That was dinner and dessert. We pulled into a state park when it got dark. The guys slept outside on the ground. Sassy and I slept in the van, which was too hot.

We arrived in Byron, Georgia, the next day.

A two-lane road led in to the campground, both lanes going in one direction: in. As we slowly crept past people walking or sitting on the side of the road, I gazed out at the sights. One guy sat on top of a car and held up a sign that said: "Welcome to Byron. Population: 350,000 freaks!" We passed people carrying backpacks and coolers. Then as we slowed to a crawl in the traffic jam, they passed us. We opened the side door of the van. Sassy and I and another girl hung our legs out the door and looked at all the people. A shirtless guy walking next to the van handed Sassy a lit joint.

"Just getting here?" he asked.

"Yeah."

"Far-out," he said with a grin.

We crawled in a long line of cars for what seemed like miles, and then we were in a camping area of tall pines trees, and the driver parked the van in a spot that would be our home for the next few days.

Sassy jumped out of the van. I followed her.

"Where do we get tickets for the festival?" she asked a passing couple.

"No tickets, man," the guy said. "They threw open the gates. The concerts are all free."

That sounded like good news to me as I had about seventy-five cents to my name.

Sassy looked a little confused.

"What's wrong?" I asked.

"I was supposed to meet someone at the ticket booth," she said.

I followed Sassy around the camping area as she got a feel

Cinnamon Girl

for the area. The red Georgia clay was dry and dusty, and soon my feet and legs were orange. I looked around at all the people as they set up their camps and mingled with each other. It seemed like they all knew each other. Sassy smiled and waved at people. She struck up conversations with anyone who walked by as if they were old friends. After a while I realized that this was simply the customary behavior of the tribe. They were friendly. Everyone was a brother or a sister. It was like Washington Square Park to the tenth power.

These girls with their long, stringy hair, their halter tops, their bikinis and blue jeans, their clean faces devoid of makeup shone with a sense of themselves as beauties. A sense I did not have. I was intimidated by their saucy smiles and their loud laughter, and as I watched them walking languidly down the road or smoking pot or even tending to the occasional little kid, I wanted desperately to be just like them.

If the girls were interesting, the guys were magnificent, walking around shirtless with their long hair and their mustaches. They could have passed for gods. I loved hearing them laugh and sensing the occasional brush of their eyes on my body. But I wished Wolfgang was with me.

"There's a lot of people here," Sassy said. "I don't know how I'm gonna find my friend." Then she turned and looked at me thoughtfully. It made me uneasy. Not to mention I was starving. A girl so skinny she looked like she was made of twigs sat over an open pit fire roasting corn on the cob. She saw me staring at the corn.

"You can have one for a quarter," the girl said.

I took one of the three quarters I had in my pocket and gave it to her. That was the most delicious corn I'd ever had in my life.

The stages were across the road from the camping area,

but Sassy seemed in no hurry to get to them. There was so much to see right in the camp and there was plenty of music from every direction. We went down to the camp stage for a while and listened to the jangly rock music, the thudding bass and the hissing of drums. I felt as if I had no identity at all. I was a piece of dust floating through the air and landing wherever I was blown. The liquid heat made it feel like being inside the mouth of a large dog. Even Sassy seemed limp and wavery like a figure from a Salvador Dali painting. Sweat and dirt marbled her neck and arms. I didn't want to know what I looked like.

Finally the sun slid down the sky, and a single breeze teased us with the hope of a cooler evening.

"Let's go hear the music," Sassy said.

"Sassy," I said, "all these guys here. How come they're not going to Canada? Why isn't the army after them?"

She shrugged. "Some of them have college deferments. Some of them got lucky in the draw. And some of them just don't give a damn."

Poor Wolfgang, I thought.

We moved in a herd toward the music. The field was amazing. Freaks and hippies for as far as the eye could see. We found a spot of ground next to a group of guys with shaved heads who had split open a watermelon. They gave us slices, and the smell of watermelon rinds and sweat and beer and mud surrounded us. It was a good smell. I didn't care that I was hot and dirty. It took my grief away. I was too busy observing this brave new world to feel the pain of losing Wolfgang and Mattie.

Sassy and I stayed at this spot for a while. A group called The Allman Brothers played and left, and the sky dimmed. I couldn't tell who was playing after that. It wasn't like I knew the music. But whoever it was played a mean guitar. Pretty soon people were up and dancing. I had never gone to the stupid dances and cotillions they had for teenagers in Augusta, but I figured out that you just had to move any way that you wanted to move. You could sway and wave your hands in the air. You could shake, rattle and roll.

Remember this, I told myself. Remember this for the rest of your life. Finally, the music ended for the night. The field was blanketed in smoke and bodies like the aftermath of a delirious battle. Sassy and I picked our way over the people lying on blankets or sitting on the grass. I passed a couple kissing and felt sad, wishing Wolfgang were with me. Though if he were, we wouldn't be here and probably wouldn't be kissing.

"We've got to get back to the van," Sassy said. All night she had been distracted, even during the music. I was worried that the friend she wanted to find was some guy she liked and then I'd be dumped again and on my own out here.

Lots of people had gone back to the campground. I smelled campfires and propane stoves. The whole place was a raucous party, music and laughter and shouts revolving through the hot night. I thought of Mattie's parties when I would fall asleep under the piano. My bare feet were tired, and I wanted to curl up on the ground and sleep like the dead.

We reached the edge of the campground and had to pass the Hell's Angels' camp, their hogs haphazardly making a barricade. An enormous biker stood up as we approached.

"You gotta pay a toll," he said.

Sassy in her ever-friendly way answered him. "Not now, okay? We're just looking for somebody."

"Well, you found him, darlin'," he said, with a cold grin

under a droopy mustache.

"Yeah, that's really cool, but you need to let me pass," she said.

"I will. I'm just asking for a toll." His eyes locked onto me and lingered on my halter top. "Just leave her with me."

Sassy shook her head vehemently. She was starting to lose some of her niceness. But the biker didn't pay attention. He grabbed my wrist and pulled me close to him. The heat and smell of his body engulfed me, and I was too startled to react.

"Let her go," Sassy insisted.

"This is my toll. You go on," he said.

I was afraid I might wet my pants in terror.

"I'm not going anywhere," Sassy said. "We have to find her father."

My head whipped around. I looked at her in shock.

"And she's way underage, so unless you want a statutory rape charge, I suggest you back the fuck off," Sassy said, her face just inches away from his.

"My father?" I asked. "Billy?"

Sassy didn't answer me. She just grabbed me by the other wrist and pulled me away. The biker let me go.

"Were you telling the truth back there?" I asked.

"Yes," Sassy admitted. "Some old lady in Rochester managed to somehow find your old man, who by the way has been frantic trying to find you."

Now, I realized that Sassy wasn't my great friend, after all. She was just trying to return to my dad.

"So you just snitched me out?"

Sassy turned on me, her face inches from mine, her long hair swaying as she spoke: "You did not tell me that your dad was Billy Burnes. He's a hero of mine. He actually saved lives in Chicago in '68, but I guess you wouldn't know about that back in your nice little safe life in Georgia."

"What are you talking about?"

"Billy Burnes is part of the Movement. Whenever someone is on the run and they go through St. Louis, he helps them find food and shelter. He is not part of the Establishment. How could you have run away from him?" Her fists jammed into her hips, and she cocked her head to the side. A musky scent emanated from her body.

"I hardly know him, Sassy," I said. "He was never around. Never."

Her lips tightened, and her dark eyes looked into mine.

"Well, he's here for you now, kiddo."

We trudged through the campgrounds without speaking. Then standing beside a beat up old pickup truck tucked between some pine trees, a familiar figure turned toward us.

"That's him," I said with a sigh.

"Thank God," Sassy said.

As we walked up to the truck, Billy's face lit up with recognition.

"Sassy?" he asked, stepping into the lane.

"Billy?" Sassy asked.

"Yep," he answered.

"It was kinda hard to find you," she said. "I walked around a lot, hoping you'd recognize your kid."

I stood back, but Billy grabbed me, hugged me hard, and whispered in my ear, "You shouldn't have done that, Eli."

"How did you find me?" I asked.

"A very kind and concerned lady called around Augusta and found someone who knew Mattie, who then gave her my number. She told me you were in Rochester, so I started calling everyone I knew and someone directed me to Sassy."

"I told you I was a messenger," Sassy said, suddenly friendly again. "You're the message this time. Don't be pissed off, okay? Your dad is a cool guy. I'm pleased to meet you, Billy Burnes. You've done some amazing shit."

"That was a while back," Billy said. "I haven't been that involved lately. You know, marriage . . . kids."

I was too tired to make sense of what they were saying. But here I was with my dad at the Atlanta International Pop Festival. Maybe it would be okay. I hoped he would want to stay to hear Jimi Hendrix play the next night. I should have known someone into music like he was wouldn't have missed it for the world.

16

The next day the heat came down on us like a busted bag of cement. People said it was 106 degrees in the shade, so I hated to think how hot it was in the sun. Billy's campsite was two rows away from Sassy and her friends. We had a sheet tied to some pine trees for shade and a couple blankets on the ground. It was weird to suddenly be with my dad at a big gathering of freaks, but with his long hair, Rolling Stone Sticky Fingers t-shirt and his faded jeans he fit right in. We stayed at our campsite that morning, eating honey buns and drinking warm cola as we watched the people pass. Once, a completely naked man walked by, droning the words, "Acid, acid, acid." Fortunately, at that point Billy was lying back on a quilt with his eyes shut. I didn't think I could stand the embarrassment of the two of us observing that tall, skinny man's penis bouncing like a windsock with his every step.

Billy didn't say anything about my going AWOL. I wondered why he didn't seem all that mad. Maybe he just didn't care. I told him about Wolfgang and he said that sucked and then he went into a long diatribe about Tricky Dick and the invasion of Cambodia.

Sassy showed up, wearing a bikini top and her long Indian-print skirt and carrying her traveling bag. She said that one of the guys among her friends had overdosed and they were leaving early.

"Stay with us," Billy said. He turned to look at me with one eyebrow raised to get my approval of the idea. Billy had this way of including you in any scheme he had, making you feel like you were in on some conspiracy.

"Okay," she said and dumped her bag of possessions in the back of Billy's truck. She must have already intended to stay with us since she'd brought her gear.

"I'm going to down to the creek," she said to me. "Want to come?"

"Sure," I said. I'd forgiven her for her treachery, and in fact, felt a kind of relief that I didn't have to figure out the course of my own life for a while. Without Wolfgang, I didn't have a reason not to go live with Billy and Cleo. Anyway, it wouldn't be for long. In three years I'd be eighteen, and I could do whatever I wanted then.

When we got to the creek, people were skinny dipping, and Sassy shucked off all her clothes, revealing her pendulous breasts, pale butt cheeks and all. Hot as hell's furnace, but I was not about to get naked around all these people so I just sank into the water with my clothes on, which probably made me more conspicuous. I looked up at the cloudless blue sky and immersed myself in the water's wet mouth.

When we got back to the truck, Billy made us peanut butter and jelly sandwiches on Roman Meal bread. I ate two and could have gone for more but didn't want to look like a pig.

Sassy pulled a strand of hair from her mouth that had gotten caught in the sandwich. She seemed so comfortable with her flesh. Billy's eyes got soft when he looked at her.

"How did a boy from Augusta, Georgia, become a radical?" Sassy wanted to know.

Billy stretched his legs out in front of him. I picked some pine bark off the tree I was leaning against and began breaking it into tiny pieces. Already the cooling off we'd gotten from our dip in the creek was fading. The air turned hot and steamy again.

"You know," Billy said, stroking his chin and looking sideways at Sassy. "I can remember the precise moment." I wondered why I had never thought to ask this question of Billy. It just seemed to me like he had *always* been different from the rest of the people in Augusta.

Sassy tilted her head.

"I was about eleven years old, and I had some money to go to the movies. But I had to take a bus to get to the movie theater. So I get on the bus and I sit down somewhere in the middle, minding my own business. There's a Black man a few seats ahead of me, and he keeps turning around and looking at me with a crazy look on his face. And for some reason the bus wasn't moving. I didn't know what the hell was going on. I saw the bus driver looking in that big mirror over his head at us. And I thought, does he know this man is crazy? Am I in danger?"

Sweat snaked along my ribs under my t-shirt. I was wishing I had a bathing suit on.

"Suddenly the Black guy gets up, and I just about wet my britches. I thought he was coming back to kill me. He had this angry, crazy look on my face. But he went right past me and sat down about three rows behind me. Then the bus started moving forward."

Billy stopped for dramatic effect. Sassy shook her head.

"That's when I realized that a grown man had to get up and move seats because of me, a little boy. The crazy look on his face had been pure and utter humiliation. That was the moment. I knew it was all wrong. Everything they were teaching us in school. Everything my father spouted about the gentility of the south – '*The*

Negroes are happy, son.' It was all bullshit."

"So you became a radical?"

"No. Not till I left. In Missouri and Illinois, I got involved in SDS and went to some communist party meetings. We marched. We had sit-ins. I got tear-gassed and beaten and jailed. Good times," he laughed.

"And what about now? What with the movement in disarray? Did you join Weatherman?"

Billy shook his head. "I help out when I can. But I've got a family now so I'm not exactly active anymore. I still go to protests if they're local and sometimes I help people…" His voice faded out and he looked away. He didn't say exactly how he helped people.

Sassy reached over and hugged him, which made me feel a little nervous. He did tell her he was married. He hugged her back, and they released each other slowly as if they were somehow glued together but the glue hadn't dried yet.

"I'm kind of tired. Mind if I take a nap in the bed of your truck?" Sassy asked.

"Sure, go ahead. Eli and I will go out and mingle," Billy said, getting up with surprising speed for such a big guy. He turned to me and said, "Ready?"

Billy and I wandered around the enormous campground. Like Sassy, Billy would strike up a conversation with anybody, asking about their music, where they were from, how were the drugs. I should have been surprised but I wasn't when Billy took a hit off someone's bong. We'd approach a group, and usually some young guy with thick hair that had to be pushed from his face would answer him, a spokesperson, a kind of philosopher. These guys seemed to enjoy talking and knew all sorts of things.

They had an amused gentleness about them that made my throat feel tight.

Eventually we sat down in front of the tent of a group of surfers from Florida. The philosopher of this group was a tall blond guy who invited us to have some hotdogs, which we did. From an 8-track player inside the car rock music poured out.

"Mitch Ryder and the Detroit Wheels," my dad said, shaking his head with a smile. "I love the way Badanjek's bass drum kicks off that song."

"You know your music, man," the tall surfer said.

"Hell, I've been in the music biz for twelve years. You ever hear of Bad Billy Burnes?"

The surfer had been knifing French's mustard on a hotdog; he stopped and stared at my dad, holding the mustardy knife aloft.

"You're shitting me. That's you? Say it again. Say Bad Billy Burnes."

"You're listening to Bad Billy Burnes on your favorite AM radio station," Billy said in his radio voice.

The surfer's cohorts were now all ears, laughing and slapping each other.

"Yeah, I heard you before. Late at night you can get radio stations from all over the place. I can get Chicago, Detroit, St. Louis sometimes. And I'm talking about from Florida."

"Cool, man, very cool."

"So are you still doing that Top-40 stuff?"

Billy finished off his hotdog, wiped his mouth and shook his head.

"Naw, man. I got canned," he said. My head swiveled toward Billy. This was news to me.

Another of the surfers leaned forward. "No way, dude."

"Yeah, it's true. I got sick of playing that payola crap day in and day out. Bubble gum for the teeny boppers. On AM a program director dictates every song. I want to put on an album and just let it play. You know? Airplane, Dead, Joplin, the good shit. Finally, one night I got really pissed off."

Billy leaned forward and everyone else leaned forward, too, including me, since this was the first time I'd heard any of this. "I played 'Revolution' over and over again. It was about midnight. I figured maybe the boss was asleep. But pretty soon the phone light started flashing in the studio. I didn't pick up. Just played the song again and again. About twenty times maybe before the engineer could shut me down."

"Far-out," the tall surfer said with a laugh.

"Yeah, but you got shit-canned," the other one said with a sympathetic expression. A wave of dread overcame me. If Billy didn't have a job, how was he going to feed his family, which now included me? He might be cool, but he was useless as a father. I began to feel really pissed off. Not just at him, but at Mattie for leaving me and Miz Johnny for not keeping me in Augusta and Wolfgang for getting busted and everyone I could think of just because.

"No big deal. AM is dead. FM is the future. Free-form broadcasting. You can do whatever you want on FM. The DJ decides the music. Even the news is better. No more rip and read from the wire." Billy settled back, and the surfers lit up a pipe, which they started to pass around. When it came to me, I passed it on to Billy. I didn't think I should smoke pot in front of my dad.

"This is my kid," he said, smoke billowing from his lung sacks. "She's not into grass."

All the attention turned to me, and I wanted to shrink into

the earth.

"Your kid? Wild!" The blond guy smiled sweetly and said, "You're a pretty cool little chick."

I couldn't find any words that seemed to be an adequate response. I was a far cry from being a cool chick, but it felt good that he said that. I probably could be cool. Like maybe I wouldn't worry about whether or not Billy had a job. He didn't seem to be worried. I stuffed my fears inside me. Maybe Cleo was working. Anyway, we had some cash from selling the antiques. I didn't know how much money you needed to live on, but surely we'd be all right for a while.

Eventually, we got up and wandered on. I thought of the naked man who had been walking down the lane earlier, calling out "Acid. Acid."

"Billy?" I asked. "Is acid LSD?"

"Yeah," he said. "Lysergic acid diethylamide. It's made from ergot. A grain fungus."

"What's it like? Doesn't it make people jump out of windows?"

"Not often. But it's best to stay on the ground if you're tripping."

What would they say back home about this, I wondered, kicking up orange dust. Here I was with a bunch of crazed hippies on drugs. I didn't know anyone else with a father like Billy.

"So you don't have a job?" I asked.

"Not right now. I've been too busy trying to find my runaway daughter," he said, lips going tight. I should have said I was sorry, but I wasn't so I didn't.

That night we went back to the festival and heard Jimi Hendrix play. Sassy came with us. She and Billy walked close together, and I stayed right behind them. Occasionally, they'd brush up against each other. I could see the dance they were doing, and I thought about Cleo back home with their two kids. Billy must not care about them any more than he ever cared about me, I thought. He probably wasn't trying to find me. That was just an excuse for not having a job.

We got as close as we could. Up on the stage, Jimi's wild head of hair waved back and forth behind a microphone. He was wearing some kind of headband and what looked like a robe. Sometime after midnight he played "The Star-Spangled Banner" with his teeth. Billy shouted in my ear: "This is it. This is the defining moment of our times." Then the fireworks started, and a single word flew up from a half million mouths: "Far-out."

This time when a joint came past me, I took a deep hit. Billy didn't even notice.

The music swept under me and seemed to lift me as if I were on the crest of something magnificent, as if I were on a mountain looking out over the world. And all the sorrow and worry that had plagued me since that night in Augusta when Mattie first pointed out the huge bulge in her abdomen seemed to float away. I felt a weird cramping in my belly but I ignored it. I was probably just hungry again.

That night the three of us fell asleep right there on a blanket on the festival grounds. I woke up the next morning. Sassy's head was on Billy's chest. He was snoring. People were just waking up and moving around. At least Sassy and Billy hadn't been able to sneak off and do anything. I made my way to a Porta John, which smelled like dead skunk and cherry candy. On my white underpants, a dark stain bloomed. It took me a moment to realize that I was having my period again. My sanitary belt and pads had been lost when the cops raided the apartment in Spanish Harlem.

I woke Sassy and told her my problem. She gave me a tampon.

"What do I do with this?" I asked.

"Shove it inside."

"Inside?"

I went back to the smelly Porta John and managed to jam the cotton finger inside me. It didn't feel good, and I thought that if sex felt like this, I might not ever be interested.

17

Billy and Sassy found me at the surfers' campsite the next morning, eating a peanut butter and jelly sandwich. Billy scowled like he thought I might have taken off again.

"C'mon," he said. "Traffic is going to be hell if we don't get out now."

I squeezed between him and Sassy in the truck. I didn't know if the two of them had done anything together after I had fallen asleep the night before.

Billy stuck a tape in the 8-track and Janis Joplin sang about freedom being just another word for nothing left to lose. If that was the case, then I had nothing but freedom.

It took a couple of hours to get out of Byron and onto the highway. It took another couple hours to get to Atlanta where we dropped Sassy off at the bus station. She was heading back to New York. She gave us each a long hug and then bounced away. If everyone in the Movement had her kind of energy, they couldn't possibly lose.

"You tired?" he asked as we drove off. I nodded. We had a long drive to Missouri, and I dreaded it. Eventually we would have to talk. Or maybe we wouldn't and that might be worse. I pretended to be asleep.

When we crossed the border to Tennessee, we stopped for gas and a bathroom break. I bought a couple of tampons from a machine in the gas station to get me through the trip.

Once back in the decrepit old truck, I looked through his

tape cartridges. I found the one that had "Cinnamon Girl" and pushed it into the mouth of the tape deck. I hoped he might feel guilty if he heard it. After all, he'd said on the air that Cleo owned his heart.

"You and Sassy sure got along," I said in a sour voice.

"Nothing happened, Eli," he said. "I wouldn't cheat on Cleo."

I scoffed and crossed my arms, listening to the music. I liked the guy's voice.

"What the hell are you mad about anyway?" he asked. "I'm the one who's been worried sick trying to find you."

"Really?" I asked. "How hard did you try?"

"I put feelers out in every city," he said.

"Well, now, you've got me," I said. "Happy?"

"Yeah," he said. "I am."

We didn't talk much after that. We stopped in Nashville for a late lunch and that took forever because Billy wanted to go by one of the radio stations and chat up the DJ. Then we were back on the road.

A sign said: St. Louis 80 miles, which meant we were 80 miles away from my new life. I felt a fluttering in my belly — a new life without Mattie, Miz Johnny, Gretchen, or Wolfgang. A life without opera, without Mattie's circle of friends. How would Cleo feel about having an extra kid in the house? I wished I'd just had a normal mom-and-dad type family. Would I find any friends? I looked over at Billy. He barely knew me. He didn't even think it was weird that I never called him "Dad."

Hot air rivered through the windows as we drove along the highway. The pickup truck was like an old man. Billy had it cranked up to about 50 miles an hour. Cars and semi-trucks barreled past us. It was late by the time we got close to St. Louis and hardly anyone else was on the highway. I'd been dozing off and on for most of the trip so I wasn't sleepy. I noticed that Billy kept looking nervously in the rearview mirror. I glanced in the side mirror and saw headlights flashing their high beams at us.

"Billy?" I asked.

He didn't answer. An arm stuck out of the window of the car behind us, and that wasn't a peace sign they were shooting. The car — a big Chevrolet — came roaring alongside.

"Filthy hippies!" a man screamed out the window. He probably didn't like the peace sign painted on the tailgate of the truck, or the bumper sticker with a picture of a crossed-out Nixon that said, "No Dicks."

I looked over at my dad with his ponytail and the red bandana around his neck. There were at least four men in that car beside us and no one else in sight. Billy slowed to let them pass. As they pulled in front of us, the bright red brake lights flashed on and off, taunting us. Something flew out the window. A bottle shattered on the windshield, and I screamed.

"We've got to get away from these assholes," he said.

They slowed way down, and Billy tried to speed past them. As we came alongside the car, one of them waved a bat out the window. They were only inches from our side, their expressions gleeful. A thud sounded against the side of the truck.

Billy stomped on the accelerator, but there was no way this arthritic old truck was going to outrace these guys. Billy pushed the truck up to 70 mph, but it couldn't keep that pace for long. They kept right alongside us sometimes veering into our lane. I was so scared I couldn't even swallow my spit.

Billy yelled, "Hang on." He turned the steering wheel

sharply to the right so the truck was going the wrong way on the highway and then he punched it down an exit ramp we had just passed. I looked around; the other car was sailing away. As we flew around the curve of the exit ramp, I slid off the seat and banged onto the floor. Billy pulled to a stop and helped me up.

"Are you okay?" he asked.

I stared up at him. The fear that had been lying like a cannonball in my gut burst through me, and I started laughing like crazy.

"Wow, Billy. Wow. That was far out. I was scared shitless."

"Me, too," he said, laughing. "Me, too."

My knees were bruised, but I didn't care. We drove away slowly, checking to make sure no one was behind us.

Billy wasn't perfect, but we might somehow make a life together. There wasn't much choice. He was all I had now.

18

Billy and Cleo lived in a small house on a gravel road in a place called Webster Groves, one of the cluster of towns that make up St. Louis County. When we arrived, two little boys tumbled out of the house, screaming. I noticed an old station wagon in the driveway and figured it belonged to Cleo.

Cleo stood in the doorway. She was thin and tall with long red hair, large lips, a snub nose and sleepy, beautiful brown eyes. I had met her only twice before – once when she was six months pregnant and she and Billy had just gotten married and once when all four of them came to Augusta for Christmas. I had not liked her or disliked her. Now, I decided I better make her my friend. I wouldn't mention Sassy.

Billy took her in his arms and swung her around while the boys screamed. I stood and watched the midnight family re-union. When Billy set Cleo down, Jake, who was almost five now, climbed onto Billy's back and Turtle jumped into Cleo's arms, pawing at her breasts.

"Sweetie, you're a big boy now," she said. "Big boys don't get num-nums. That's for babies."

"I'm a baby," Turtle cried.

"Baby! Baby!" Jake laughed.

A pang of jealousy cut through me as I watched Cleo dote on her boys. I felt large and conspicuous, an imposer. Cleo led me into the small gray house. The first thing I noticed was a big poster on the living room wall of two babies, playing together — one

Black and one White. In the dining room was another poster for something called the La Leche League, and it showed a woman breast-feeding a baby. I figured the posters were Cleo's. Cleo saw me looking and said, "Breast milk is the best milk." So Cleo was an activist, too, in her own way.

Billy disappeared into the bathroom while Cleo and the kids showed me into a room in the basement. A single bed occupied one corner, and a cheap-looking dresser stood against the wall. It had no carpet on the concrete floor. I thought about my canopy bed back home. Cleo pointed out a clock radio on an overturned crate and an afghan she'd made that I could use. My trunk full of my belongings waited at the foot of my bed.

"You can put posters on the walls and make it look cool," Cleo said brightly. Two of the walls were paneled wood and two were cinderblock. It was a makeshift room, I realized, but it was mine, and she was right. I could decorate it. Maybe get a lava lamp or a black light.

"It's great, Cleo," I said. Above the bed a row of windows was level with the ground outside. I liked the idea that if I needed to leave in a hurry, all I had to do was open a window and scramble out. I unlatched one and pushed it open. A big furry gray dog came ambling up, stuck her face in, and licked my cheek.

"That's Heidi," Jake yelled. "Go away, Heidi."

I wiped the dog saliva from my cheek. I'd never had a dog before. Ever since I'd read *White Fang*, I always wanted a dog at my side. Maybe she would come sleep in my room at night.

As I unpacked the trunk that Billy had brought back with him after the funeral, I found my treasure box and looked inside. I'd forgotten that I had stashed a bottle of Mattie's Estée Lauder perfume. I took out the perfume and put the box with Mattie's tape, my picture of my mom and dad, and the other keepsakes inside the top drawer of the dresser where prying little hands couldn't get to it.

When Cleo finally herded her kids out of the basement and back upstairs, I looked around the basement itself. Billy's workshop on the other side of the stairs was cluttered with protest signs, radio equipment, records and tools. He had a long desk made of a door on two wooden horses. Newspaper clippings about the war, about protesters and about music were thumb-tacked to the wall. A big picture of a distraught girl standing over a dead student – the Kent State shootings – hung in the middle.

I continued searching through the basement. A short flight of steps led to a storm door. When I opened it, Heidi wagged her whole body in greeting. I let her in and she followed me around, stopping to lick my toes if I stood still. There were pipes, a hot water heater, storage places and boxes scattered around. A musty smell hung over the place.

I went back to my haven and spritzed a shot of perfume on my arm so I could smell it as I slept. It smelled like Mattie and while I slept, a light tickling voice in my head sang, "hush little baby, don't say a word, Papa's gonna buy you a mockingbird."

Mattie had had her "set" and I soon got to know Billy and Cleo's friends and co-conspirators. First and most unforgettable was Jeremiah, a slight man with a scraggly gray beard and long, stringy brown hair. He wore a beret most of the time and a pair of baggy corduroy pants that looked like they had once belonged to his grandfather. People who casually saw Jeremiah might think he was a crazy street bum. But as soon as you started talking to him, you realized he was probably the sanest person you ever met.

Just looking into his deep brown eyes was mind-altering. It was like looking into raw genius without any of the usual masks. He laughed frequently, and his laughter, a loud "ha-ha-ha," spread like a contagion. Most of the other people in the anti-war movement seemed to be uniformly pissed off, but Jeremiah had a way of being angry and happy at the same time.

I met Jeremiah and the others: Mike and Janet, original members of Students for a Democratic Society, which apparently was no longer a functioning organization. Mike was now studying for a Ph.D. He was going to be college professor. The other couple was JoAnne and her husband, Stump, a Vietnam veteran who had lost his right leg in a minefield. It seemed in major bad taste to call him "Stump" but he wouldn't let us call him anything else. Stump spoke in a quiet voice. He was not a tall guy, less than six feet, I guess, with long blond hair that he kept in a braid. He looked like he had been cute once, but the war had scrubbed all the cute out of him. JoAnne was a large earth-mother, whose lap was often occupied by one of my little half-brothers.

Every weekend would find them, sitting on the patio of my dad's house where they had get-togethers, drinking beer and bitching about the government and planning "actions" against the war.

They argued a lot. Janet and Stump seemed to be in favor of planting bombs in the United States in retaliation "for the terrorizing of Hanoi." Mike, JoAnne and Jeremiah didn't think that violence was the answer. Billy could see both sides of the issue, and Cleo kept her thoughts to herself.

"It's not like they don't warn people before they set off a bomb," Janet, the attorney of the group, said. She had thick curly black hair, a sharp chin and murky eyes behind a pair of granny glasses. "There is always a communiqué. No one has been killed or even injured."

"Except for the townhouse in Greenwich Village where they blew themselves up!" JoAnne said.

"True," Stump interjected. "But that was a mistake. And they learned their lesson the hard way. How else are you gonna make these assholes listen? I've been to Vietnam. I've seen what we're doing to those people. It isn't pretty watching a little girl with her intestines spilling out of her belly die."

His voice was bitter. Everyone grew quiet for a moment as that image seeped into our brains.

"He's right," Janet said finally. "We've tried being peaceful."

"These actions are against the law, dear heart," Mike said putting his hand on Janet's. "And as an agent of the court, you should not be in favor of illegal tactics."

"Weathermen's hearts are in the right place," Billy said, "But you have to be very careful when you turn to violence that you don't lose your soul in the process."

"You will always lose your soul," Jeremiah insisted. "You become violent then you become like the enemy. Nonviolence is the only way. Gandhi proved it."

Janet had tears in her eyes. "But, Jeremiah, they're killing children in our names. Blood is on our hands. My hands."

I listened to these endless debates without ever saying anything. The war didn't make sense to me. The only thing I really understood was that young Americans were being shipped overseas and coming home in body bags. When we weren't hosting the weekend parties, I didn't have much to do – no friends my own age to hang out with, no operas to help put on, no boyfriend to daydream about. Cleo gave me chores around the house, and I helped Billy with his garden. Otherwise I read a lot — especially after I discovered Billy's Tolkien stash. I was finally able to finish *Lord of the Rings* and still pictured Wolfgang as the wizard Gandalf. At night, Heidi, part Schnauzer and part Shepherd and part something else, would come and put her shaggy head on my knee as if offering herself to my lonely little heart.

Summer in the Midwest was just as muggy and thick as it was back in Georgia. Shortly after we got back from our sojourn in the south, Billy got a job at the hottest FM radio station in town, but because he was new to FM, he got stuck in the overnight shift.

"The music part is easy, but I've got to create a whole new persona," he said. "I can't be 'Bad Billy Burnes' anymore. I've got to be mellow, converse with my listeners. Like that, man."

Sometimes I'd wake up and listen to him. Gradually he grew into the new role. He became "Bill Burnes" with a softer voice. At first he sounded stilted, but before long, he was rambling away, even letting some of his political views come out, which I thought was probably not a good idea, and Cleo said as much.

Cleo and Billy grew tomatoes that were fat and juicy. I had never liked tomatoes before but my mind was changed when Cleo pulled one off the vine and told me to take a bite. As the juice ran down my chin, I shuddered with delight.

On Sundays I was allowed to call Gretchen. I still sometimes felt a hollowness in my chest that only seemed to be alleviated by those phone calls. I missed Gretchen, and I worried about Wolfgang. I missed Miz Johnny's dinners, and I imagined Mattie's voice singing me to sleep.

Labor day weekend I called Gretchen on Sunday afternoon. Gretchen sounded like she had just woken up. Actually, she had been crying.

"Wolfie got back from bootcamp. He's leaving this week," she said.

"Leaving for where?"

"He's going to Vietnam."

"Shit."

Gretchen was silent for a minute.

"Maybe it's not so bad. He says if he lives through it, the army will pay for him to go to college. He wants to be a philosopher."

I was sitting at Billy's desk in his basement office with the phone clutched to my ear, wishing I could crawl through the wire and hold onto Wolfgang, tie him up, kidnap him, anything to keep him from going to war. Once again, there was nothing I could do. I would have to let him go like I let Mattie go. But while Mattie had lived a full life, Wolfgang's was only beginning.

Gretchen and I hung up. It took me forever to fall asleep. In the morning Jake and Turtle tumbled into my room. They bounced on the bed while Heidi, who had taken to sleeping on my dirty clothes, barked at the three of us.

"Get up, Eli. Mama says we're having a cookout today. You got to help. Get up right now."

I struggled out of bed and shooed the boys out of my room.

Cleo cleaned the house and I mowed the lawn. Then she made beans, macaroni salad, and homemade bread while I kept the boys out of her hair. Billy went outside and lit the grill. People started showing up in the early afternoon. Though the house was small, we had a big backyard, and people brought their own chairs.

Jeremiah showed up first with some middle-eastern mixture he said was for the vegetarians though I think he might have been the only vegetarian there. Janet and Mike brought a cherry pie with a tiny toy soldier stuck on top. Others showed up with beer or wine or cokes.

"Viva la revolución," Jeremiah said and then ha-ha'd in a way that made the rest of us giggle.

Mike strolled over to Billy and said, "You know, I'm pretty sure I saw an unmarked cop car around the corner when I was driving up. They're hip to you, man."

Billy glanced around. He had a slab of ribs on the grill along with some hotdogs.

"We're not doing anything illegal," he said. "Just having a cookout."

"Your phone has to be tapped."

"I don't say anything on the phone," Billy said.

Janet put a hand on Billy's arm. Janet had graduated from Harvard Law at the top of her class, and Billy often spoke about how smart she was, which elicited a jealous smirk from Cleo. Cleo had met Billy when he was on the campus of SIU organizing an anti-war rally. It was her first year. She never went back for her second year.

"Billy, they know that you know," Janet said. She had a beer in her hand and reminded me of Fallene when she had one too many.

"Know what?" I asked.

She turned to me with her blinking murky eyes and said, "Nothing."

Billy's right eyebrow went up.

"Loose lips, Janet," he said.

A nervous shiver passed through me. What did Billy know and why wouldn't Janet tell me?

"Still working the night shift at the station?" she asked.

"Yep," he said.

"Good," she answered.

This conversation baffled me.

Cleo hurried outside, followed by Turtle.

"Has anyone seen Jake?" she asked.

"He's around here somewhere," Billy said.

"Where?" she asked insistently, pulling Turtle up onto her hip.

"Um," Billy looked around and called out "Jake?"

"I'll find him," I said, rising from the chair where I'd been sitting. I couldn't believe Billy didn't even seem worried. Then again, he'd left me, hadn't he?

Cleo handed Turtle off to Jeremiah, and we split the search. She took the house, and I went to the basement. I checked my room and then under Billy's desk and the nooks and crannies where a mischievous kid might hide. Heidi followed but she was no bloodhound. Then I went out the storm door to the garden, but he wasn't out there. Cleo came back onto the patio.

"He's not in the house," she said, a note of panic in her voice.

A look of annoyance crossed Billy's face.

"Jake?" he called out again. "Jake!"

Most of the guests had stopped talking and were glancing around, unsure what to do. Billy went into the house to check it again. Janet and JoAnne were peering into the surrounding back-yards.

"I'll check the front," I said.

Cleo's panic had infiltrated my brain. I hurried down the gravel road, calling Jake's name. I could hear Billy calling for him, too. Maybe Jake went down to the IGA store, I thought. He was an enterprising kid. Maybe he found some change and went to get candy. But everywhere I looked, I saw nothing but houses and trees and cars. The gravel road was only a block long. I turned at the corner and headed down to the IGA, but the parking lot was empty. It was closed for the holiday.

I headed back to the house, hoping someone else had found him. Sweat trickled along my back and it felt like I was blind, like Jake was standing right in front of me but I couldn't see him. How could a kid just disappear? When I turned back onto the gravel road, I saw Stump at the other end of the street and there beside him was Jake's small form. Relief rushed over me, followed by chagrin that I had been so worried in the first place. Yet still I found myself running toward them. Cleo had spotted them as well and she was dashing across the front yard to get to him. She swept Jake in her arms, and I saw her shoulders shaking from behind as I trotted up to them.

"He's all right," Stump said in a reassuring voice. "He just wandered off."

"A man gave me a truck," Jake said, holding out his fist.

By now Billy, Mike and Jeremiah, still holding onto Turtle, had joined us. Jake was smiling, all his baby teeth showing, as he reveled in the attention.

"What man?" Billy asked him.

"A man in a car. He came out of the car and said was we having a party? Then he said I could have this truck."

Jake opened his hand and inside was a tiny army truck.

"What did the man look like?" Stump asked.

"He was tall."

Stump said, "Anyone would be tall to a little kid."

"Never mind," Cleo said. "Jake, you aren't supposed to leave this yard without us. Do you understand?"

Jake nodded soberly. Billy hoisted Jake onto his shoulders and galloped with him to the backyard. Cleo took Turtle from Jeremiah and followed. I stood with Stump, Mike and Jeremiah. They were silent. Then Stump said, "That was the pigs, man. Trying to interrogate the little boy."

Mike nodded. Jeremiah didn't say anything, just bowed his head as if in prayer. A sliver of anxiety cut through my belly. I thought about how the cops had taken James and Val away and then gotten Wolfgang. Maybe I was a jinx.

The party resumed with Jake's return but Cleo didn't let him or Turtle out of her sight. We sat in chairs eating dinner off paper plates, and people traded stories about marches and demonstrations and going to jail.

"What people don't seem to know about Kent State is that the National Guard were actually using bayonets on people," Janet said in her crisp smartest-girl-in-the-class voice.

"You're not serious," Cleo said.

"I am. They stabbed Mike," she pointed at her husband. He shrugged and nodded.

"In the leg," he said.

"Let's see," Stump said.

Mike rose and unzipped his jeans. "Don't worry. I'm wearing underwear. But you gotta see this."

He lowered his jeans, his t-shirt hanging down past his underwear, and showed us a puckered patch of skin—pink as a rose.

"Bled like a stuck pig," he said with a laugh. I looked

down at the rib I had been chewing, and my appetite disappeared. He pulled up his jeans and sat down, having silenced the group.

During the momentary silence, I spoke up. I had never said much more than hi or bye at these gatherings, but now I couldn't stop the words from coming from my mouth.

"I saw a Black man get shot by the police in Augusta."

Billy leaned back and turned to me with a puzzled look on his face.

"You never told me about that."

"It was during the riots last May right before Mattie died. Wolfgang and Gretchen and I went to see what was happening. We got trapped between the rioters and the fires so we went to hide at Miz Johnny's, but on the way we saw the police shoot down one of the rioters. Another man was screaming because it was his brother. And there wasn't anything we could do."

Everyone was quiet. Jeremiah's soft eyes watched me. Janet shook her head. Stump crossed his arms and his face took on a masked expression.

"Now Wolfgang's been drafted into the army and he's going to Vietnam, and I'm scared for him." They didn't know who Wolfgang was, but I knew that they would understand. Stump reached over and patted me on the shoulder. Jeremiah stood up and came close to me. Then he squatted down and took my hands. He didn't say anything, but just looked at me with moist brown eyes full of kindness.

To be honest, I had mixed feelings about this war that my father and his friends hated. I knew I was supposed to agree with them, but it was hard to believe that the president of our country didn't know what he was doing. Why would he and the Congress send Americans to die unless it was important? I mean, this was

America. We had stopped the Nazis, and the communists were just as bad, weren't they? As I sat there in the cooling twilight with Jeremiah's warm damp hands on my own, I realized that whatever the reason, it was not good enough for Wolfgang to lose his life.

19

*M*y first day at Webster Groves High School. What the hell was wrong with me? I was living with my long-haired, war-protesting hippie dad and my 24-year-old hippie stepmom, but I was still dressing like the bookworm girl from Augusta. Well, actually I was trying to dress like the cute popular girls at my old junior high. I had on a gray dress with white polka dots that flattered my budding figure and a pair of strappy black shoes with a slender two-inch heel. I thought, this is high school. I need to dress like I'm grown up now.

So there I sat in my homeroom class surrounded by kids in jeans and t-shirts, sneakers and flip-flops and Candies. I was like a Martian. No, that planet is too close to Earth. I was like someone from Uranus, yeah, the butthole of the solar system.

Each class was steadily more painful. Everyone was friends with everyone else. At least back home I had Gretchen I could sit with at lunch. But here no one. During lunch period I traveled to different bathrooms from the third floor to the first. I spent about ten minutes in each until thank god classes started again.

Finally it was over. The day was not eternal, after all. When the final buzzer rang, I made my way through the jostling kids in the halls and out the nearest exit. Too late I looked around. Perched on the stone rail and sprawled over the steps were a strange breed of teenaged adults. They stared at me.

"This entrance is for seniors only," a voice informed me as I hurried down the steps. On the last step, the heel of my right shoe broke off. I hobbled to Cleo's old station wagon amidst a roar of laughter.

"How was your day?" Cleo asked.

I wiped away a tear and said, "It was really cool."

That weekend I took all my old clothes to a thrift store and traded them in on used jeans. Then Cleo showed me how to make roach clip earrings with beads and feathers in Billy's workshop.

I didn't immediately start winning friends and being a bad influence on people, but at least no one laughed when I walked past.

"*I*'m going to a consciousness-raising meeting tonight," Cleo said, wiping off Turtle's dirty hands with a washcloth. The boys and I were sitting at the table waiting to eat the grilled cheese sandwiches that Cleo had fixed for dinner. Billy did that thing with his eyes and eyebrows, looking at me with a sly expression that managed to say Cleo was up to something he thought was silly but he wasn't saying anything.

"What's a consciousness-raising meeting?" I asked.

Cleo poured milk for all of us and then put the milk carton away. I loved milk, but she never let me have more than a glass with dinner. Milk was expensive.

"It's where a bunch of chicks get together and talk about how bad men are," Billy said.

"That is not true," Cleo said. "You of all people should understand women's desire for equality."

"I do understand it, darling. I do. It's just that I think the war and racism are more important issues right now," he said. Cleo deposited the sandwiches on our plates with a spatula and then walked briskly back into the bedroom. She came out, draping a shawl over her shoulders.

"If women were truly equal, there would *be* no war," she said.

"Can I come?" I asked with a mouthful of grilled cheese.

"Really?" she said. "You want to?"

"Yeah," I answered.

Billy's lips were pursed as if he was about to say something but then changed his mind. Instead he abruptly changed the subject.

"You know who Timothy Leary is?" he asked, pouring some Lay's potato chips into a bowl.

I shook my head.

"A former professor at Harvard. They fired him for using LSD," he said.

"He didn't just use it," Cleo said. Clearly she didn't approve of this man. "He promoted its use to everyone, including students."

"What about him?" I asked.

"He just escaped from a prison in California with the help of some friends of mine," Billy said.

"Why was he in prison?"

"Marijuana," Billy said.

At the moment Turtle started singing "Mary had a Little Lamb."

"Shush, Turtle," I said. "Where's he going to go?"

Billy shrugged. "Cuba, maybe. Algeria."

"As long as he doesn't show up here," Cleo said.

Turtle continued singing, and Billy held a fork in front of the kid's mouth as if it were a microphone.

"Sing it, Turtle," he said, laughing.

It scared me that Billy knew the people who had helped someone escape from prison.

"You'll have a great career in opera," I told Turtle, which made Jake laugh and spit milk all over the table. Jake found everything funny even if he didn't understand why he was laughing.

"Are you ready?" Cleo asked me. "JoAnne is picking us up."

I bolted down the rest of my grilled cheese and the milk, wiped my face and got up. Cleo kissed the boys and Billy.

"We won't be late," she said.

"Don't run off with a lesbo," Billy said.

Cleo's eyes narrowed. "Why do men equate feminism with lesbianism?"

"Because you got to admit a lot of them are man haters."

"With good reason," Cleo said and turned her back on him. We walked outside and waited for JoAnne.

JoAnne drove. Janet sat in the front passenger seat, and I sat in the back between Cleo and a big-breasted woman named Nancy. Everyone was talking all at once it seemed, and the conversation revolved around one topic—sex. I didn't have anything to add, but I sure did listen.

"We balled for three days straight," Nancy said, laughing, her peppermint breath wafting across my face. "God, I was so sore I swear I couldn't walk."

"Use K-Y jelly," Cleo advised. "Your labia skin is very tender. You need to keep it lubricated."

Nancy asked, "Is it true that men like their balls licked?"

Janet cracked up, and I thought I would choke I started coughing so hard.

"Are you a virgin?" Nancy asked me.

I hesitated. I was so embarrassed already I wanted to wither to the floor, but I finally said, "Yes."

JoAnne interrupted the conversation. "Why is it that we're talking about sex? Why can't women get together and have an intellectual discussion?"

"Because we've been repressed for too long, JoAnne," Nancy said. "Men talk about sex all the time. Men sleep with whoever they want to. They're admired for their prowess, but if a woman wants to have sex with different men, then she's a slut."

Cleo put her two cents in: "We need to stop being ashamed of our bodies. We need to be able to talk about anything and everything, including sex."

"Yes," JoAnne said, "but how about not limiting it to sex. How about talking about equal pay, equal opportunities, exploitation, rape, domestic violence."

"We'll talk about those things at the meeting," Nancy said.

"Well, all I can say," Janet said, "is who cares if men like their balls licked. It's time for them to do the licking."

They all burst out laughing. Lick what, I wondered.

The meeting was held in the living room of a nicely furnished house, which was owned by two women. I figured they were the "lesbos" that Billy was worried about. Their house was filled with books, real art hung on the walls, and it smelled clean and childless. They definitely weren't hippies.

The talk centered around the fact that there were no "women's studies" courses at the local universities, whether the issues they were concerned about were also issues that Black women had, and about various stories of injustices that each of the women had experienced.

"It's worse in the Movement," JoAnne complained. "Women's opinions are discounted and devalued. These men are supposed to be progressive, but only when it comes to their causes."

JoAnne turned to Cleo and asked, "Honey, why don't you go back to college? I know that you want to."

Cleo pulled herself up straight and said, "Well, I will when the boys are a little older."

"That's right. You, as the mother, have to stay home, don't you?" Nancy asked.

Cleo stammered.

"But Billy has a job."

"So what?" JoAnne said. "His schedule is flexible. Cleo, don't wait too long. Don't put your life on hold forever."

I was stunned by the turn of the conversation. I never dreamed that Cleo might want to go back and finish college. She seemed so happy being a mom and a wife and doing her work for the La Leche League. She looked down at her sandals and didn't say anything. I felt sad for her.

"I can babysit more often," I said, "if you want to go back to school."

The rest of the women erupted in cheers and one of the "lesbos" kissed me on the cheek, which made me feel wonderful. I was glad I had come to this meeting and met these women. For a second I wondered about my mother. If she was alive, was she somewhere in a meeting like this? Talking to other women about equality? Maybe she was telling them to abandon their children. And maybe that had been the right thing for her. Cleo laughed. Without the boys hanging on her, she looked like a teenager.

20

*7*he weather changed. Mornings were brisk, afternoons balmy, and nights downright chilly. Billy and his friends were planning a big demonstration against the war. Several of the ringleaders congregated over at the house one Saturday night: Jeremiah, of course; Mike and Janet, Stump and JoAnne.

While they were hatching plans in the living room, I was in the kitchen, eating a piece of carrot cake that Cleo had made. I loved food and couldn't get enough sweets. I would have eaten the whole cake if she'd let me, but Cleo kept a close watch on food consumption in that house, and I was always just a little bit hungry. Stump came in and searched the refrigerator for a beer.

"How ya' doin'?" he asked. "You coming to the protest?"

I shrugged my shoulders. "Probably not." After my experiences in the Augusta riot, I wasn't that interested in mob scenes.

Stump maneuvered himself into the chair across from me. He generally wore a metal prosthesis, but today he was on crutches instead. He opened the can of beer, throwing the pop-top on the table. I broke off the tab and slipped the ring on my finger.

"Now, we're married," Stump said with a laugh. I laughed, too.

Then I asked him a question that I'd been wanting to ask ever since I met him.

"What was it like? In Vietnam, I mean?"

Stump took a long slug from the beer and then wiped his mouth with his hand.

"Here's a tip for how to make your own luck, kid. When your government comes to you singing 'My Country Tis of Thee' and waving those pretty stars and stripes in your face and tells you to come be a hero, saying you gotta go halfway across the planet – 9,000 miles – and kill people you don't even know, you tell them to kiss your ass. 'Cause even if your ass winds up in jail for a few years, you will still have more luck than those sumbitches over there. If you listen to them, then the rest of your life you'll have the stink of blood on you. And that stink draws bad luck. Don't go. No matter what. No matter how bad they say it will be if you don't go, it will be worse if you do. If you go, then it's always with you, always. Ever wonder why guys don't talk about the war. Even the guys been back a few years like me? They can't make their tongues do it. The tongue is too thick in the mouth, swells up with blood. Think about that." He closed his eyes and took another swig of beer.

I didn't say anything. Stump wasn't much of a talker, and yet he had damn near delivered a Shakespearean monologue. Jo-Anne's voice called from the living room, "Stump, honey, come on and help us get this thing figured out."

Stump winked at me and pulled himself up on his crutches.

"Duty calls. Remember what I told you."

"I will," I said. "I won't ever forget it. Thank you."

I thought about Wolfgang, surrounded by the stink of blood, and I wanted to weep.

After they left I went into the living room where Billy kept the little stereo and a stack of records. I put on Jefferson Airplane's *Surrealistic Pillow* and lay down on the carpet, looking up at the white ceiling. Grace Slick's voice washed over me and I fell down Alice's rabbit hole.

21

Like all high schools, Webster Groves had its various cliques and tribes, and I had to decide which one I wanted to try to infiltrate. A girl named Martha Lyons had befriended me early on in gym class, but she soon realized I didn't fit the profile of a Lyons' groupie. She was like the girls I knew back in Augusta, the ones I called the 'nail polish girls' since they started dolling themselves up in the fourth grade. Martha was rich, a judge's daughter, and she liked to have an entourage, but I couldn't be obsequious enough to join.

The brainy kids seemed kind of boring. The sports enthusiasts were definitely not my crowd. That left the freaks and hairies. But I was too shy to talk to them. Since I had no one to eat with, I never saw the inside of the cafeteria. Rather I brought an apple or some other snack to the courtyard every day and that was my lunch.

I'd been at the school for more than a month. As usual, I sat on the wall by myself, eating my apple, during lunch. I observed the cool kids, hanging out in the smoking section. In Augusta there had been no "smoking courtyard." In fact, girls caught smoking in the bathroom were regularly suspended. Here, no one seemed to care. I wished that I liked smoking.

These kids were so wrapped up in each other they didn't even know I was there breathing their smoky air. I suppose I could have bummed a cigarette from someone but then what do you say? Maybe this would be just like Augusta. I just wouldn't have friends my own age.

But on this day the kaleidoscope of my life shifted. As I tossed my apple core into the trash, I locked eyes with one of the more popular guys. You could say he was "stocky" but that implies muscles, and this guy had a teddy-bear physique, thick curly hair that hung in his eyes, and a sheepish, mischievous smile. The other kids seemed to like him. From what I could tell, he was a bit of a class clown. I wandered back to my wall.

"Nice earrings. Smoke much?" I looked up and there he was, the teddy bear, looking at me with bulging hazel eyes. I thought he meant cigarettes, so I played it off, saying, "I'm trying to quit."

He tilted his head and looked perplexed.

"Why?" he asked.

I scratched my ankle and tried to think of an answer. Then I realized he didn't mean cigarettes. He had noticed the earrings. The roach clip earrings that Cleo had taught me how to make.

"Oh, you mean . . ." I touched the earrings and grinned.

"Yeah, now you get my drift," he said with a grin. "My buddy Todd's got a doobie. Want to come out to the tree with us and enjoy the pause that refreshes?"

I giggled.

"Sure," I said. Wolfgang's misgivings aside, it was time for me to start acting like every other American kid who had the tiniest shred of cool. After all, even my own dad smoked pot. I'd seen a few drunks in my time. Pot provided a mellow high. It was the love grass that Steppenwolf extolled, the green-leaf symbol of freedom, defiance, nonconformity and independence of mind. Also, it made you laugh a lot.

My new friend had puppy dog eyes, and his lips sidled into

a near constant grin. I hitched my leather purse over my shoulder and walked with him out of the courtyard and along the back of the building. The other kids glanced at us as if seeing me for the first time.

"Where's your buddy?" I asked.

"He'll be here," he said. Then he stuck out his hand and said, "I'm Dave."

"Eli," I said. "Eli Burnes."

"Cool name."

"Thanks."

"Hey," a voice called out. Dave and I turned around. A thin, red-haired boy came loping toward us.

"Hey," he said to me.

"Hey," I answered.

"You're the new chick," he said. "I'm Todd."

"Her name is Eli," Dave leaned forward and said.

"Oh," Todd nodded. "You know, all the guys have been asking who the cute new chick is. No one knows you."

I was stunned. No one had ever called me "cute" before. I managed to stammer, "I'm from Georgia." I didn't add, *where everyone thinks I'm flat chested and ugly.*

"Damn. All the way from Georgia?" Dave said in a pseudo-southern accent. "Hotlanta?"

"Augusta. But I was born in England," I said, imitating a British accent.

"Really?" Todd asked.

"No," I said. "I just say that sometimes because my grandmother was British. Actually, my step-grandmother. She raised me. It makes me sound more interesting."

Dave looked at me with a grin and said, "Don't worry,

you're plenty interesting."

"Why are you living here now?" Todd asked.

"Came to live with my dad. She died. My step-grand-mother, I mean."

"Bummer," Dave said. "But we're glad you're here."

We started walking again. An autumny glaze shined the air as we climbed a small hill up to a bright green playing field. An enormous elm tree threw a shadow over the closest corner. That, I gathered, was "the tree."

We glanced around and saw that no one was spying on us. So we headed toward the tree where we positioned ourselves so we could be half hidden in order to smoke the doobie and watch the school at the same time. It wasn't really that I wanted to get high. But I did want to become friends with these two guys, who had fun oozing out of them. I took a hit off the joint, and I was no longer the lone stranger.

"Okay, here's the best part," Dave said after we'd finished the joint. He led us to a water fountain. "Fill up your mouth with water, and then we see who can hold it the longest without laughing."

I lost. The water burst from my lips and hit Dave square in the chest. I couldn't remember laughing that hard in my life. They didn't last much longer, and I got drenched.

When I got home that afternoon, an unfamiliar Volkswagen Beetle was parked in the yard. People were always coming over to hang out with Billy and Cleo so I didn't think much of it. It might have been one of Cleo's La Leche friends. Inside I found the boys on their bellies in front of the TV set, watching PBS. Turtle looked like a miniature version of Jake.

"Hey, little dudes," I said. Their brains were locked by

some kind of tractor beam emanating from the television, and they were unable to respond.

I heard voices in the kitchen, so I headed that way, hoping for an after-school snack that sometimes awaited me, if the boys hadn't scarfed everything like locusts. If there was nothing to eat, I'd have to go down to the IGA and get a Three Musketeers Bar, which I'd been able to eat again after my illustrious New York boosting career.

Cleo leaned against the kitchen sink, arms crossed. Billy sat at the table and there was Sassy and some guy with his back to me. Sassy jumped up and hugged me.

"Hi," she said and smiled enormously at me. "Hi, hi. hi."

"Hi yourself," I said, hugging her back. "What are you doing here?"

"I'm on my way to 'Frisco. Did you see my car? Isn't it cute? Frank's gonna stay here in the Midwest. Lots of people needing to go underground these days. This is a good stopping-off point."

Sure enough, the guy at the table with his back to me was Frank with short hair and wearing a button down white shirt.

"Hey, Frank," I said.

"Hey there, kid," Frank smiled at me. "I'm *incognito*."

"*Incognito?* What's that?"

"In disguise. He has to look straight these days," Billy said.

Seeing Frank reminded me of James and Val and David. I asked Frank what had happened to them.

Frank shook his head.

"James got 25 years in the penitentiary," he said with a shrug. "They pinned some bank robberies on him."

"Oh," I said, stunned.

"But Val's okay. She's running a day care center. No one knows what happened to David."

I tried to fit this information about James with what I had seen in New York. Granted I hadn't known him long, but he just didn't seem like the type of person to go out and rob a bank.

"Did he really rob a bank?"

"James' only crime was being a Black man who didn't want to be doormat," Frank said.

Cleo had her arm around Billy as if she instinctually knew a threat. But there was something else going on with Cleo. Her smile looked like it had been pinned on her face.

"We read about the courthouse bombing in Long Island City," Cleo said in a tight voice. "I would have thought after those kids blew themselves up in that New York apartment, you people would stop bombing buildings."

"Has America stopped bombing villagers in Southeast Asia?" Frank asked.

"No one was hurt," Sassy said.

Cleo started putting away dishes.

"So, Frank, you've got a place to stay?" Billy asked. "You can always crash on the couch."

"Jeremiah's coming to get me," Frank said. Then he leaned in confidentially to Billy and said in a lower voice, "I know how important you are to the leadership, man. Everyone speaks highly of you."

There was something in Frank's eyes and Billy's set of his mouth that told me things were being unsaid. Sassy hugged me once again and hugged Billy and then hugged Cleo. She was soon in her Bug and on the road.

Frank and Billy shot the shit for awhile, and I went downstairs to do my homework. I was still a little high from the pot and from the fact that I actually had found a couple of friends. Dave and Todd *felt* like friends at any rate.

"Where's Frank?" I asked after dinner while I helped Cleo clean up. The boys were in the living room watching TV. "He sure looks different. All straight-arrow."

"Jeremiah took him to stay at his place," Billy said, drinking his coffee, "and he has to look straight. He's looking for a new safe house for some of our friends who happen to be on the run."

"I don't like it," Cleo said. She put the leftovers in the fridge. I poured Ivory dish soap into the dish pan.

"No need for you to worry, sweetie."

"I know that you help those people. You can't hide it from me," she said. "It's dangerous. I wish you wouldn't do it."

She scraped off the boys' plates and handed them to me.

"I just do what I can to keep people from spending their lives in prison or getting killed for doing the right thing," he said.

"They won't get killed," she said. "They have rich parents. They might serve a few months in jail. That's all."

"You don't know that," Billy said. "Look what happened to Freddy Hampton in Chicago. Feds busted in and shot him while he slept next to his pregnant girlfriend."

"I'll admit, Black activists sometimes get killed, but most of these Weather Underground fugitives are the sons and daughters of rich white people." I remembered once again the man I had seen shot by the police in Augusta, and I knew that Cleo was right.

Cleo went into the living room and turned off the television. "Eli, can you make sure the boys take their baths tonight? I have a headache."

I got the boys undressed and into the tub. They each had rubber duckies, and, of course, the duckies had to do battle, and water had to get all over the floor. I couldn't stop thinking of the man who had been shot while his pregnant girlfriend lay next to him. What had happened to her, I wondered, and her baby? Was he in a bathtub somewhere, playing with a rubber duckie, and did his mother have a headache that had never gone away since the night the father of her child had been murdered next to her?

22

$\mathcal{B}$y November, I was hanging out with Dave and Todd nearly every day. They were fascinated with my stories of running away with a draft dodger and hearing Jimi Hendrix play. I just wished I had a girlfriend, too, like I'd had in Gretchen, to complete the picture.

We'd just finished our cream sodas at the Squeeze. The real name was the Velvet Freeze. Dave had dubbed it the Squeeze. All the cool kids went there after school. I had eyed them enviously for the first few weeks of my non-existence at Webster Groves High School, and now here I was, doing something so mid-western – hanging out in an ice cream parlor – so unlike my strange sequestered life with Mattie back home in Augusta.

It got dark earlier these days, and I was eager to get home, take off my boots, and sprawl on the floor by the stereo and listen to King Crimson, imagining life in his court. As I walked through the parking lot, I glanced up and noticed a girl on the other side of the street. Skinny as a praying mantis, she had a long sheath of platinum blond hair hanging halfway down her back. She wore light blue jeans and a jean jacket. I stopped and stared at her, she was such an unusual looking creature. At that moment Martha Lyons came walking alongside me.

"That girl is a skank," she said and kept walking.

Martha Lyons seemed to be the type of person whose life was scripted out for her. She would never have to ad-lib a moment of it. If she thought the platinum-blond girl was a skank, then probably the platinum-blond girl was a fascinating and worthy companion. But I had never seen her before so she probably didn't even go to our school.

At home Billy and his friends were freaking out because three members of the Weathermen were now on the FBI's Most Wanted List. What I found interesting about this news was that they were all three female. Three chicks on the FBI's Most Wanted List. I wondered if Billy was helping them in any way, but I knew better than to ask.

Friday Dave and Todd and some of the long-hairs from school decided to play a game of football.

"You wanna play?" Dave asked me.

I shook my head. I had played tackle loco back home, but that was just a free-for-all for kids.

"I'll come and be the cheerleader," I said. We all got a good laugh out of that.

"You can wave a joint and be like *don't hurt 'em, team. Don't hurt 'em.*" Todd said. So then we started making up stoner cheers and amused ourselves all the way to the field.

"W-E-E-D! What's that spell? Weed! What's that spell? ... Uh, I forget."

Or

"Two, four, six, eight. Why the hell am I doing math?"

We thought we were funny enough to be on the *Johnny Carson Show*.

Through my association with Dave and Todd, I had gained acceptance into the cool kids' crowd. They were pretty nice overall. Not like Martha Lyons and her posse, who were always talking about someone behind their back. *She fucks like a fish,* Martha said about one chick, and I had wondered if fish were especially promiscuous.

I sat on the bleachers enjoying the chilly air, my arms wrapped in a big sweater, Dave's jacket over my knees, when a girl came loping up and sat down beside me. I looked over at her matchstick legs and the white-blond blanket of hair — the girl I had seen walking down the street a few days earlier.

"What's happening, Toots?" she said.

"Not much, Jellybean," I answered.

And that pretty much settled the whole matter.

Jellybean went to a private school, but she didn't like the kids there, so we started hanging out after school and on weekends. Dave and Todd liked her, too. She was a comfortable addition to our group. My life felt just about perfect. I had three of the best friends I could imagine. A lot of girls at school were already locked into steady relationships with guys, but that was the last thing I wanted. Or at least, that's what I thought.

One Sunday afternoon Jellybean and I thumbed out to Forest Park. Hippies still flocked there to gather and flaunt their freedom. The guys with their bushy hair wandered around shirtless, flinging Frisbees into the sky, and the women lounged on the grasses or danced, their long hair flying about like so many silk scarves. And everyone shared—their blankets, their pot, their music and laughter. Jellybean and I strolled among the tribe, breathing in the fragile moments, sweet as maple syrup. Jellybean ran into a guy she liked, and we got involved in a Frisbee game with him and some of his friends. After the game Jellybean sat down in the grass with the guys, and I wandered around by myself. I grew thirsty and headed toward the stone pavilion to find a water fountain. I ascended the long granite steps of a Parthenon-like building, feeling like the Goddess Athena, and saw the water fountain across the court. I walked toward it. A thin, tall figure leaned against the wall. His head was turned the other way but as I got closer, he looked over and we saw each other.

We stared. A smile pushed its way across my lips. A floppy suede hat topped his six-foot frame, and under it he had a bushy afro. He had light-brown skin and deep thoughtful eyes. As I got to the water fountain, he reached over and turned the handle for me. I leaned forward, holding my hair back with my hand, gazing into his eyes for a moment before I looked down at the clear fluid rising toward my lips. It twisted and reflected and caught the contours of the chrome spout like a Dali painting. I bent my face closer and closer until the cool water splashed against my lips and rushed over my tongue, gathering in my mouth before I swallowed. Patchouli oil wafted from his hand. I stood up, drops of water clinging to my lips, and said, "Thanks."

He smiled. I turned and walked away.

23

St. Louis is a pretty big place, but when you're destined to fall in love, it doesn't matter what kind of odds are against you. The next time floppy hat and I saw each other was December tenth at a Moody Blues Concert at the Arena. Jellybean, Todd, and Dave, and I had the worst possible seats in the house, the nosebleed section.

We watched the tiny figures on the stage below and wished we were high in the other sense of the word. For some reason no one had any pot. The second song was one of my faves, "Tuesday Afternoon." Dave finally bummed a joint from someone next to us. The band had just started "Melancholy Man" — another one that I absolutely loved — when I realized I had to pee bad. Thus began the long trek down to the lower level. I found the bathroom. A girl was vomiting in one of the stalls.

"You okay?" I called to her.

"Yeah," she said. "I just did too many 'shrooms."

"Okay," I said. "Far-out."

I came out of the bathroom, wiping my hands on my jeans because the paper towel dispensers were empty when I saw him walking toward me, as if he'd been looking just for me.

"Hi," he said with a slow grin. I said hi back.

"Where you sittin'?" he wanted to know.

"Nowhere," I said, which was stupid, but I didn't want to admit that we were in the worst seats possible.

"Come sit with me," he said. He took my hand and led

me down to the seats in the second row of the orchestra section. About five of his friends were sitting there, and they all watched me silently.

"Where will I sit?" I asked.

"Right here," he said, patting his legs. I lowered myself onto his lap, leaned back against his silky shirt, felt the heat of his chest against my back, and knew I would never hear "Nights in White Satin" like that again for as long as I lived. The music rolled across us like ocean waves.

"So where do you live?" he asked after the concert. We were standing in the refreshment zone, waiting for one of his friends to come out of the bathroom. I needed to find Jellybean and the guys.

"Webster Groves."

"Hey, that's where our shop is. Come by and see me."

"What shop?"

"The headshop where I work. All of us work there," he said, nodding to the group of guys behind him. "Have you seen it? We just opened a couple weeks ago. It's called Illuminations. How do you think we got second-row seats?"

"I know the place you mean. On Old Orchard, right? I haven't been in yet." At school I had heard talk about the head shop. The freaks were in awe of the water pipe collection.

"Well, come and see me. Okay?"

"Okay," I said, just as Jellybean came storming up to me.

"Where have you been?" she said in an exasperated voice.

The guy from the headshop was already walking off.

"Wait a minute," I called. He turned and looked at me. "What's your name?"

"Zen," he said.

"I'm Eli," I answered.

He smiled. Then the crowd pushed between us, and he was gone.

"I'm in love," I said to Jellybean.

"You do know he's Black, right?" Jellybean asked.

"Yeah," I said. I had noticed his beautiful brown skin.

"He's cute," Jellybean admitted.

"He's beautiful," I said.

When I came home that night, I was surprised to find someone sleeping on the couch in the living room. All I could see was a head full of dark hair and a body encased in a blanket. I tiptoed past and went downstairs to dream of nights in white satin.

24

I walked along Big Bend to Old Orchard, a little section of Webster Groves that I guess was once an orchard of some kind and now was lined with shops and restaurants. Illuminations was in a brick building on the left hand side of the street. When I walked into the headshop, a little bell tinkled. The aroma of incense spread over every inch of the place. I turned around in a circle like Alice when she falls into Wonderland. Posters and black lights on the walls, glass cases filled with various styles of water pipes and beaded necklaces and earrings and tie-dyed clothing and everything the aspiring hippie could ever desire. I felt as if I were seeing color for the first time.

Zen leaned his elbows on the counter and smiled at me.

"Eli," he said.

I floated over to him. I don't remember what we said. It was nonsense, but I gave him my phone number, and he said he would call. Then he handed me a peace sign on a silver chain and wouldn't take any money for it.

"It's a present," he said, dropping it into my palm.

When our hands touched, the bell on the door rang to indicate someone had entered. It was magical. It was first love. I'd had a crush on Wolfgang, but that was a little kid thing compared to this. I swore to myself I would never take off that peace sign necklace.

Zen called every night before eight because Cleo said I couldn't talk on the phone after eight. I didn't mind. There hadn't been any rules with Mattie, but having a few rules made me feel like I was a regular kid. Zen went to a different school from me. He told me that Jimi Hendrix was his idol, and he was dumbstruck when I mentioned that I'd actually seen Hendrix play. Hendrix had ODed in September, and Zen couldn't get over the fact he would never get to hear him play live.

"You wanna go out with me?" he asked.

"Like on a date?" I asked. I'd never been on a date.

"Yeah."

When I told Billy and Cleo, I was going to the movies with a boy, Billy looked at Cleo for guidance. He had no idea what to say.

"Okay," Cleo said, trying to be an authority figure, "but you need to be home by eleven."

"But the movie doesn't start till midnight," I said. "They're called the Midnight Flicks."

Cleo sighed.

"Then come home as soon as the movie is over," Billy said. I mean the fact that I'd been out in the world for a month on my own meant they were sort of late when it came to imposing curfews.

"Why are they called flicks?" Cleo asked.

"In the old days movies used to flicker because filmmakers hadn't yet figured out they needed to be shown at 24 frames per second in order to create persistence of vision," Billy explained. He never graduated from college, but he was the smartest person I knew besides Jeremiah.

1 went to Illuminations after school to tell Zen I could go to the midnight flick with him. He went to the clothing rack and

pulled off a slinky black shirt with tiny buttons going about half-way down the front.

"Wear this," he said. "You'll look foxy. I mean, you're foxy anyway, but this will look really good on you."

I thought my heart would erupt from my chest. He'd said I was foxy!

"I can't afford it," I said.

"It's an early Christmas present," he said.

I stood in the bathroom trying to hold my hand steady as I applied a black line to my eyelids. Jake stood on the toilet seat, watching me. I could smell his milky breath. Turtle sat on the floor and hummed.

Cleo suddenly appeared at the door.

"He's here, Eli," she said in a whisper. "He's a Black guy."

I glanced over at her, holding the eyeliner brush in my hand.

"I know that," I said.

She grinned, raised a fist, and said, "Power to the people."

I grinned back. How lucky I was. In Augusta, the color of his skin would have meant a burning cross in the yard. But in the world of Billy and Cleo, it was a trivial, but interesting, detail.

Zen was 17, but his friends from the head shop were older. I stayed mute around them, relying on my instincts to hide my ignorance. I wasn't sure how I had gone from a homely flat-chested girl trapped in a jungle gym to being with the most audaciously gorgeous dude alive.

We saw *Easy Rider* in an old movie theater sitting in front of Zen's boss, Gordon, and his girlfriend, Zen's arm draped over my shoulder. His boss and co-workers eyed me with amused tolerance. They had no idea that I had hung around adults most of my life. To them I was just a school girl with a crush, and they thought it was cute. I did not enlighten them.

Zen wanted to go out again the next Friday night but I had to babysit.

"I'll come over there then," he said.

I didn't mention to Cleo and Billy that Zen was coming over. They might not have cared, but I couldn't take the chance that they would say no. So about a half hour after I got the boys in bed, Zen showed up at the door.

My dad had this strange paisley couch. He had sawed the legs off it and so it was a long drop down. Zen's lanky body folded up like a grasshopper as he sat. I went to the kitchen and brought out a couple of milkshakes and sat next to him. It was the first time we were actually alone.

"So," he said, licking chocolate ice cream from his lips, "what was it like living in Georgia?"

"Weird, I guess," I said.

Then for some reason, nervousness maybe, I began to tell him all about Mattie and Miz Johnny and the operas and even the riots. Memories thronged through me, each one leading to another when suddenly Zen leaned over and planted a kiss on my lips. I was so startled I knocked over the chocolate milkshake. But the kiss continued and drained every memory down, down, and away. Then a small but insistent voice broke through the spell. I pulled away from the lip lock and looked up. Jake stood there with his feet in the chocolate milkshake, telling me he had gone pee-pee in his bed. Zen peeled himself off me.

"I guess I better go," he said. We said good-bye about 37 times and then finally he was gone, and there was milkshake all over the floor, and I didn't even mind changing and washing the sheets and I promised Jake I wouldn't tell his mother ever. And he promised he wouldn't tell on me either.

"God damn it!" Billy said at breakfast the next morning. He was reading the *St. Louis Post Dispatch*. Fortunately, the boys were in the living room watching cartoons or Cleo would have knocked him in the head with one of her wooden spoons.

"What is it?" I asked.

Billy pointed to an article in the paper.

"They arrested Judith," he said.

"Whose Judith?" I asked, but then I remembered the sleeping body on the couch. "Wait? Was she here?"

Billy nodded.

"What did she do?" I asked.

"Nothing really. The indictment is for 'mob action,'" he said. "She was in Chicago during the so-called Days of Rage. They arrested hundreds of people."

"Then how can they arrest her now?" I asked.

"She jumped bail," he said. "They're trying to kill the Movement, and they're closing in on everyone." He frowned, and his eyebrows furrowed.

I took his hand. He was smart. He wasn't involved in any bombings. I believed he would be okay. I hoped he would be okay.

Cinnamon Girl

25

*C*hristmas came. I had made some money babysitting the boys and I spent it all on presents for them. Billy said not to get anything for him and Cleo, but I did spend the day before Christmas cleaning the bathroom, and that made Cleo happy. I'd also purchased a brass incense burner on sale at Illuminations for Billy. Billy gave me a stack of used books wrapped up in a black ribbon, Cleo gave me some of her prized concert t-shirts from back when she 'had a life,' and I couldn't have been happier.

I remembered the Christmas dinners with Mattie when all her "orphans" would come over to feast and sing around the piano. Billy's friends were scarce on Christmas, but Jeremiah did come by with some hashish brownies for Billy and Cleo and some regular brownies for me and the boys. Zen had to visit his grandparents so I didn't see him, which was good as I had no idea what to get him for Christmas. I mean we'd only known each for a couple of weeks.

On New Year's day, Zen picked me up and took me to a party at his boss's house in a rundown neighborhood called Lafayette Park. The neighborhood looked like a surreal slum with big, once-handsome houses now boarded up and covered with graffiti. Gordon's house was a large two-story square. It had obviously once been a mansion with large rooms, high ceilings and a gorgeous staircase. Gordon had fixed it up into a showpiece.

"This used to be the most fashionable neighborhood in the city," Gordon said when he saw me admiring the molding around the ceiling. "I got this place for fifteen thousand dollars."

That sounded like a ton of money to me, but by the way Gordon smirked I figured he'd gotten a bargain.

"Most people think this neighborhood will never come back," Gordon said. "They're wrong."

The party was kind of boring. People sat around, drinking wine. A bong was passed around. Emerson, Lake, and Palmer's prog rock came out of the speakers. I found a cache of *Rolling Stone* magazines and parked myself in the den.

After the party, we drove to Forest Park. I still had an hour before I had to get home. It was cold out. I jumped out of the car and ran across the field. I felt alive, alive, alive—air licking me, the sky stretching blue-black overhead. A shock of white moon dangled above us.

And then Zen caught me. I sank to the ground. He lay on top of me, the sides of his fringed suede jacket hanging to either side like the wings of a hawk. My bones sang; blood rushed through my veins like neon. The sky stretched limitless and black and unknowable above us. I felt the velvet taste of his neck against my lips. Our bodies were pulled together by a force stronger than gravity.

But it was getting late, and Cleo already had her eye on the clock in the kitchen.

"I have to go home," I whispered. We peeled our bodies apart, and walked to his car slowly.

"Will you be my girlfriend?" he asked once we were in the car.

"Yeah. Who else's girlfriend would I be?" I asked with a laugh.

"So we're copacetic," he said.

Cinnamon Girl

"We are copacetic."

Then my boyfriend kissed me and I kissed him back for a long time. When we were done, he turned the key and gunned the engine.

At school word got around that I was going out with one of the guys who worked at Illuminations. My status among the cool kids in the courtyard rocketed. I was still best friends with Dave and Todd, but now the others made a point of including me in their conversations and asking if I wanted to get high after school. Usually I said, no. Like Wolfgang, Zen wasn't much into drugs, and I didn't want him to think I had some kind of problem.

Not everyone admired my new situation. In the locker room after P.E. Martha Lyons and her flock eyed me curiously. Finally, walking between the lockers in her white bra and her gym shorts, Martha Lyons approached me.

"So, I hear you're going out with a Black guy," she said.

I shrugged. I didn't think of Zen as "a Black guy." He was just Zen. Hippies, freaks, whatever you wanted to call us—we were our own race. Not Black, not White. I had grown up in the deep south. In Augusta there was a line, a barrier, a brick wall between Whites and Blacks that would have taken a stronger heart than mine to scale. But I wasn't in Augusta anymore.

"What's it like? I mean, do you kiss him? Aren't his lips really big?"

I turned to Martha with my hands on my hips. I didn't dislike her, but she was definitely showing her ignorance.

"Yes, I kiss him," I said. "It's amazing. His kiss is like drinking a really fine wine. A Beaujolais, say, from 1959."

I was completely bluffing, recalling conversations from

Mattie's dinner table, but since Martha Lyons had never had a fine wine, I knew the right superior tone to invoke, the way to toss it out as if I knew what I was saying, as if it were I who had traveled the world and sung in Italy and Brazil.

"Oh, my," Martha Lyons said, pretending to make fun of me, but she didn't have much else to say after that, and she and her minions went about their business.

26

*O*ne school night I decided to sneak out of the house. Billy was on his shift at the radio station so I made sure Cleo was asleep, and then I closed the basement door and left through the storm door. Zen was waiting for me in the backyard. We climbed over the fence and strolled through the neighbor's yard in the moonlight. He had left his car a couple blocks away.

"Give me a piggy back ride," I said.

He was so tall, I had to leap up to get on his back. I draped my arms over his shoulders and smelled the scent of incense and sweat in his thick hair.

"Have you ever been to the Arch?" Zen asked.

"No," I lied. Once when I first came to live with my dad, he and Cleo had taken me and the boys to the arch. We'd gone up inside it all the way to the top where we could gaze over half the world. I remembered thinking that Mattie with her claustrophobia would have been climbing out of that little tram car like a cat trying to claw its way out of a bath.

"Then let's go," he said.

"Won't it be closed?" I asked.

"Doesn't matter."

He was right. What mattered was that he and I were out together alone in the night, and being with him made me feel happy. I let my fingers crawl across the front seat toward his hand. Our fingers just touched, and we left them like that as he drove along the dark, empty streets into downtown St. Louis toward that sluggish dark vein, the Mississippi River.

As we walked across the park with that totally weird structure looming over us like the metal legs of a giant whose body disappeared into the clouds, Zen started acting the fool, dancing like Fred Astaire and saying, "Ginger, how lovely you look in the moonlight." Pretty soon I was giggling, caught up in the game, twirling and saying, "Oh, Fred, darling, you are simply dashing."

Except for a rumpled bum trying to sleep on a wooden bench and a bored security guard who may or may not have been on duty, we had the place to ourselves.

Once we had stopped dancing and had reverted to our former selves, I asked, "Can you swim in the Mississippi?"

"Hell no, girl," Zen said. "That thing is brown. Water is supposed to be blue, don't you know? You can't swim in brown water. Didn't your momma teach you anything?"

"I don't have a 'momma' to tell me that kind of stuff, Zen," I said, pretending to be hurt, but he knew better, and that's one thing I liked about him. He had no problem translating the language of me.

"Oh, that's right," he said. He pulled me close to him as we walked side by side toward the whispering water. "How about if you let me be your momma? I'll teach you all the things you need to know about life."

"Like what?" I asked with a laugh. We had reached the edge of the park, and I leaned back against the railing that separated us from the wide river, sloshing its way past us. The night sky hung dusty gray-orange over our heads. He pressed close to me. The heat of his body surrounded me like a cloak.

"First of all, I want you to stay away from boys," he said.

"Then you better get off me," I said.

"I said boys, not men."

I laughed again and punched his arm. He pretended that I had broken it.

"And don't have sex," he said, his voice dropping low. "Not until you're at least . . . sixteen."

"You mean, I have to wait . . .?" I asked, letting my fingers rove along his thighs.

Zen looked into my eyes and nodded. "There's a clinic that gives birth control pills to girls as long as they're at least sixteen."

My birthday was in early June. I shivered. I realized if I didn't want to go through with it, I could break up with him before then. And if I didn't break up with him? My arms locked around his waist. His heart thrummed against his rib cage—a tall, skinny boy. I had not known it was possible to feel like this.

"Okay. I'll wait."

Something broke free like a pigeon suddenly fluttering to the sky.

"I better get you home, Cinderella, before your wicked stepmother turns into a pumpkin."

"Cleo isn't wicked, and that's not the way the story goes anyway."

"I know that," he said. "It's Cinderella who turns into the pumpkin."

"You are crazy," I said. We swung hands as we walked back to the car. On the way back to Webster Groves, I laid my head against his shoulder with his arm draped over me and fell asleep.

As usual Jellybean met me, Todd and Dave at the Squeeze where we jammed ourselves into a pink-cushioned booth, pictures of cows and heaping bowls of ice cream painted on the wall. Dave bent over his root beer float and slurped. Jellybean twirled a strand of her long platinum blond hair while Todd tried not to stare at her. Todd may have been the most normal of the four of us, but his crush on Jellybean had nearly debilitated him.

After we'd sat there and methodically tortured and killed the afternoon, Jellybean and I walked to the corner separating poor Webster Groves from rich Webster Groves. I went one way. She went the other.

"See ya, Toots," she called after me. "Don't call me tonight because I'll be busy studying." Then she laughed like a lunatic because Jellybean never studied. Still, somehow she made straight A's.

On weekends, I would wander down to the main street where I'd stick out my thumb and catch a ride to Jellybean's house—a big, brick two-story that reminded me of the house where I had lived with Mattie back in Augusta. If Jellybean was one of the skinniest girls I'd ever known, her mother was the fattest woman. Her mother would waddle from the front door and call upstairs to Jellybean that I had arrived. Jellybean's mother couldn't say anything, not even one word, without Jellybean rolling her eyes and sucking her teeth and muttering something like, "shut up, stupid."

Her mother ignored the muttering or maybe she couldn't hear it. I liked her because she always offered me something to eat—something sweet and unhealthy and, unlike her own daughter who never ate anything from her mother's table, I was a willing recipient of Twinkies and ding dongs and homemade chocolate chip cookies because God knows Cleo wasn't feeding me much.

My friends couldn't get over the fact that my dad had once

been "Bad Billy," whom they'd grown up hearing on their AM radios, or that we lived in a tiny house on a gravel street.

"I thought you'd be millionaires," Dave said the first time he saw the house, peering out of the car window at the gray wood house.

"He works the graveyard shift on FM now," I said. I didn't mention that although they might be famous, radio DJs didn't make all that much money, and Billy was currently supporting a wife and three kids. "Also he hates money. He's always giving it away. To his causes."

"Is he a commie, Eli?" Todd asked.

I shook my head.

"Just because he hates the war and doesn't want to see guys like you get your faces blown off doesn't mean he's a commie," I said, annoyed. Sometimes I was so angry with my dad for being who he was. His shitty old truck embarrassed me, and I wouldn't have minded living in a nicer house. On the other hand, he truly believed the war was evil, racism was wrong, and that most rich people had sold their souls. In my heart I believed he wasn't wrong.

Todd and Dave had the accessories of the hippies, but it was already 1971 and the 60s were over in their minds. They didn't get what the Movement was all about. They were still a couple of years from being draftable and they probably didn't get lectures at their dinner table about the evils of McNamara, Kissinger and Tricky Dick. They probably hadn't heard about LBJ's treachery, didn't know that the Gulf of Tonkin crisis was a big lie and didn't realize that American tire companies were salivating over Vietnam's rubber crops.

I knew more than I'd ever wanted to know and the more I

learned, the more I felt that it felt it was futile to even give a damn.

I usually hung out in Billy's workshop at night while Cleo bathed the boys and tucked them into bed. Ostensibly I was doing homework but really I was sitting there after my allotted 30 minutes on the phone with Zen or Jellybean, looking through my dad's stuff or reading his science fiction books while I rocked to and fro in the big office chair he'd gotten at some garage sale.

There were plenty of interesting things to look at—National Geographics, old records, protest flyers, posters of rock and roll bands from the early 60s—The Beatles, The Shondells, The Supremes. Before things went psychedelic. There were also books of all kinds, including a book called *Siddhartha* that I read, and halfway through I remembered the guy in the turban in Rochester who had mentioned it to me. He had been right in a way. Things turned out okay for me, not so much for Wolfgang though. The last time I talked to Gretchen she said he was in the 12th Infantry Regiment, which had just been in a bad battle, but that he had managed to survive. *Stay alive, Gandalf,* I thought, *please stay alive.*

*Z*en was seventeen and when he came to pick me up on dates, he would stop and listen to my dad for a while, and I could tell he was wondering what he would do if his draft number was low. From his occasional comment, it was obvious he was wondering about career opportunities for headshop clerks in Canada. College deferments were no longer an option. Supposedly the U.S. was withdrawing forces from Vietnam, but that hadn't stopped the body bags.

It was Monday morning, and I was going to be late to school. I wanted breakfast but Cleo and Billy were having an argument in the kitchen. Billy squeezed his fists on the table. His July-green eyes looked like shut doors.

"I'm going, Cleo. We won't lose the damn truck."

"I hope not," she said. "It's not like we can afford to lose it, you know."

"Um, I'm gonna be late to school. Can you drop me off?" I asked Billy.

"Sure," he said.

Billy and I left the house. We got into his rusty blue pick-up truck. A row of rainbow peace symbols lined the bumper and probably held it on to the truck. He had bumper stickers on the gate from the '68 election that Hubert Humphrey lost—probably because his first name was Hubert, which is, I'm sorry to say, even worse than Dick.

Billy pulled his hair into a ponytail and grinned at me.

"Don't go to school today," he said.

"Really?" I asked.

"Come to the demonstration with me," he said.

"On a Monday?"

"This is not the kind of demonstration that can be undertaken on the weekend. About two hundred of us are going to park our vehicles in front of a major corporation that builds weapons for the U.S. military. We're going to block off the exit from the freeway so the workers can't get in," he explained.

"Billy, do you think any of this does any good?" I asked.

"Yes, I do. I know it doesn't look like it. But we are making an impact. Public opinion is turning against the war," he said. "Change takes times. Sometimes centuries. Look how long it took to end slavery. How many people had to die. Blacks in the south are still fighting for equality. But you can't give up. You can't ever give up."

When we got there, there must have already been fifty parked cars, building a metal blockade. Jeremiah hurried over to us. He wore jeans with two long Indian-bead lanyards dangling from his belt loops. Instead of his usual beret, he wore a baseball cap over his stringy gray hair.

"It's like in the Civil War," Jeremiah explained to me. "When the North blockaded the ports of the South."

Frank joined us a few minutes later. Janet and Mike followed. Janet wore a jacket and skirt because she had to go to court later.

"Look who's skipping school," Mike said and tousled my hair.

"She'll get a better education here," Jeremiah said. "Civil disobedience is what Thoreau believed in. Eli, have you read *Walden Pond* yet?"

I shook my head and promised that I would. Someday.

"Have you heard from Sassy?" I asked Frank.

"Yeah, she's in the Haight right now," he said, chewing his Juicy Fruit. His hands were jammed in the pocket of his jeans. His hair had grown longer and he was starting to look like his old self. He glanced at me and while Billy was off passing out protest signs, Frank leaned close and said, "You're growing up, aren't you?"

His eyes lingered on my breasts. My face prickled in embarrassment. I didn't know what to say. Billy returned, and Frank looked away, stroking his mustache.

"You ready to go to jail for the cause?" Frank asked me.

"If I have to," I answered. Which I really hoped wouldn't happen because Zen and I were going to the Grateful Dead concert that weekend.

"She doesn't know any secrets, does she?" Frank asked Billy.

"What secrets?" Billy said. Frank laughed knowingly.

The demonstration felt more like a big party than anything else. Our side was happy. No one was building weapons at this particular plant today. The cops who showed up were friendly. Billy said they were called the Red Squad because they had to be at all the demonstrations. It was as much protection for the demonstrators as anything else, Billy explained to me. He even stopped to talk to them. By now the regular demonstrators and the Red Squad knew each other by name.

"Not all cops are pigs," he said as we drove home. "They've got families, too."

"Since when was that so important to you?" I asked.

"What's that mean, Eli?" he asked. The hurt in his voice surprised me.

"Nothing, Billy," I said. "I didn't mean anything at all."

I decided to change the subject.

"What did Frank mean about secrets?"

Billy sighed. "The way it works is this. I may know something and you may know something, but if I don't know what you know and you don't know what I know then whatever it is we know is safer than if we both know everything. Like say I know half the combination to a safe and you know the other half, then no one can get the full combination from either of us."

"Okay," I said, "so what does that have to do with you?"

"There are some things that I know and only I know. But because I'm just a D.J. in St. Louis with a family no one thinks I know anything."

"Except Frank."

"Yeah, except Frank."

"And Cleo."

"And Cleo."

"And Jeremiah and Janet and Mike and Joanne and Stump."

He laughed. "Well, none of them know what I know, so it's all good."

Later that night I heard voices upstairs. I should have been asleep but I wasn't. I opened the door of my basement room and out of curiosity, sat on the steps, and listened.

"Wait! His tag was too dirty?" Cleo's voice.

"That's what they said." A woman's voice. Janet?

"Then they pushed him and when he tripped and fell, they said he was resisting arrest?" Billy's voice.

"That's what Mike told me, but there were no witnesses." It was definitely Janet's voice. And it sounded like she was crying. "They're going to try to railroad him."

"Isn't there anything you can do? Are you even allowed to defend him?" Cleo's voice.

"A friend of mine will do it, but I'm worried," Janet's voice. "Judge Lyons is the most conservative prick on the bench right now. He will take a bribe, but I don't play that way. They'd love to find a reason to disbar me."

"It's harassment, pure and simple," Billy said.

Judge Lyons? Martha's dad? It didn't surprise me that he was "a conservative prick." But a bribe taker? I suddenly felt sorry for Martha.

I surmised that Janet's husband, Mike, had gotten arrested after the demonstration. America was not the pretty purple-mountained place of my youthful fantasies. It was Mordor. But I was tired, and I had school the next day. And it was hard to have all this stuff in my head and just try to live a normal life, as if I even knew what "normal" meant. I crept down the stairs and went to bed.

27

*T*he Grateful Dead were coming to the Fox Theater. Illuminations, the headshop where Zen worked, had tickets for sale and that meant that Zen and I would be in primo seats. It was a Monday night, but Cleo and Billy said I could go this once. Billy said he wished he could go but he had a shift that night.

"They may or may not get to the concert," he said. "I heard they got arrested in New Orleans and all their equipment impounded."

Cleo let me borrow her white lace peasant blouse which showed off my silver peace sign necklace. She looked at me wistfully as I gazed in the full-length mirror hanging on her closet door.

"God, what I wouldn't give to be young again," she said.

I stared in surprise because she was only nine years older than me. Just then Jake jumped onto her back from the bed and yelled, "Let's go, pony!" and Turtle let loose with an ear-piercing shriek that could split atoms. So I understood what she meant.

"Hey, Cleo," I asked. "What happened to Janet's husband? Did he get sentenced yet?"

"Not yet," she said. I could tell from the look on her face that she was scared. If Janet's husband could get arrested, and she was an attorney, no one was safe.

*Z*en had never looked so beautiful, his smooth brown skin and his fro like a fluffy halo around his head. He wore a purple shirt, blue jean bell bottoms that covered his feet, and a single silver chain around his neck. When he smiled the flash of his large white teeth made me want to swoon.

Cleo practically did somersaults as she offered everything in our kitchen—soda, beer, animal crackers, cereal—anything he wanted. I slid a hand around his silky waist and tugged on him, and in a moment we were out the door and riding to the concert in the back seat of his boss's VW.

"Don't drink the Kool-Aid," Zen advised as we walked through the chandeliered lobby. The glamorous old building made me think of Mattie and how she would have liked to sing in a place like this and probably did back when she was young. As we crossed the red carpeted floors, I gazed up at the enormous dome of the gilt-trimmed ceiling.

Then I asked in a perplexed voice, "What Kool-Aid?"

"The Kool-Aid that's gonna be passed around the auditorium tonight."

"Why not?" I asked.

"It's electric," Gordon wheeled around to inform me.

"Electric?"

"That means, little chick, that you'll be tripping your brains out approximately twenty minutes after your first sip."

"They put acid in it?" I asked, incredulously. "Far out."

Zen gave me a razor glance. He was strictly against alcohol and not fond of drug use either, which I thought was odd since Jimi Hendrix was his idol. Zen was like his name, sort of Jesus-like. I didn't know why I kept getting involved with these guys who didn't like to get high. But Zen was different in a thousand ways. Sometimes when we were alone he would read snippets of the *Tao te Ching* to me. Other times we would devote to my favorite activity: kissing. I could lock lips with Zen for hours, panting in between kisses in the back seat of his mom's Pontiac, our bodies pressed against each other so hard it was as if we were welded together. Zen said the worst thing that could happen to either of us would be for me to get pregnant and looking at Cleo's life I concurred, so we kept our clothes on. But sometimes I felt they'd burn off our bodies from the friction, and we definitely indulged in what Cleo called "petting," his fingers roving up under my shirt. Sometimes I purposely didn't wear a bra so I could feel his hands squeezing my small breasts.

Since the concert was part of St. Louis University's homecoming, the crowd was a weird mix of straight-looking college kids and full-on hippies in thrift-store regalia.

We sat in the ninth row, and after what seemed like hours of music from some other band, called Aorta, which I thought was a pretty awful name for a band, and Frisbees being tossed and lighters being flicked and the hazy aroma of reefer settling over the entire auditorium, the Dead emerged. I guess they'd gotten out of the New Orleans with their equipment, after all. There were six of them. They had long hair, beards, tie-dyed t-shirts and their instruments. The crowd grew quiet and then suddenly the guitarists like pied pipers struck their chords and started singing. At first, it sounded like country music to me, but then it got bluesy, and when they played "St. Stephen," the audience came to life, out of the seats, dancing and waving their arms.

By the time whoever was singing got to the lyric about some chick's finger dripping moonlight, a plastic carton of grape Kool-Aid was passed to me by a laughing barefoot hippie girl. I didn't stop to think. I just raised it to my lips and gulped. Zen was so engrossed in the performance he hadn't seen me do what he

Cinnamon Girl

expressly warned me not to do.

I didn't notice anything until they started "Turn on your Love Light" and then everything turned purple and electric, and I felt a tingling sensation as if all my hair was standing on end.

Since it was a school night, I would have to go home as soon as the concert was over. Zen's crew was staying to party with the band, and I could tell Zen wanted to drop me off and get back there as soon as he could.

As we drove home, snow began to fall. It rarely snowed back where I was from, but this was a full-bodied Midwestern snowstorm. I was amazed at how quiet it was. The earth thrummed. My mind opened like a starfish as the universe flowed freely in and out of my head. I sat in the front seat hypnotized by the enormous snowflakes flying at the windshield in the white glow of street lights.

"You sure are tripping on this snow, Eli," Zen said. My heart lurched as I wondered what he meant by that. I glanced at him but realized he was just talking. He had no idea that when he moved his hand, five thousand hands followed. When we got to the house, I kissed him quickly and said I'd see him later. For once, there'd be no groping in the dark. The idea of making out made me feel clammy and gross. Fortunately, he wanted to get back to the party. I felt guilty for drinking the Kool-Aid and hoped he wouldn't find out and hate me.

Cleo had fallen asleep in front of the Johnny Carson show. The Smothers Brothers were on, and the laughter followed me like a clanking skeleton. The kitchen appliances were breathing as I tiptoed past them to the basement door. Slowly I maneuvered my way down the flight of steps, which seemed to go on as far as the Grand Canyon. My legs stretched down for miles to reach each step. Finally I reached the bottom.

I sank into the papasan chair and tried reading an R. Crumb comic book, but nothing made sense. The walls of the room were breathing. I was afraid I was losing my mind. Heidi's fur grew longer and longer in a disconcerting way. I started to shake. I didn't like this. I didn't like losing control of my mind. What if I went crazy? What if this didn't end?

Then the door opened and I heard footsteps. I jumped up and saw Billy. He looked kind of normal except his face was pink.

"What are you doing here?" I asked.

"I live here," he said.

"But...work," I said.

"I only had to do a half shift. How was the Dead?" he asked.

For a second I thought he was asking how was Mattie, but then I remembered the concert and that jug of Kool-Aid. How I had tipped it to my mouth and gulped.

"They were great, man. It was totally far out. They sang for a long time, and I drank some Kool-Aid and now everything is all weird. And I'm scared shitless."

Billy's pink face was soft and doughy, his voice echoey and strange.

"Wait right here."

Billy returned and opened up an old turntable he kept down there with other old radio equipment. He put on the Beatles *Sgt. Pepper's* album and handed me the cover.

"Sit down," he said. "Look at the cover. You'll be amazed at what you can find in there."

"I can't. I can't sit," I said, pacing around the room.

Billy took my hand and held it. "You'll be fine. I promise

you."

"All these friends of your going to jail. What if something happens to you? What if they put all of us in jail? Zen told me not to drink it, but I did."

Billy talked to me softly and slowly, and finally convinced me to sit down. For hours I sat in the bean bag chair as the secrets of the cosmos, which had somehow been hidden in the cover of *Sgt. Pepper's Lonely Hearts Club Band*, revealed themselves to me in an exotic language that amazingly I understood. My dad sat in the room with me reading comic books as reality wobbled and dissolved and took shape again.

When I woke up, it was almost noon and I was in my bed, still wearing my clothes. I staggered upstairs and found a note from Cleo that said, "Eli, hope you're feeling better. Your dad said he thought you had a stomach flu or something and that you shouldn't go to school today. I'm at the store. Back soon. C."

I dropped the note back on the table and sank into one of the cushioned metal chairs. Sunlight shone on the stones of the patio and a red cardinal with a black mask over his eyes nibbled at some seeds on the ground.

Billy had taken care of me last night. I had needed him, and he had been there for me.

28

If I didn't go out with Zen, I'd usually go riding with Todd and Dave in Todd's old Rambler, and we'd cruise through the Steak 'n Shake. Dave would pretend to be all tough and might yell out the window to someone he knew, "You cruisin' for a bruisin', boy? Packin' for a smackin'?" Then he'd laugh and you'd have to laugh with him because Dave had never been in a fight in his life.

One night the three of us went to Larson Park to have a bottle rocket battle. In spite of the fact that they were major potheads, Todd and Dave were terminally wholesome. So we drove to the park and spread out each with a dozen rockets and created our own version of the Mekong Delta, puncturing the cold night air with sparks of light and the loud cracks of our fireworks. We took off running across the fields, shooting at each other and diving on to the brittle brown grass as we dodged the incoming missiles. I had just reached the shelter of a tree and fired when Todd suddenly yelled, "Shit!"

I ran toward him. The sleeve of his jacket was sparking in a variety of bright colors and Dave was weeping with laughter.

"It's not funny," Todd said, beating his jacket. When I got up to him, I could smell the charred leather. "My dad is going to be so pissed."

"Uh oh," Dave said, glancing toward the parking lot. Just then we heard a whoop, whoop and a voice came over a speaker: "This is the Webster Groves Police. You are violating the law. Come here now." All three of us charged in the other direction like scared rats before he had even gotten to the word "Police."

"Over here," Dave said, pointing to a little knoll. We dove behind it and peered over the edge into the dark.

"Oh man, we're going to jail," Todd said, wiping the sweat from his forehead.

Dave glanced into my eyes, and we both started giggling so hard it was almost painful. Todd, however, was breathing hard and looked like a hunted animal, his thin freckled face pale as a ghost.

"My car," he whimpered. "They'll impound my car."

We digested that thought and all its implications. Finally, Dave heaved a sigh and said, "All right. Let's surrender to the pigs. We can't let you get in trouble by yourself."

So we stood up, brushed the wet grass from our jeans and walked back to the gravel lot where Todd's rambler waited alone. We could see the tail lights of the cop car as it drove away.

Dave puffed himself up and yelled, "And don't come back either, suckers."

Todd got on his knees and kissed the door handle of his beloved old beater. We squeezed into the front seat, me between the two of them on the bench seat with my feet up on the hump. Dave had his window open, gulping the cold air.

"Roll that up, moron," Todd said.

"I'm sorry but your jacket stinks," Dave said, but he rolled up the window. It soon got steamy inside from our breaths. I felt great and was secretly glad that I was out with my friends. It was only later, much later, that I realized how safe we had felt as white kids, even with the police after us. What was the worst thing they would do? Call the parents.

When I got home, I joined Cleo on the low couch to watch

a Tammy movie on TV: *Tammy and the Doctor.* I always loved the Tammy movies though it's not something I'd admit to anyone. Tammy was incredibly naïve, and for some reason I thought I was worldly, so I watched her with a feeling of superiority and no idea of the log in my own eye.

29

I was washing the dishes after supper, and Billy sat at the table, reading *Steal This Book*. Billy chuckled and read aloud: "Free speech is the right to shout 'theater' in a crowded fire."

"Huh?" I said.

"It's backwards, don't you see. The Supreme Court debated whether shouting fire in a crowded theater was considered free speech. But the yippies take those ideas and turn them around completely. They want you to reconsider all ideas. What's right? What's wrong? I mean, we're fed a line of bullshit constantly, so you have to learn to question everything. The publishing establishment won't publish this book, so Abbie Hoffman raised his own money to print it. This copy is hot off the press."

"Oh," I said.

I could hear Cleo in the boys' room, reading "Peter Rabbit." Another revolutionary, I thought, Peter Rabbit stealing from the man.

A knock-knock rattled the window of the back door. I turned and looked at Billy who seemed as perplexed as I was. Who would be coming over on a Wednesday night and why would they come to the back door?

I walked across the kitchen and opened the door. Janet stood on the concrete stoop. She stepped inside. Her hair was pushed up under a baseball cap. She was a bony woman with an always serious expression on her stern face.

"Janet, hi," Billy said. "Dropping by for dessert?"

Janet sat down at the table across from Billy. I sat down at the end between the two of them. The dishes could wait.

"Could I have some coffee?" she asked me.

"Sure." I got up and put the coffee pot on the gas flame.

"How's Mike doing?" Billy asked.

"Okay. We managed to get a new judge. The resisting arrest charge didn't stick, and so he just had to pay a fine."

"That's good," Billy said. "Then why are you here?"

"There's a problem," she said.

Billy leaned his elbows on the table. "What kind of problem?"

She didn't answer right away. She seemed to be thinking, worrying. I poured some coffee into a chipped St. Louis Cardinals mug, placed it on the table in front of her, and sat down.

"Is it all right to talk in front of her?" Janet said, indicating me.

I gave Billy a look that said I wasn't going anywhere. Instead I passed her a spoon and the sugar bowl.

"Yeah, it's okay," he said.

"I have to get a message to Jeremiah," she said.

"What kind of a message?" Billy asked.

Janet shook her head. "I can't say. And I can't deliver it myself. I need to hunker down after this thing with Mike. My phone is tapped. And they're watching me. Right now, Jeremiah seems to be the only one who's safe."

"Maybe I could call him from the radio hotline," Billy suggested.

"No," Janet said. "It has to be delivered to him in person."

"I'm probably as hot as you are," Billy said.

"I can do it," I said.

They both turned toward me in surprise.

"You can't get mixed up in this," Billy said.

"Why not? You want me to care about the war. You want me to care about the Movement. I won't be doing anything dangerous. I'll skip some classes tomorrow and take a bus to Jeremiah's. It'll be easy."

Janet looked at me hopefully. Her face was one of studied composure, but her eyes were bright.

"You're perfect," she said. "No one would suspect you."

"I can do this, Billy," I said.

"No," Billy said.

"Stop being so stubborn, Billy. I'm doing fine in all my classes. And Janet needs me to do this. You get to help people. Why can't I?"

He stared at me. He didn't really have an argument.

"Okay," he said. "Just go there and go right back to school. I'll write a note that says you have a doctor's appointment. And wear something straight-laced. Don't look like a hippy."

I smiled in triumph.

"Trust no one," Janet said as she handed me a sealed envelope. "No one but Jeremiah."

"How do you know you can trust him?" I asked.

"There are a few people – a very few people in the world whose moral center is so firm that it permeates every aspect of their lives. Jeremiah is one of those people," she said, standing up. She shook Billy's hand and then shocked me by reaching out and hugging me.

"Little soldier," she said with a dry laugh and slipped out the back door.

I left school after first period history. I hoped I would make it back in time for geometry. It was the one class I really liked. I had been to Jeremiah's place enough times with Billy that I knew the roads to get there and though I said I would take the bus, it seemed more efficient to thumb over there. I probably looked strange in my white shirt, my navy blue skirt and pumps with my thumb out, but within 45 minutes I was on the corner next to Jeremiah's print shop. I went to the front door, but it was locked and a closed sign hung in the window. I walked around the back of the store to the alleyway where the fire escape led to his apartment. I didn't see his car, but he could have loaned it to someone. Jeremiah had a very loose sense of property.

It was a cool spring morning with a tang in the air. The potholes in the street were filled with puddles from an early morning shower. The windows at the backs of the buildings were barred, and the trash cans full. A tabby cat slunk between the cans. I climbed up the fire escape and knocked on the door. Someone stirred on the other side. I was relieved that I hadn't made the trip for nothing. The curtain was pushed aside, and a pair of eyes glanced out at me. Then the door swung open.

Frank stood in the doorway.

"Hey, kid," he said.

"Hey."

He opened the door wide, and I entered Jeremiah's kitchen.

"Is Jeremiah around?" I asked.

"Nah, he's gone out for a few hours. I'm just hanging out, listening to some music." I followed him into the living room where jazz was playing on the stereo.

The blinds were down in the living room; it was dim and comfortably warm. Records and books were piled on the tables and in the corners. One wall was covered by shelves. Framed black and white photos hung on the other walls. A few throw rugs brightened the room.

I sat down on a worn-looking couch. Frank sat about a foot away from me.

"What brings you over here?" he asked.

"Skipping school. Didn't have anything else to do. I thought I'd see if I could help Jeremiah print up flyers or something."

"Skipping school. Won't you get in trouble?"

"No. My grades are pretty good," I said.

He reached over and lifted a strand of hair that had fallen in my face.

"Pretty girl," he said.

"Thanks," I said.

"That was a bummer about Wolfgang getting nabbed. Do you have a new boyfriend?" he asked.

"Yes," I said.

The record ended, and Frank got up and turned it over.

"Who is this?" I asked.

"Stan Kenton," he answered.

The music had a seductive quality, and I sensed that Frank's intentions were shady. I could have left, but I didn't want to come all the way here and not complete my mission.

"Are you and your boyfriend having sex?" he asked.

I shook my head. "I don't want to get pregnant."

He chuckled.

"There's lots of ways you can please each other without

getting pregnant," he said.

I was silent. Zen and I hadn't done much beside kissing. He'd touched my boobs, but never went below the waistline.

"What do you think when you see a guy with a lump in his Levi's?"

"What?" I asked. It had never even occurred to me to look at a guy's Levi's.

Frank's lips curled up in a look of amusement.

"How about a lesson in sex education? Jeremiah won't be back for another hour at least," he said.

"No thanks," I said.

"I won't hurt you. I won't even touch you. You need to learn a few things about the male anatomy," he said.

Frank went into the bathroom. I wondered what in the hell I had gotten myself into when he walked back out wearing his t-shirt and underwear. There was no one here but the two of us. He pulled out his penis and began stroking it slowly. He knelt down a few feet in front of me. He had a towel draped over his shoulder.

"Unbutton your shirt," he said.

"No," I said.

"That's okay," he said. "I'll use my imagination. You have so much power and you don't even know it."

He began to stroke himself harder and faster. I watched in horror and fascination and then he grunted and clamped the towel over the thing. He sank down to the ground breathing heavily and blinked up at me. "See, you can do this to a guy even just sitting there, doing nothing."

He got up and went into the bathroom. He hadn't touched me, and yet I felt sordid.

When he came out, he grinned and said, "Girls can have

orgasms too, you know."

"I think I'll let my boyfriend teach me that lesson," I said, wishing he would go away.

He leaned over, kissed my forehead, and brushed his hand against my thigh. I jerked my leg away from him.

"He's a lucky guy," he said, leaning closer. "This won't hurt."

I knew I should stop him. I didn't want him touching me, but I was petrified. His hand moved from the outside of my thigh to the inside. Then it moved under my skirt and soon he was rubbing his hand against my underwear. Why couldn't I move? Why was my body betraying me? I felt absolutely powerless.

Footsteps sounded on the metal stairs outside. Frank's hand stopped moving. He pulled my skirt down and stood up. I gazed up at him. He'd won something from me, and I was ashamed. I should have made him stop. What was wrong with me?

"Maybe we'll finish this later?" he said and put his hands in his pockets.

"No, asshole," I said. "We won't."

I looked away, my cheeks blazing.

Jeremiah came in and tilted his head in curiosity when he saw us.

"Hello?" he said.

"Hey, man. I need to borrow your car," Frank said. "Thought you'd never get back."

"Take it, take it," Jeremiah said and tossed him the keys. He turned to me. "Are you with him?"

"No," I said. "You promised you'd show me how to print flyers. I need to make some for school."

After Frank left, I gave Jeremiah the letter, and he gave me a peanut butter sandwich and some juice. I choked down the sandwich as I watched him read the message. His face conveyed nothing. Then he rummaged through a drawer and pulled out a lighter. He opened a window and held the piece of paper by the corner as he set it afire. I watched it disintegrate into ashes and blow away.

He turned to me with a gentle smile. "Are you okay?"

"I'm fine," I said. I stuffed down the guilt and shame of my encounter with Frank and grabbed my book bag. "See ya."

When I got back to school, it was time for dismissal. I had missed geometry. I walked in to Mrs. Martini's classroom. She was just starting to erase the scrawled figures from the blackboard.

"Wait," I said, sitting down in one of the wobbly old desks with curse words gouged over the top and old gum stuck to the bottom. "I want to write down those formulas."

Martini smiled at me.

"I'll go over the lesson with you."

She was the kindest teacher in that school, and for an hour I lost myself in the properties of triangles and spheres and cubes. And I purposely wiped out the earlier lesson of the day.

30

*S*pring arrived like a newborn filly. The hard winter air gave way to softer breezes, and I put away my camel coat.

Saturday night Zen came to pick me up in his mother's old Pontiac for the Jethro Tull Concert. He was early so Cleo invited him in for a pop.

She poured our drinks into colorful aluminum tumblers — a purple one for him and a gold one for me. We sat down at the rectangular kitchen table. Cleo had tried to make the kitchen a homey sort of place with copper decorations on the wall and a ceramic salt-and-pepper set shaped like a chicken and a rooster. A stack of paper napkins was in easy reach. But the cabinets were old and dingy looking and the wallpaper faded. Zen seemed perfectly comfortable. I'd never been to his house, but I don't think their kitchen was any better. His father had lost his job as a bus driver after he had a heart attack and his mom cooked for a school cafeteria.

Cleo had a stack of Ball jars by the stove that she was boiling to sanitize for tomato sauce. Billy came in, dressed in jeans and a t-shirt for his shift at the station. He'd grown a beard and looked like a pirate.

"Zen, my man," he said. He and Zen did the brother handshake and he sat down with us.

Cleo brought over a cup of coffee and Billy dumped a

spoonful of sugar into it.

"How did you get the name Zen?" Billy asked.

"Real name's Zeke," Zen said. "After my great uncle. Gordon's the one who gave me the name Zen."

"Gordon your boss?"

Zen nodded.

Of course, Billy wasn't going to pass up the opportunity to find out what Zen thought about 'current events.'

"Do you know who Angela Davis is?" Billy asked.

"Is she a singer?" Zen asked.

I vaguely remembered Wolfgang and Val talking about her in New York, so I knew she was some sort of revolutionary.

"No, she's an activist, a member of the Communist Party, and now she's in jail," Billy said. "People all over the country are raising money to pay for her legal expenses. In fact, I'm helping to organize a benefit for her this summer. We might even get John & Yoko. "

This was the first I'd heard of a benefit concert.

"Wow, that sounds cool," Zen said.

"Maybe that store you work at would want to get involved," Billy said.

"Gordon's not real political, but I'll ask," Zen said.

"Thanks, I appreciate it," Billy said. "This may sound like a stupid question but what do you plan to be when you graduate high school, my man?"

"A business man."

"A what?" Billy's eyes went wide.

"I want to have my own business like Gordon does. I like business. I like selling things and making money," Zen said.

Billy stared at him in surprise. Here was this young Black

man with a bushy Afro and puka beads. And he wanted to go into business? Billy had been born into money, but he'd rejected it and everything it stood for. He didn't get that Zen had grown up poor and had no intention of staying that way.

The Jethro Tull concert was fabulous. First Procol Harum came on, and the audience went wild when they played "Whiter Shade of Pale." I never understood what the words meant, but it didn't matter. It was the mood that the music put you in, especially the electric organ as if you were in a psychedelic church service.

During the break Zen and I walked around, hand in hand, looking at the freaks and hippies. Both of us in our bell bottoms and head-shop gear, we fit in perfectly. We had seats in the fourth row and I felt like we were hippy royalty, which is what my English teacher would have called an oxymoron.

Then Ian Anderson bounded out on the stage, flute in hand. He was all bushy hair and red beard, wearing a long coat that looked like something out of a medieval fairy tale. The band members fiddled with their equipment and Ian paced like a tiger while the audience grew antsy. "Get it on!" a guy yelled impatiently. The band pretended not to hear them. Just when it felt like the tension would explode, the music erupted — Ian Anderson's deep voice telling us that "Nothing is easy." He stood at the mic, blowing his flute, one leg up like a stork, bouncing his dangling foot to the beat of the music. We encountered no jugs of electric Kool-Aid at this concert but a cloud of pungent reefer smoke hung above the audience.

I realized, sitting next to Zen, listening to "Cross-Eyed Mary" that I loved my life. Sure I still missed Mattie, and I still worried about Wolfgang, but I had a new life now — concerts and school and friends and Billy and Cleo and kids. In a couple months I'd be sixteen. I leaned into Zen's shoulder and wondered what it would be like when we finally made love. That's what he had said, "I can't wait to make love to you." But we were waiting. I don't know what was so special about turning sixteen, but Zen had some old-fashioned ideas. He kissed the top of my head.

As we drove home through the city, passing through pools of light, we talked about how cool the concert had been. Zen mentioned that Gordon had talked about making him assistant manager of the store that summer.

"That's amazing," I said. His face shone in the headlights of the passing cars.

"Do you think your dad is really going to get John and Yoko to come?" he asked.

"I don't know. People are pretty mad about them locking up Angela Davis. She was some kind of college professor but she got fired. I don't really know much more about it. Are you going to go to college?"

He shrugged.

"Not right away. I got to make some bread, baby," he said. "But, yeah, I'll probably take some business courses some day. I'm gonna be a millionaire."

I laughed.

"Zen, the capitalist pig," I joked.

"Oink, oink," he said. He reached over and squeezed my knee. "Mule munching corn."

I laughed and pulled my knee away.

We had turned on Rock Hill Road and were about a mile

away from the turn to my house when we passed a cop car going in the other direction. We didn't think anything of it until a few minutes later when the whoop whoop of a siren sounded behind us.

"What the hell?" Zen said. "I wasn't speeding."

He pulled over as the flashing lights whirled behind us. For an ominous minute or so nothing happened. My heart began racing and my legs shook. For the first time since we'd been dating, I saw Zen the way the police would see him: a Black man with a white girl. I heard something break and turned around to see the police man stride along side the car, slapping a billy club in his palm. Zen rolled down the window.

"How can I help you, Officer?" Zen asked. His voice was calm, even. I couldn't breathe. Memories whizzed through my brain — James being brought out of the apartment in Spanish Harlem on a stretcher, the smell of smoke from the riot in Augusta, the loud shot, the body crumpling to the ground, the man wailing for his dead brother.

"You've got a broken tail light," the cop said. He was a big, clean-shaven man, the black leather belt around his waist heavy with weapons.

"What?" Zen asked in shock.

"See for yourself," the cop said.

"No, Zen," I whispered, but he didn't hear me. He opened the car door, and the cop stepped back.

"It wasn't broken when we left." Zen walked to the back of the car and then looked at the cop. "You did that, man."

"What are you doing out here with a white girl, Negro?" the cop said, his voice dripping with disrespect. He made the word "Negro" sound just like that other word. Funny how they could make any word sound hateful.

"Negro?" Zen asked in confusion.

By this time I was trembling all over. I had to think. I had to think quick. What would Billy do in this situation? I had no idea.

As I turned to look out the back window, the billy club landed on Zen's head. Zen yelped and stumbled to the ground. I yanked the car door open and ran to the back. Zen lay on the ground, looking up at the cop, his hands raised up to shield his body from the blows. The cop's partner — a skinny guy with a sick grin on his face — had gotten out of the police car. He leaned against the hood of the cop car, watching, arms crossed.

The club landed on Zen's ribcage. He screamed.

"Man, what are you doing?" Zen managed to gasp. The club landed over his eye.

I ran to the other cop and got in his face, fists clenched.

"I am Judge Lyons' daughter. My name is Martha Lyons. I go to Webster Groves High school. This is my friend. If you don't stop your partner right now, I will turn you in and both of you fuckers will be out of a job." I said the word "fuckers" with the exact same inflection that I'd heard Martha use it when she was pissed off at the football players for destroying the volleyball net in one of their stupid pranks.

The second cop stared at me for about thirty seconds. Now the first cop was kicking Zen who was grunting and crying in agony.

"Stop it!" I screamed.

The second cop walked over and pulled the first one away.

"Hey, come on, buddy. Leave him. She's a judge's daughter."

The first cop looked at me in confusion, face covered in

sweat. He sneered and got behind the wheel of his car. Everything went still and quiet except for Zen's whimpers.

Then just like that they were gone. I bent down and touched Zen's face and felt blood on my fingers. He groaned. I didn't know what to do. I had not learned how to drive a car yet, and Zen was in no shape to drive.

"Zen, baby, we got to get you out of the road."

He crawled on his hands and knees over to the grass and slumped down with a groan. My heart ripped in two. I didn't want to leave him. What if someone else stopped and hurt him? But I had to get help.

"Wait here," I said. "I'll be back. I promise."

I took off running along the side of the road. It was uneven and gravelly, no sidewalk. My boots were not cut out for running and my breath burned in my lungs, but I kept going. I reached the pool of light from the streetlight at the corner, turned and puffed up the hill, ignoring the stitch in my side. I ran all the way to the little house on Clairmont, and banged into Cleo's bedroom.

"Zen's hurt," I said.

The boys were asleep. Cleo got dressed and came back to the car with me.

"Jesus," she whispered when she saw his face was covered in blood, his lip was swollen and there was a cut over his eye. We got Zen in the car and took him to the house.

"You have to stay here tonight," Cleo said, washing the blood off his face and examining the cut above his eye. "I'll call your parents and tell them it's okay."

She gave him a bag of corn from the freezer and told him to hold it over the lump over his eye.

Zen fell asleep on the couch. I slept on the floor next to

him. Every time I closed my eyes, the memories of the riot in Augusta came back to me: the body in the road, the man's brother crying. What a fool I had been to think that things were different outside Georgia. Look what had happened to James in New York. Look what happened to Angela Davis in California.

When Billy woke me up the next morning, I knew what I had to do.

31

9 didn't see Zen that week. I told Cleo to say I wasn't home when he called. I didn't go to Illuminations after school to see him. The next weekend came, and I hung out with Dave, Todd, and Jellybean. We went to Forest Park, where I had first seen Zen, and played Frisbee. They didn't ask me what happened to Zen, and I didn't want to talk about it anyway.

Late Saturday night a knocking on the window woke me up. I glanced up. Zen's face loomed in the glass. His lip was no longer swollen but there was a purplish knot over his eye. He wore an old navy pea coat. Heidi tried to nuzzle his neck.

For a moment I lay in the bed watching him. Then I pushed off the covers, knelt on my bed, pulled the latch and swung the window open. I moved aside and he wiggled down through the window onto my bed. I shut the window. We leaned back against the cinderblock wall.

"Are you okay?" I asked.

"Yeah. He cracked one of my ribs, but it'll heal."

Night pawed at the window above us. Jimi watched us from above my headboard. My pale bare legs stretched out next to his long, jeaned legs, and the denim felt soft against my skin. Our breaths were synchronous, and I could see my pulse beating in my wrists.

He took my hand in his. His hand was brown, the fingers long and gentle. Mine were white and small. I sighed. His other hand brushed against my cheek. A heavy sadness filled the room.

"Zen," I said. "I'm breaking up with you."

"Why?" he asked.

"You know why," I said.

"Because I'm Black?"

"Because I'm White," I said. "And you could get killed being with me."

A tear snuck out of the corner of my eye, but I wiped it away. He pushed his shoes off with his feet and peeled off the coat, dropping it on the little rag rug on the floor. Then he put his arms around me. He smelled like wool and sweat and something else, something sort of like licorice.

"How can I change your mind?" he asked.

"You can't," I said.

Zen pulled me tighter to him, his warm mouth against my ear, but my body was stiff and unyielding so he stretched his lanky body along the length of my bed, resting his head on my pillow and I slowly collapsed beside him.

We lay there like a couple of spoons tossed into a drawer. I pulled the blanket over our bodies. When the pale light of morning spread across the windows, I woke him up.

"You have to go. And you can't come back," I said. "I mean it."

He searched my face, then kissed my nose.

"I'll miss you," he said.

"Go become a millionaire," I said.

He crawled out the window and was gone.

Friday after school, Jake, Turtle, and I sat at the table eating a snack. Life had lost a lot of its luster.

"What are you doing tonight?" Billy asked.

I shrugged and took another bite of cinnamon toast. I wasn't going out with Zen, so what difference did it make.

"Want to come to the station with me? My shift ends early tonight."

I shrugged again. Then Jake began to cry.

"I wanna go. Why are you taking *her*?"

Billy scowled, his big bushy eyebrows twisting ferociously. Jake shut up immediately. Billy never spanked those boys. All he had to do was scowl like that and sometimes add a growl, and they straightened up. I could see that he was a pretty good father to them. But it was too late for him to step into that role with me. So he tried to be my friend instead.

After supper, Billy kissed Cleo, who was busy wrangling the boys into the bathtub, and we left to go to the radio station. We got into his battered blue pickup truck and headed out to the station, which was in one of the other cities that make up St. Louis County.

"Radio's one of the greatest forces of democracy," he told me.

"Why?" I asked.

"Because it's something everybody can listen to, and just about anyone can make themselves a little old radio station. The day that radio no longer belongs to the people is the day democracy will die in this country, mark my words." He had the window rolled down and the wind blew the hair from his face, revealing his widow's peak. I studied his profile. He had a strong-boned face, a copper beard, and a high forehead. In some ways our features and coloring were similar. But our eyes were different.

I said, "All you do is play music."

"Good music. I also read the news," he said. "That's one of the best parts. At the Top 40 station I had to rip and read, right off the wire. But on most FM stations you can actually clarify what's going on." It amused me how formal Billy sometimes spoke, as if he were a professor and not a hippy DJ. "And as for the music. It's not all 'do wah diddy' anymore. These are songs of the revolution. You have to listen carefully. We're changing people's minds one song at a time."

"Okay, but why do you keep doing the night shifts?" I asked.

"That's when I can do the most good," he said.

"How can you do any good if you're just sitting there playing Humble Pie or whatever?" I asked.

He looked over at me.

"In most major cities, the hip FM radio stations have a hotline. It's for people to call to find out where the demonstrations are, what concerts are coming up, what to do if you get arrested, where to crash if you need a pad. During the day, there's a secretary to answer the hotline. But at night, the DJ answers it," he said.

"So you want to answer the hotline?" I asked.

"Have you ever looked at a map of the U.S. of A.?" he asked.

"Of course, I have."

"Well, if you draw a line from San Francisco to New York City, about halfway, you'll find St. Louis. A lot of people in the Movement come through here. And they know I'm on the air. They know they can call me on the hotline and it's a safe line. And

I know where the safe houses are."

"The Feds can't wiretap it?"

He shook his head.

"Look, it's not much, but I do what I can," he said. "Some of these folks are going to be on the run for a long time."

We pulled up to the station. It was in a strip mall and didn't look like much.

I swiveled back and forth in a black leather chair in the studio while he sat at the control panel, the mic hanging in front of his lips as he cued records and carts for commercials. While he played music, I looked through the thousands of record albums, reading the liner notes. I read a long essay full of praise for Joan Baez by a man named Langston Hughes. I stared at the orangish red cover of Janis Joplin's album. I loved the way her wild hair swirled in a blur. Too bad she had died—just a couple weeks after Hendrix. I wondered why such talent had turned on itself. But then maybe we didn't deserve to have them with us. Maybe they were sacrificial lambs.

I had to be quiet when Billy flicked on his mic. The needles on the meters bounced with every word he spoke.

"That was from *Electric Lady Land* by the late great Jimi. Ashes to ashes, dust to dust. He will not be forgotten anytime soon. Carole King and 'It's Too Late' up next."

When it came to time to do the news, Billy informed his listeners that Tricky Dick had commuted Lt. William Calley's life sentence to three years of house arrest. Then he put on Peter, Paul & Mary's song, "Where Have All the Flowers Gone?"

Billy only got two calls on the hotline that night. One was from a kid wanting to know if the Beatles were going to get back together, and one from a girl who needed a place to stay because her step-dad had tried to crawl into her bed. Billy told the first kid no and he gave the girl the address of a refuge for abused kids.

"Take a cab there," he said. "They'll pay for it. You'll be okay. And call me back. Let me know how you're doing."

His voice sounded warm and comforting. In spite of everything, I felt grateful to be his kid.

32

*B*illy was in his workshop in the basement, making a drum out of elk hide. The room had that weedy smell that indicated he'd probably been indulging earlier even though Cleo didn't like him to smoke pot in the house. I was still down about breaking up with Zen.

"How should we celebrate Bicycle Day?" Billy asked me.

"Bicycle Day?"

"That was the day that Albert Hoffmann discovered acid," Billy said. "April 19, 1943. It was the first time he tripped. He was riding his bicycle and suddenly started seeing colors and trails and all kinds of cool stuff. Remember when you drank the electric Kool-Aid a few months ago?"

"Yeah. It was kind of scary, especially the part where Heidi looked like a wolf."

"Did you ever think that you were seeing the true essence of Heidi? You saw the wolf inside her."

I was sitting in the big papasan chair by his work table. I scratched my ankle and said, "You think so?"

He shrugged. "Maybe. Maybe it's opening up the doors of perception. You know where The Doors' name comes from, don't you?"

He didn't wait for a reply. "From the poet William Frank, who wrote *if the doors of perception were cleansed, everything would appear to man as it is, infinite.*"

Often I could not think of a response to my dad's pronouncements. This was such a moment. He was pulling the hide tight over the drum head while it was wet. It would dry that way and tighten up on the rim.

"Aldous Huxley wrote an essay called 'The Doors of Perception.' And in it, he said something like the man who comes back through the door in the wall will never be the same as the man who went out."

"What does that even mean?" I asked. Conversations with my dad made me feel like I was walking through a darkened maze. He answered my question with a question of his own.

"Do you think that the only reality is the one you can pick up with your five senses? What if I told you there were people who could materialize in another place."

"You mean like, 'Beam me up, Scottie'?" I heard Cleo clunking around in the kitchen upstairs. She never allowed the boys to come down the basement steps by themselves—too many death hazards down here, so Billy and I were relatively safe.

"Not like that. On 'Star Trek' they're using technology. I'm talking about the technology of the mind."

"Oh," I said. Sometimes I figured he was just plain crazy.

"Are you two coming up for dinner?" Cleo called down.

"In a minute," Billy said, looking over his drum.

I got up to go upstairs. I was always ready for dinner, but Billy was looking at me with a sly expression.

"Cleo is taking the kids to her folks' place this weekend," he said.

"Yeah?"

"A friend of mine just gave me some psilocybin mushrooms."

I was still confused. I had no idea what that was.

"It's a hallucinogen, only not manmade. Cow-made. Not quite such a drastic experience as regular acid. The problem with your earlier trip is that you were alone for most of it. You had the wrong set and setting."

"The wrong—?" I asked.

"It's a hypothesis that Timothy Leary developed. In order to have a transformative experience when taking a hallucinogen, the set and setting are crucial. By 'set,' he means your mindset. Like are you prepared? Do you feel good about what you're doing? Do you feel safe? You didn't feel good because you were afraid your boyfriend would be mad at you, and you weren't prepared to trip. It was an impulse."

"True," I said, remembering how I'd taken the jug of Kool-Aid and swigged from it without a moment's hesitation.

"Setting refers to where you are. You were in a loud environment surrounded by thousands of strangers. That did not get you off to a good start," he continued.

I had to admit I didn't enjoy the concert as much as I wanted to.

"So what I propose is this. You and I do some of these mushrooms while Cleo is out of town. And we make it mellow and wonderful so you can get the full benefit. And you promise me you won't do acid again and you won't take any hallucinogens unless you're with people who love you, people you can trust."

I was stunned.

"You mean, you and me together. Tripping?"

"Yes." He tilted his head, one eyebrow cocked, his finger tapping the drumhead.

"I guess," I said and turned to go upstairs for dinner.

Sunday morning. I slept late till the morning light shoved its fingers under my eyelids and pried them open. Outside the trees were shaking in the spring breeze, vibrating tiny green leaves. It was still chilly in the mornings, and I was grateful for the little throw rug on the concrete floor. I pushed it with my feet over to the corner where I had tossed my jeans the night before. I grabbed them and jammed my legs into their cold corridors, found a sweater and some socks to pad upstairs in.

The Beatles were playing on the living room stereo. Billy was shirtless, wearing a pair of sweat pants as he cooked breakfast on the gas stove, brown egg shells broken in half and lying empty on the kitchen counter.

"Smells good," I said, sitting down at the linoleum table. He had poured orange juice into the jelly glasses, decorated with pictures of Fred Flintstone and Wilma and Dino the dinosaur. The orange juice felt good in my sleep-furred mouth.

Billy slid a plate in front of me and dropped a piece of toast onto it.

"What is it?" I asked.

He sat down across from me with his own plate.

"Omelet," he said. "Cheese and mushroom."

"Yum," I said and took a bite.

"You like?" he asked.

I nodded and then stopped mid-chew.

"Did you say this was a mushroom omelet?"

He grinned and lifted a big cheesy bite on his fork.

"They don't taste so great by themselves," he said and inserted the fork into his mouth.

I swallowed.

"Bon appetite!" he said.

Cinnamon Girl

"Back at ya'," I answered, and we ate our omelets and our toast and drank our orange juice. As we ate, I thought that even though Billy and Mattie were not related by blood, they had in some ways come from the same mold, or else they were aliens who had come from the same solar system. I wondered how my ordinary, stuffy old grandfather had managed to have two such unicorns in his life. Maybe there was more to the old man than met the eye.

We cleaned up after breakfast and were sitting outside on the back patio when Billy said, "We've got to go somewhere. We must experience the world."

"Where?" I asked. My stomach felt queasy, and my skin had started to feel kind of squishy.

"Forest Park."

I realized at this point that my father was a genius. Such a brilliant idea that only the most brilliant mind could have conceived of it. Forest Park. We would lift our bodies from these plastic chairs and advance out — out into the wide world.

I nodded and said, "The deep, dark Forest Park."

"Yes," he said. "We'll slay dragons, drink gin with ogres and rescue fair princesses." Billy's face folded upwards in a huge grin. He had a big, expansive way of moving his arms and his head as if he needed lots of space just to be.

I discovered by the ache in my cheeks that I was also grinning. Involuntarily. Why, I wondered, did this silly psilocybin open such vats of golden joy inside me? What was wrong with our species that we didn't grin uncontrollably all the time? Instead we frowned at each other and snarled and beat innocent young men with billy clubs for no reason at all. What if we could somehow put this in the water supply? Would the war and brutality end then, everyone giggling and admiring the pretty colors?

"It makes no sense," I said to Billy. We had somehow donned our jackets and were walking out the front door. He shut it with a click that sounded like a cannon going off.

"I know," he said. He was, of course, completely able to read my mind.

"Why do we make it so hard when it's all so beautiful?" I stopped in the road, tilted my head back, and saw the sky running like water overhead. "Hey, where are we going?" I asked when I realized that we had walked past his truck in the driveway and were now on the gravel road. "Are we walking to Forest Park?"

Billy laughed so hard tears sprung to his eyes, and I caught it, the laughter I mean, though the only funny thing was absolutely everything. Billy's copper beard had flecks of purple in it. I wondered how I'd never seen that before.

"We're taking the bus," he said. "Driving would just be too weird."

"I see what you mean," I said.

So we walked through the air as if we were moving through some material that crackled with every motion. I imagined that brittle pieces of plastic were snapping as I pushed down the road. It didn't hurt, but I could definitely feel the air and it wasn't soft like air is supposed to be. Fortunately there wasn't much traffic when we got to the main road or else we would never have gotten across. As it was, we made it over just as the bus rounded the corner and headed toward us.

The sight of the bus slowly rolling down the gray stretch of road mesmerized us. We were amazed when it stopped and opened its maw for us to enter. Billy stepped in first.

"Hi there," he said to the driver in a ridiculous attempt

to appear normal. He looked at me and his thoughts entered my brain: *See how well I'm doing. Follow my lead, kid.*

The bus driver kept his eyes straight ahead. He didn't want to see us.

"Exact change only," he said in a monotone voice.

"Oh, yeah, change," Billy said, panicking as he dug into his pocket. I giggled helplessly. Finally he pulled out a handful of change.

"Is that a quarter?" he asked me. I nodded, not daring to open my mouth, and he just poured the changed into the metal box. The door closed behind us and the bus rocked forward. We lurched down the aisle feeling as if we must be invisible, then tumbled into a seat at the back.

"This time is different than the other time," I said.

"Really?"

"More fun. Not scary," I said.

"Different stuff. This is what the Indians use to go on vision quests," he said.

"Yes," I said.

"Yes."

"Yes," I said again with a contented sigh.

When I moved my hand across the window, I saw trails – copies of my hand – following it, but they were rainbowy and blurred, not the stuttering film strip effect that the electric Kool-Aid had produced. When that had happened, I thought I was in a painting by that French guy Marcel somebody who did a picture of the nude chick going down a staircase. I had seen the picture in one of Mattie's art books. Now I realized the artist may have been doing a few hallucinogens himself when he came up with that picture.

We floated off the bus when we got to the Forest Park stop. The blue sky welcomed us. The sun spilled its warm white light all over the place. The grass of the park looked green and wet.

"Eli," Billy said, motioning toward a strange warping point in the air.

"What is it?" I asked.

"It's a . . . butterfly," he said wonderingly. As if we were pulled by a string, we followed the wavering spot of air. He was right. A bright yellow butterfly beat its wings in front of us.

"Come on," Billy said. We followed the flitting butterfly across the expanse of lawn next to the museum.

"Is it possible to see into other dimensions?" I asked.

"Absolutely."

We passed people, families with kids, freaks with Frisbees and couples with their hands entwined. Everyone seemed to be enjoying the bright birthing of spring.

"Hey, brother, can you spare some change?" a guy with filthy clothes and a hungry look in his black eyes accosted us. To me he seemed some strange apparition out of *Lord of the Rings*, but Billy smiled and said, "Sure, brother."

Billy pulled out his wallet. All he had in it was a ten-dollar bill. He gave it to the man, who was so shocked, he dropped it and the bill floated like a butterfly between the two of them before the guy recovered himself and snatched it out of the air.

"Thanks," he mumbled, stuffing the bill in his pocket and hurrying away.

"What a beautiful man," Billy said. Beautiful had always been his favorite word. Now it was mine, too.

We sat on a bench near the lake, which rippled under a

breeze the way a cat's skin will ripple under your fingers. The museum stood like a Greek temple.

Not far away a long-haired guy sat on a different bench. He had a guitar and was singing to no one. It took a moment but then I recognized the song.

"Billy, that's yours and Cleo's song," I said.

Billy listened and started singing along.

"Who else would I be chasing after moonlight with?" he asked. Then he laughed and turned to me, his eyes wet, and said. "That's not Cleo's song. That's your song. That's the song I always played for you."

"For me?"

"Yeah, I imagined you back in your bedroom in Augusta listening to me. I played that song for you," he said.

I stared at him. All this time, I was the Cinnamon Girl. Not Cleo. Whatever happiness I had been feeling before exploded.

The song ended, and the guy eventually packed up his guitar and walked away.

"Billy," I asked. "Is there such a thing as God?"

"What do you think?" He gazed out at the lake.

"Well, if there is, why can't we see him?"

"What if God isn't a him?"

"Why can't we see her then?"

"What if God isn't a her either? What if you are seeing God all the time, but you don't know it?" He leaned forward as he said this, and the purple words slipped across his lips in strings. Then we gazed into each other's eyes. I saw the gold flecks gleaming in his green eyes, the black pupils large and round like dimes. I thought I heard an engine humming all around me; at that moment infinity shot from his eyes and engulfed me. I shook like a fish on a hook. Billy smiled. I didn't see God. I saw something else. I saw my father and his father and his father and all the fathers all the way back to the Cro Magnon man. Then time zoomed back to the present, and a feeling I couldn't define washed over me.

"I see all the dads in the universe in your eyes," I said.

"I see the cosmos in yours," he answered.

Then we laughed, and we couldn't stop laughing for a long time.

We passed the rest of the day, wandering through the park, enjoying the sensations, seeing figures in trees, patterns in the grass and designs in the sky. The years we had been apart disappeared.

The afternoon grew chilly. Slowly the colors that had been so bright began to fade.

"How are we going to get home?" I asked.

"I don't know," Billy admitted. He had given away all his money.

We walked across the dulling grass that before had looked like freshly washed emerald. On the museum steps we saw a small bearded man with scraggly gray hair, hands deep in the pockets of baggy corduroy pants. Billy chuckled.

"Is that who I think it is?" I asked.

"Jeremiah!" Billy called out.

Jeremiah turned and saw us. I recognized the smile, the beaming eyes, the ecstatic wave.

Jeremiah gave us a ride home in a big old Buick his grandmother had left him in her will. Before she died, he had always refused to own a car. But now it was his grandmother's wish that he have a car so he said he would drive it but none other. He was not a good driver. He liked to talk, one hand flying up to emphasize his point as he looked over at my dad. But some angel would always take care of Jeremiah. It was the least God could do for the troubled world.

"Hey, Billy," Jeremiah said. "Be careful."

"I'm always careful," Billy said.

"Be extra careful," Jeremiah said.

When we got home, I was tired and yet happy – the way you are when you've gone on a long journey and had innumerable adventures. Cleo and the boys were back, and the boys climbed all over Billy, establishing his body as their territory once again. Cleo offered me some Hamburger Helper, but I shocked her by saying I wasn't hungry.

I went to my room, and as I fell asleep, I wondered if that Huxley guy was right about how you're different when you come back through that door in the wall.

33

A few nights later, the scraping sound of the storm door on the other side of my thin paneled wall woke me up. I pulled myself out of dreamworld, suddenly alert. I listened. Voices. I got up and went to my bedroom door. Quietly, I opened it just a crack.

"Man, you don't know how much we appreciate this. It's for a good cause, you know. The Movement needs money bad. Too many people on the run." A man's voice, talking fast.

"I'm with you, man." That was Billy. "But you've got to get it out by this weekend. I've got kids in the house."

"I can dig it. We're cool. It'll be gone by Saturday. I swear. You won't regret it. And I'll pay you. I know you need the bucks."

"Yeah, I do, but still . . ."

"Look, we gotta do what we gotta do, man."

"Keep it down. My daughter's asleep."

"Oh, sorry."

I thought I recognized the other voice, but I couldn't be sure. It sounded like Frank, and I suddenly felt guilty, remembering that day when he had put his hand under my skirt and I hadn't stopped him. The voices moved to the far side of the basement, and I couldn't hear what they said anymore.

A few minutes later the storm door opened again and then shut. I heard Billy cough and imagined him standing out there, his big hand rubbing his thick beard. Then his footsteps slowly climbed back up the stairs, and the basement door closed. I quietly stepped out of my room. I waited to make sure he wasn't coming back down, and then I turned on a lamp. I looked around and didn't see anything different. I went over and looked behind the hot water heater. A panel was loose, so I pulled it open. There was a big duffel bag. Damn it, I thought. What if there's stuff for a bomb in there? I didn't touch it. I put the panel back, went to bed and hoped Billy knew what he was doing.

Dave, Todd, Jellybean and I were playing badminton, yes badminton, in my backyard a few days later. None of us was much good at it, but is anyone really good at Badminton? Jake and Turtle had their own game going, which entailed hitting each other on the head with their badminton rackets.

"That looks like fun," Dave said.

"You kids want some pop?" Cleo asked, poking her head out the back door. I thought it was weird that she called sodas "pop," but the others didn't think anything of it. They all turned on their speaking-to-a-mom charm even though Cleo wasn't even ten years older than any of us. She brought out some drinks, and Dave and Todd started laughing and cutting up like they always did when Cleo was around. I think they were smitten with her.

So we took a break from our vigorous game and gathered around the currently fire-less fire pit, sitting in the plastic webbed chairs. Summer was already sniffing around, getting ready to pounce.

"There ain't no time for the summertime blues," Dave sang and shook his big head.

"Speaking of summer, what's everyone doing?" Todd asked.

"I thought I'd be a camp counselor," Jellybean said.

We snapped our heads in her direction. She burst out laughing.

"Yeah, right."

I thought about the previous summer: Mattie's death, the bus trip to New York, James getting shot, Wolfgang getting busted.

"A nice boring summer sounds great to me," I said. "I'm sure we can find a lake to go swimming, right?"

"Camping in the Ozarks!" Dave suggested.

We all agreed that was a fab idea.

"I wonder if I shouldn't have broken up with Zen," I said. "I miss him."

"We are way more fun than some stupid boyfriend," Dave said. I thought that Dave wouldn't have minded being someone's boyfriend, even mine, but he wasn't going to admit it.

"You definitely did the right thing," Jellybean said, draining her Coke. "You don't mind if I go out with him, though, do you?"

My mouth dropped open, and I ogled her. She giggled.

"Kidding, Toots," she said, but I wasn't sure that she was.

Maybe I had been too hasty. Maybe it was cowardly to have broken up with him because of the race thing. Maybe that meant letting the racists win. I hadn't thought of it that way. I'd seen myself as sacrificing my own happiness for his safety, but the more I thought about it, the more stupid it seemed. Besides, who was I going to lose my virginity with when I turned sixteen in a few weeks.

After a while, Todd drove us to the Steak 'n Shake, and then we invaded a local playground and jumped on the carousel thing. We raced around in a circle, hung on to the bars and jumped on. I leaned back, looking up at the dark sky whirling above me. Jellybean wound up puking up her vanilla shake, which the rest of us thought was hilarious.

When I got home, I went to bed, feeling happy. I had made a plan. I would call Zen the next day, see if we could give it another go. I fell asleep, my giant Jimi Hendrix silk banner watching over me like a guardian angel. I dreamt of Mattie, and in the dream she wore white pearls and her crimson gown. She sat at her mirror, worried about something, and I stood behind her brushing her thick, golden brown hair, trying to soothe her but she wouldn't be calmed.

Then the noise began. Thudding on the stairs woke me hard, my heart thudding like a racer in the last lap. I heard Cleo scream, "Damn it! We have children here."

My first thought was that we were being robbed. Then I heard someone banging on the storm door. I sat up, clutching the blanket. I heard men's voices, but it was impossible to make out what they were saying. My bedroom door swung open, and a flashlight beam danced across the room until it landed on my face. I squinted.

"Who's this?"

A light came on in the other part of the basement. Men were mingling in there.

"That's my daughter," Billy said. "She's only fifteen. Leave her alone. I'll show you where it is."

"I want to talk to her," the man said.

My father's radio voice took over as he planted himself in front of the flashlight. "No. She's just a kid. She doesn't know anything. Do you want the stuff or not?"

Then Billy shut the door to my room. My throat felt tight like someone had a noose around my neck. I threw off the blanket and slid into my jeans. Pulling on a t-shirt, I went to the door and cracked it. An army of cops converged on the far end of the basement.

"Dad?" I said.

He turned and looked at me. His lips were tight, and his eyes glimmered with tears. He shook his head and waved his hand at me to shut the door. But I didn't shut it.

"Got it," one of the cops said, pulling the duffel bag from behind the paneled wall by the hot water heater. The other cops leaned over the bag so that each one could inspect it.

"William Burnes, you're under arrest for possession of marijuana with intent to distribute," a short man, sweating in a coat and tie, said to my dad. The suited man grinned at my dad, as he hung his head. My whole body shook as they led him up the stairs. So it hadn't been explosives, after all. It was just reefer. Enough for them to throw a dealing charge.

Cleo and I stood on the front lawn under the elm tree in the swirling blue-light night and watched as the police shoved my handcuffed father into the back of the patrol car. He glanced at us just once and then the car pulled away. The police ignored us and loaded the duffel bag full of pot into the trunk of another car. Cleo clutched me. I had finally stopped shaking, but my breath was hard to find.

We stood there even after the police were gone in the silence of the cool morning as the sun slowly aimed its rays in our direction. A morning breeze stirred the full branches of the tree.

"Did you know?" Cleo asked.

"I didn't know it was pot," I said. "I just knew somebody came by and asked Billy to hold on to something."

The screen door creaked open and Jake came out onto the

front steps.

"Mommy?" he said.

Cleo slowly walked inside the house. She didn't seem so young anymore. I sank to the ground and leaned back against the trunk of the elm. I didn't think I would ever get up. I'd been living with my dad for nearly nine months but I'd never told him that I loved him. It seemed like I was just getting to know him, to understand who he was. I thought of when we were tripping in Forest Park and how I looked into his eyes and felt that unspoken, unbreakable connection to him. Now I was bereft. Mattie was gone. Wolfgang was gone. Billy was going to jail. I was completely alone. I could stay there and melt into the tree, become hard like the wood and forgetful of everything except the way the ground tenaciously held on to me.

34

Billy's picture appeared on the front page of the newspaper. Cleo sat with her cup of coffee staring at it while I fed the boys and got ready for school. I glanced over her shoulder at the picture. He looked maniacal like the long lost brother of Charles Manson.

"Where did they get that photo?" I asked.

"That's a publicity shot from a few years back," Cleo said. "They were trying to promote his 'Bad Billy' image. You know, he was supposed to be the next 'Wolfman Jack.' But if you look at his eyes, you see how gentle he is." Cleo started sniffling as I took the boys in their room to get dressed.

When I walked the halls of Webster Groves High School, people pointed at me and whispered behind my back. Martha Lyons pretended to be sympathetic, but she couldn't hide her smirk. I wondered if her dad would be my dad's judge. Dave and Todd took turns accompanying me between classes and I think that kept anyone from outright saying anything to me. The "heads," of course, all raised their fists when they saw me as if having a dad go to jail was the ultimate act of revolution. I knew that, in a sense, Billy was a political prisoner. He never would have been targeted if he hadn't been active in every demonstration, protest and hippie bake sale in the county. But conveniently he had gone and broken the law by letting someone hide pot in his house, so in another sense he was just another criminal.

My teachers all paused after calling my name for roll call

and glanced up to look at me curiously with their eyebrows raised. Except for Mrs. Martini, my geometry teacher. For Martini nothing much existed outside the realm of geometry. Sometimes, if I came to school early, she and I would go over problems and proofs together. She would show me advanced stuff that you learned in calculus and trigonometry and together we would marvel at its beauty.

That day after class, she asked me to stay for a few minutes. She asked me if I planned to major in mathematics in college. I hadn't even considered college except as a place to have sit ins and protest the war. Dad said that Berkley was the best place for radical action. I looked at her. She had a squarish, pleasant face and wavy dark blond hair cut short. She was ordinary in every way except for her eyes that shined with theorems and proofs and isosceles triangles.

"I like math, but I'm going to be a lawyer," I answered, surprising myself, and yet nothing had ever felt so right. Of all the women I knew, Janet with her big funky glasses and her nervous energy, seemed like the only one who could actually exert some control in the world. And in this chaotic life, it felt like if you didn't have at least a little control, gravity might stop working and you could fly off the face of the spinning planet.

Every moment, every conversation, every glance between me and Cleo circled around my absent father. How could we get him back, we wondered. Could we raise the money to bail him out? Could he go on the run and get away?

"I don't think it's fair to the boys to raise them in Mexico," Cleo said.

"It would be better for him to go on his own," I said. Cleo

and I had both watched *Butch Cassidy and The Sundance Kid.* Getting gunned down in South America didn't seem a pleasant prospect. "I could go with him."

"No, Eli, you can't throw away your whole life to be a fugitive. And he can't spend his life hiding. It won't work." She tugged at the roots of her hair.

"Then we have to hire a lawyer," I said. "Where is Janet? Why hasn't she called? Have you tried to find her?"

"I don't know where she is," Cleo said. "I called her office but no one answers. We might have to use a public defender."

After school I went out looking for work. But IGA wasn't hiring anyone under 16.

"No openings any way," the manager said.

Finally, Jeremiah called, and Cleo and I took the station wagon and drove into downtown St. Louis to find his print shop. When we got there, he shuffled to the door and smiled that big wide open smile of his, his eyes all bright like a squirrel's.

"Come in," he beckoned. The back room behind the print shop was full of stuff—old broken chairs, paintings of wide-eyed children that nobody could ever want, bales of wire, boxes filled with toothpaste and mouthwash. There was even a box of old troll dolls. Jeremiah saw me looking at it and insisted I take a troll. I wasn't a little kid. I was there on business, important business. I grabbed one with long green hair sprouting from its ugly little head and stuck it in my pocket.

Once we got past the junk room, we took the stairs to his apartment. Sitting at a table in the kitchen were Janet and Mike.

"Oh, thank God," Cleo said as she hugged Janet.

We sat down at the table. Mike took Cleo's hand.

"Sorry to hear about your old man," he said.

"They'll most likely try to give him an extremely stiff sentence, make an example of him," Janet said, sadly. "The real criminals, of course, those murderers in Washington will ride home tonight in their limousines and eat dinner with their spoiled, narcissistic families and sleep the deep sleep of people born without consciences."

Mike nodded and said, "The U.S. is a police state. The only way to deal with it is through revolution. Until then, most people just go underground."

Cleo scoffed. She had become fairly disillusioned about 'the revolution.' She believed in the core values of the peace movement. The other stuff – guns, kidnappings, bank robberies, and drug dealing! – she said that was "pure testosterone-driven bullshit."

"Can you help him, Janet?" Cleo said.

"I would love to, but I've been hired to work on the Pine Street Bomb Factory case in Frisco," she said. "I leave tomorrow. But I know someone who would be perfect. Allen Schwartz. We went to school together. Brilliant guy. And sympathetic to the movement—for a price."

Cleo cleared her throat. She looked so tiny now. "I can sell Billy's truck. Maybe get another three or four hundred dollars."

"If he's that good of a lawyer," I said. "He should be able to figure out how to get my trust money free."

Cleo looked at me with her pink lips open and her brown eyes round.

"You can't!" she said.

"He's my dad," I said.

Cleo bit her lip and drummed on the wooden table with a long fingernail.

"Give us his number, Janet. We might as well talk to him," Cleo said.

Janet rummaged through her purse until she found a business card for the lawyer.

"By the way, Frank has disappeared," Jeremiah said.

"Has something happened to him?" Cleo asked.

Janet spoke up, "Eli, remember when I sent that note to Jeremiah? I was telling him that we had an informant in our midst. I didn't know who it was. I think we have the answer now. It was Frank. I believe he's a fed."

Jeremiah nodded.

"I told Billy to be careful," he said.

My jaw dropped. It suddenly became so clear. James. David. Val. Wolfgang. Billy. All of them — Frank's victims.

"He set up my dad. That was him who brought the pot over," I said. "I heard him say it was just for a couple of days."

Jeremiah reached over and patted my shoulder.

"Please don't worry," he said.

When I looked up, I could see the couch in the living room where I had let Frank touch me. Violence squeezed my gut. I excused myself to go to the bathroom where I threw up.

When we got home, I went down to the basement and found a battered leather address book that Billy kept in his office. Sassy's name was on the last page next to the words "San Fran" and a phone number. I dialed the number.

"Hello?" I asked. "Is Sassy there?"

Sassy came to the phone, her voice full of its usual enthusiasm.

"Hi, chica!" she said, her voice like a wave of love.

"Sassy," I said. For a moment I forgot why I was calling;

it was so good to hear her voice. Then I remembered. "Listen. My dad got busted."

"What? What happened?"

"They found some pot in the basement." I figured it didn't matter if the cops were listening. They'd already busted him. "And there's something else. You know our friend, the one who was with us when Wolfgang got busted and James and Val. You know who I'm talking about?" I was trying to be circumspect but if they were listening they wouldn't have much trouble figuring out this conversation. Still the information needed to get across.

"Yeah, I know who you mean," Sassy said.

"He was involved. Like maybe he had something to do with it."

"Oh," Sassy said. "He's supposed to be on his way here. Wow. Thanks for the tip, Eli. You're a good chick."

"Be careful," I said.

"I will," she said. "I've got friends in Seattle I can go visit."

I knew that was a lie for the benefit of the "party line." I wondered if I'd ever see her again as I hung up. I probably wouldn't.

35

$\mathcal{B}$illy was in the county jail. Allen Schwartz had not been able to get my money out of the trust fund, but he agreed to let me pay him when I turned eighteen. Who needs college anyway? He arranged for us to be able to see my dad in a little room where at least we didn't have to talk through a thick screen, but we could only see him one at a time. So Cleo went in first.

When Cleo came out, her smile was hard like it was set with plaster of Paris. The guard motioned for me to enter the room. My dad sat in a wooden chair by a table. I sat in the other chair. He didn't bother to put a fakey smile on his face. He had bags under his green eyes and his lips were pursed tight against whatever he was feeling. An obnoxious clanging sounded beyond the door.

"Baby, you shouldn't have done that. You shouldn't have spent all your money on me."

"It wasn't all of it," I said, though it would be a big chunk. "I'll figure out how to get to college. Besides, what is money? Look at what it does to people. It makes them greedy and crazy. It causes wars. It makes people mean."

He stared at me.

"You're right," he said. Then he looked even sadder if that was possible. He took my hand and slowly stroked each finger. "Eli, I haven't been much of a dad to you. I was so young when you were born, I didn't understand what it meant to be a father. But I love you. I love you more than anything on this planet."

I wasn't sure if he was including Cleo and the boys in that "anything" but it didn't matter.

"I'm glad you are who you are," he continued. "I'm glad you understand what this has been about it even if it turned out so fucked up. Peace. Compassion. Love — those are the only things worth believing in."

"I know."

"For a moment a whole lot of us believed in that. But those days are gone."

"No, they aren't."

"Yes, they are. You don't know it yet, but they are. I've seen the signs. Money and power – they're making a big comeback. Mark my words."

"Please don't tell me that. What about the revolution?"

"Eli, there's only one truly revolutionary act," he said, leaning close and speaking in a hoarse voice.

"What?" I asked.

He smiled, and looking into his summer green eyes I remembered the two of us tripping on psilocybin and the moment our minds seemed to meld.

"Stay true," he whispered.

I felt his fingers on mine, and I got a feeling like colors swirling as those words, "stay true" were road-mapped into me.

I hugged him and said, "I love you, Dad."

The morning of my dad's trial, I didn't go to school. Instead I went with Cleo to the courthouse. Dad didn't have a jury trial. It was actually a fairly quick process. While Cleo and I sat on the hard wooden benches like sinners in church, a bunch of men clustered together and talked in low voices, sometimes laughing and sometimes looking all serious. My dad sat in a suit that one of the radicals had given to Cleo. His beard was shaved and his hair cut.

He looked at us and tried to smile as if everything was gonna be okay. Then his lawyer came over and whispered something to him and his smile fell apart.

"Ten years," the judge said with a bang of his gavel.

Apparently, Billy hadn't told the feds anything. And now he was paying the price. Cleo didn't say anything. I didn't say anything. We sat there like we were statues. I looked over at Allen Shwarz. I had given up my future for my dad to get a ten year sentence?

Later, the attorney told Cleo he would file an appeal, but he warned that the wheels of justice turned ever so slowly.

"Could be a few years before we can get him out," he said.

Cleo dropped me off at school so I could go to my afternoon classes. Todd and Dave understood when I explained I didn't want to go to the Squeeze that day. Instead I walked to the headshop to see Zen. I wanted to tell him what happened. And I hoped, maybe we'd get back together. I could sure use an ally about now.

As I got to the store, I glanced in the window past the display of brass incense burners, posters and black lights. Zen leaned on the counter, talking to a beautiful girl who looked like she probably went to Webster College. She ran her hand through her black hair. Her boobs were big, barely concealed by her midriff top. Zen smiled and she smiled. Why shouldn't he smile at her? Was he supposed to ignore a girl if she was pretty? And yet I wanted to plunge my head through the plate glass window. I had given him up for the stupidest of reasons.

I turned around and began the half hour walk home. I walked along the main street through town, passing the Squeeze as quickly as possible. No one noticed me. I turned at the hill and walked down, remembering how hard it had been to walk up that hill during the icy winter. A southern girl, I had no idea how to deal with ice until I finally figured out I should hitchhike up the hill. Now summer had emerged from its shell. It was a good long walk and I liked best of all just being by myself. Occasionally some car would honk at me but I kept my eyes straight ahead. I passed the spot where the policeman had beaten Zen. Then I passed Larson park, drenched in green leaf, turned right and climbed the hill to the gravel street.

When I walked in, I was astounded to see the living room full of boxes. Cleo was on the phone in the kitchen, opening cabinet doors and pulling pans and Tupperware containers out and placing them in a box.

"Yeah, Ma . . . Saturday . . . I don't know, Ma. Okay, yes. The boys are fine. I'll talk to you later."

When she hung up, she turned around and her eyes did a funny zigzag before landing on me. She wore pink lipstick, and her long hair hung in two braids on either side of her pretty oval face.

"What's going on, Cleo?" I asked.

Her hands held her hips as if holding on helped her stand. Jake and Turtle came running through the kitchen, Turtle holding a matchbox car and making siren noises as he chased Jake.

"I don't have any money left, Eli. Nothing. I'm going to have to get a job, and I need to someone to watch the boys. I can't afford the rent anymore."

"Well, where are we going to live?" I asked.

Cleo hesitated and shifted her eyes to look out the window.

"The boys and I are going to Springfield to live with my parents until I can get on my feet," she said. Then she met my eyes, and her meaning sank in. I felt like I was in a long tunnel. I couldn't hear anything but the loud humming of blood in my head. Everything outside of Cleo's face got blurry. I was wondering how to breathe when Cleo walked out of the room.

"What about me?" I asked the empty space where she had been standing.

She came back in, holding an envelope.

"Billy should have told you about this," she said and handed me the envelope.

"What is it?"

"A letter. From your mother. She's not dead, Eli."

Cleo opened the refrigerator and started rummaging around while I pulled out the letter. Jake and Turtle ran from room to room screeching like deranged eaglets. The letter was dated October, 1970.

I stood in the bright kitchen and started to read:
Dear Billy,

> *I just found out that Mattie died recently. I know I promised her I would never try to contact you or Elisa, but I do not think I have to keep that promise now that she is dead. Billy, I have been sober for seven years now. Seven years. Every single day I long for my daughter. I know that what I did was unforgivable. But God has shown mercy on me by giving me a new life. I have a job as a bookkeeper for a good firm here in Miami and I started painting. I have even been able to buy a house.*

> *I just want to be able to write to my daughter, maybe to see her if you think she would want to see me. Does she know what happened? Does she know about the baby? Does she know how sorry*

I am for everything? I'm not asking for much. Or maybe I am. But even just a letter from her. A picture? A phone call? Please.

Carmella

I looked up at Cleo. I could tell she was tired and had already left this part of her life behind. But she opened her arms for me, and I stepped into them.

"When are you leaving?" I asked.

"Saturday," she said. "I'll take you to the bus station."

"Who will visit Billy in prison?" I asked.

"I'll go when I can. And Jeremiah will go. Janet said she's already working with Allen on an appeal. Billy will be okay," she said.

Turtle came crashing into the room, tripped over the box of pans and started crying. I went downstairs to my room, clutching my mother's letter in my hand. Heidi crawled onto my bed, and I cried into her fur. Then I remembered something. I went to my dresser and searched through the drawers until I found the square box. I opened it. Brown magnetic tape was coiled around the plastic spool.

I went into my dad's workshop and found his old reel-to-reel tape player. It wasn't heavy so I brought it into my room. I placed the tape on one of the spindles and threaded the end of the tape around the empty reel. I brought in a set of small speakers and hooked them up. When I pushed the button, I heard the soft whisk-whisk sound of the tape rolling and then the grave released its hold on Mattie's voice. As she sang for me, I fell asleep on the floor, imagining I was under the piano looking up at its glossy wooden underbelly.

36

*9*f Cleo had been older, less preoccupied by two little savages and less broken up by my father's arrest, she might have waited around to see me actually get on the bus. But the bus wasn't leaving for an hour and Cleo was desperate to get out of town. She wanted to shake Webster Groves off her like a dog getting out of a bath.

The day before, Cleo had asked me if I wanted her to call my mother, but I said no. I lied and told her I had called her. I assured that everything was fine, that my mother said I was welcome to come live with her. Actually I wasn't sure I wanted to give my mother a chance to tell me no.

We went by Jellybean's house early that morning and I left her my posters and my blacklight. "See ya, Toots," she said in a quiet voice as I walked out of her nice brick house to Cleo's waiting station wagon.

9 stood by the door of the bus station next to my duffel bag. Cleo handed me the ticket to Miami. Turtle was in her other arm, and Jake stared up at me with wide eyes. Like me he was getting to learn about the kaleidoscope turns early in life.

Cleo squeezed my hand, tears gathering in her pretty, almond-shaped eyes.

"Take care, Eli," she said. "As soon as you're settled I'll ship your stuff to you."

I bent down and gave Jake a hug. He smelled like milk and

Cheerios, and I knew that smell would always remind me of him.

"Bye, sissie," he said. I kissed the tip of his nose.

Then I tried to give Turtle a kiss but he buried his face in Cleo's shoulder.

"Okay, well then, be good," she said and started to turn away. But then Turtle started screaming with his arms out to me. Cleo brought him close to me so he could plant a sticky kiss on my cheek. That seemed to satisfy him. Then the three of them walked back to her old station wagon, Jake turning to wave good-bye before she put him in the car. I watched as they drove away. Heidi's head hung out the back window, her pink tongue lolling in the wind. I couldn't believe they were leaving me, but it was the pattern of my life, wasn't it? Hello, goodbye.

My mother's letter was jammed into the back pocket of my jeans. In the corner of the envelope was her address in black ink. I looked down at the bus ticket in my hand. I didn't want to go to Miami. I wasn't ready to see this woman. What if she had changed her mind since she wrote the letter? Even if she hadn't, she was a stranger to me. She was some kind of boring bookkeeper. I ignored the fact that I had recently discovered the soothing power of numbers myself.

Where I really wanted to go was home—to Augusta. Mattie wasn't there to spill her perfumed love all over me, but Miz Johnny was still there. And I needed her. She hadn't ever been the gentlest person on the planet. But her stern wisdom had felt like a kind of love, the counterbalance to Mattie's extravagant affection.

I walked back to the ticket window of the grimy bus station, asked for a refund, stuck the money in my purse and got a map showing the bus route. I stopped in the diner, got a Coke, and studied the map. It looked like Highway 40 would take me out of

St. Louis toward Louisville, and then maybe I could take an Interstate south. Of course, the Interstates were tricky as sometimes they would just end in one place and start up somewhere else. I figured as long as I was heading south and east, I'd wind up somewhere close.

My first ride was with an older couple. You could tell they were religious types who wanted to do a good deed. The woman was a plump, bright-eyed lady with her hair in curls as if she went to the beauty shop once a week for a shampoo and a set. The man was bald. I was scared they were going to try to convert me or adopt me or something.

"Where are your parents?" the woman asked me after a lot of small talk about the weather.

"My dad was in prison. But he escaped," I said. "He murdered some people. Said Satan told him to do it. It could be true. My mom is in a coven."

I figured this would either make them more determined to save me or scare the hell out of them. Fortunately, it was the latter. The woman got quiet and we rode in silence for a while.

Outside a town called Mt Vernon, the man slowed down at a big intersection.

"This looks like our turn," the man said. "Guess we better let you out."

"God bless you," the woman said as I stepped out, tugging my duffel bag after me.

"And may Lucifer bless you, too," I said with my sweetest smile. Their car left me in the dust.

I had only hitch-hiked around Webster Groves, and it occurred to me as I stood on the side of the road in the hot sun, observing the cigarette butts, drink bottles and random pieces of paper dotting the landscape, the smell of exhaust roiling around me, that maybe it wasn't such a smart thing to do—thumbing across the country by myself. I realized I hadn't told anyone of this plan, which I had only formulated about the same time that Turtle was screaming to kiss me goodbye.

Semi-trucks passed me at a million miles an hour. And I noticed thunder clouds building up in the east—just the direction I was heading. It was funny to watch the grass bend in the wake of the trucks. Truckers were said to be the best rides because they were lonely and usually going long distances, but I was scared of them. I waited till they passed before sticking out my thumb.

I got a ride from an Asian-looking guy in an old Ford. He drove ten miles under the speed limit and had the air conditioner running as cold as he could get it. His name, he said, was Michael, but I figured it was really some unpronounceable foreign name. He was a small man with a thick accent and I had to lean close to hear his soft voice as he spoke.

"I from Vietnam," he said. Then he smiled very big. "South Vietnam. Not Viet Cong."

"Oh," I said. "I'm sorry about the war."

"War very bad," he said, nodding his head. "U.S. soldiers save my life."

"Really?" I asked.

"Yes, we very happy to see soldiers. So glad when they come. Communists killed my family. But I was saved. Got papers to come here. This great country."

"Yes," I said. "I guess it is."

All my preconceptions were suddenly shattered. I knew

Dad was right. I knew that LBJ had escalated the war, and Tricky Dick was keeping it going for his own purposes. I knew that young men were dying for a lost cause. But if I lived in South Vietnam, I realized that I might feel differently. It was not easy to know what was the right thing to do. We humans were such odd beings, each walking around with our separate version of reality. How could there be such a thing as truth?

Michael pulled into a gas station when we got near Louisville. He was turning north, he said, but needed to get gas first. I found the bathroom behind the gas station. When I came out, Michael gave me a 7-Up and a bag of peanuts.

"Good luck getting home," he said and bowed to me. I bowed back. Then he got in his Ford and drove off.

As I walked up the entrance ramp to the Kentucky Turnpike, I felt a drop of rain on my head. Then another and another. By the time I got to the top of the ramp, the sky was practically black, and thunder mocked me for the peon I was. I glanced around for shelter, but there was none. Cars sped past me. The rain slammed the pavement in a torrent. I couldn't even tell that I was crying.

I stuck out my thumb, not caring who picked me up. I just wanted out from this canopy of pounding rain. But no one stopped, no one wanted a soggy waif in their car. Water seeped through my sneakers. I hoped my duffel bag was keeping my stuff dry. I wished so hard then that Mattie had never died, that I had never left Augusta, that none of this had happened. I just wanted to be home in my big four-poster bed with Mattie downstairs singing Puccini and Carl's long fingers dancing on the keys, Miz Johnny quietly moving around the house, dusting, rearranging the knick-knacks and figurines, maybe some collards and fat back boiling on the big gas range in the kitchen. I thought of all the good food I hadn't tasted since I'd left—cornbread, grits, fried fish.

A car slowed down, and I was just about to pick up my duffel bag and run to it when it picked up speed again and kept going with a spray of water from the back tires.

"Rednecks!" I shouted over the rain, spattering and splashing against the pavement. Another car sped past, and I watched its tail lights disappear in the gray rain.

I felt like falling to the ground and sobbing. Instead I turned back around and nearly jumped out of my skin. Just a few feet in front of me on the shoulder of the road was a VW van. The windshield wipers knocked back and forth, and in between their metronome arms I saw the face of Jesus behind the wheel. He seemed to be watching me, waiting to see what I would do. I stood there, the rain sweeping across me, and he beckoned. Snapping out of my stupor, I grabbed my duffel bag and hurried over. He reached over and pushed open the passenger side door. Squeezing my duffel bag over the seat into the back, I hopped in and slammed the door behind me.

Water dripped from my hair, my face, my fingers, my clothes. My feet made a sloshing sound on the floor of the van.

Jesus grinned and said, "I think there's a towel in the back there."

He shoved the long-handled gear shift into first, and the VW engine chugged as we pulled onto the road.

$\mathcal{W}$e were silent for a long time. The 8-track tape deck played Leon Russell. He had a case of tapes on the floor that I started looking through for something to do. Zeppelin, Cream, The Doors, Sgt. Pepper's Lonely Hearts Club Band. I knew them all from my dad's collection. What an education I'd gotten in the past year.

I was excited about seeing Gretchen and Miz Johnny again. The further I got from Webster Groves, the more Zen, Jellybean, Todd, and Dave started to shrink into the past. What was the point of meeting these people, making these friendships that felt so intense, so important at the time as if no one else ever mattered and now they were gone from my life just like Mattie, except that somehow Mattie seemed more real to me than ever? Sometimes, I'd swear that I could smell her perfume, and I would remember the way she smothered me in her plump arms.

I glanced over at the man who looked like Jesus—or at least like all the paintings of Jesus because who the hell knew what Jesus really looked like? It's not like anyone took Polaroids of the guy.

"What do you want to listen to?" he asked. "Got some Airplane down there on the floor."

I leaned over and found the tape. "I love Surrealistic Pillow," I said.

He grinned. "You look like you'd be a Grace Slick fan."

"I look like a drowned cat," I said.

"Cold?" he asked.

"I'm warming up."

He took the tape and shoved it into the deck. I noticed he hadn't asked where I was going, and I hadn't volunteered. The rain was still falling, and the windshield wipers were slapping time as Janis would have said. Maybe this guy really was Jesus, and I'd gotten hit by a truck on the highway. Maybe I was dead. I wondered if he would take me to heaven or hell, but since he was Jesus, he must be taking me to heaven. Besides, I hadn't lived long enough to do anything to get to hell, which – if I did happen to be dead – really pissed me off.

"So where you headed?" he asked.

"South," I said.

"Anywhere in particular?"

"I'm supposed to be going to Miami to live with my mother," I said, noticing how weird the words 'my mother' felt in my mouth.

"But . . . ?"

"But I need to go to Augusta first. I need to see Miz Johnny and Gretchen and find out if Wolfgang is okay and figure out some other stuff too."

"All right," he said.

"All right?"

"I'll take you to Augusta and then on to Miami on one condition."

I looked over at him. Don't tell me Jesus is going to want to have sex with me, I thought, although he was a good looking god for sure.

"I want to hear your story," he said.

"Oh." He wants some kind of confession from me, I figured, still thinking I might be dead after all. "All right."

"By the way, I'm Jackson Hartman," he said and held his right hand out to me, driving with his left. I shook it. It was definitely a real flesh and blood hand.

"Eli Burnes," I said.

"Do you?" he asked.

"Do I what?"

"Burn?"

I blushed and didn't answer.

38

*H*e turned the tape deck off and I started telling him my story. I didn't leave out much. I told him about Wolfgang and my first kiss, told him how Mattie died without letting anyone know she was sick, told him about my dad getting busted and going to jail. I even told him about Zen and how I had thought he was the love of my life. Then I read him the letter that my mother wrote.

"What baby? What did she do that was so unforgivable?" he asked.

"I don't know. That's why I need to see Miz Johnny. She'll know what happened. Miz Johnny knows everything."

"What makes you think she'll tell you?"

I laughed. "Miz Johnny can't lie. I learned that when I was a little kid. But back then I didn't know what questions to ask. Now I do."

We had finally traveled through and out of the storm. The sky was a deep azure blue. By my Timex it was almost six o'clock and my stomach was starting to growl. According to the road signs we were close to Nashville, and I remembered stopping there with Billy last summer.

"Hungry?" he asked.

I nodded.

"Looks like there's a truck stop up ahead."

I suddenly got a creepy, scared feeling. There were still lots of places where a long-haired guy and a girl decorated in peace signs might get their heads bashed in. Maybe things were different where Jackson came from. I could hide the peace sign necklace under my shirt. Unfortunately, the other peace sign was sewn on to my jeans.

The van chugged off the highway and pulled into the truck stop – a small place, painted pink with a green neon sign: "Truckers welcome." Jackson got out and stretched. He was about six feet tall and had long, lanky arms. The air was warm, and I was just about dry. Jackson smiled at me. I didn't know a damn thing about him, but I felt like I'd known him all my life. He looked like he could defend himself (and me, I hoped) if the need arose so I followed him inside. Booths with plastic seats lined the walls, each one with its own little jukebox. After we sat down, I immediately started flipping through the pages of the juke box. The pages were behind a clear case and you used these metal levers to move the pages to see the titles of the songs. D4, for example, was something by Hank Williams. I had never heard of Hank Williams or Conway Twitty or Loretta Lynn.

"What kind of music is this?" I asked.

"Country and western," Jackson answered.

"I only know rock music," I said. Then I added, "And opera."

Jackson took out a dime and put it in the jukebox. He pushed D4—Hank Williams and I listened.

"Kinda like opera," I said. "Thematically at least."

He shook his head at my weirdness as a surly waitress with bleached white hair and two-inch black roots dropped some menus in front of us.

Jackson ordered the Brunswick stew and I got a hamburger. When she brought them over to us, she slung the plates on the table with her fleshy red hands.

"Thank you very much, ma'am," Jackson said and smiled that warm smile of his. I was ready to sling the food right back into her porky little face, but when Jackson smiled at her, I saw her grimace falter. She must have thought he looked like Jesus, too.

"You're welcome," she said grudgingly. Then she hesitated and asked, "Can I get you anything else?"

"Not for me, thanks. This looks delicious," he said.

"I would like some catsup," I said. She sneered at me, but reached over to another table, grabbed a bottle and then plopped it in front of me.

After she left, I took a bite of my burger.

"So, you know a lot about me," I said, before I had even swallowed my food. "Tell me about you."

He wasn't being any daintier than I was. Miz Johnny would have been appalled at our lack of manners, talking with food all stuffed in our cheeks like chipmunks, but we were both famished. Standing in the rain will do that to you. I didn't know what his excuse was.

"What do you want to know?" he asked.

"Where are you from?"

"Michigan. I'm a graduate student at the University of Michigan at Ann Arbor."

"Oh. Good protest school, right? What does that mean? Graduate student?"

"Means I don't have a lot of time for protesting. I've already got one degree and now I'm there to get my master's."

"You mean, you can just go to college forever?" I asked.

He shrugged. "Beats working."

He talked some more as we made quick work of our meal.

As we left our table, a lean trucker wearing big, brown,

shit-kicker boots and a cowboy hat looked Jackson up and down and then whistled like he was whistling at a girl. Jackson bent close to my ear and whispered loudly, "He must like boys."

I felt the temperature of my blood plummet.

"What the hell did you say, punk?"

"Me?" Jackson said, whirling around. He had that warm friendly smile on his face, but I thought something dangerous flickered in his eyes for the tiniest fraction of a second. Then he seemed to think better of whatever he was going to say.

"I was just asking my sister here if she'd like some toys."

I nodded in agreement.

"Get the hell out of here, scumbag," the booted man said.

"Thank you. I think we will," Jackson said. Just then the waitress came up and glared at the man in the boots. She turned to us and said, "Y'all drive safe now."

"Yes, ma'am," Jackson left, leaving some money on the counter before we skedaddled out of the door.

"You should have beat his scrawny old truck-driving ass," I said.

"You've got to know which fights to pick and which to walk away from, Eli Burnes," he said. "Besides, I'm a peace lovin' hippie freak, don't you know?"

"Well, so am I," I said. "But I'd still like to see that redneck get the shit beat out of him."

We drove through Nashville and on south.

We drove till dark. The Interstate ended around Murfreesboro, Tennessee. So then we took Highway 41 south and east. Jackson stopped at a small white wooden church in the middle of nowhere. He drove around the back and turned off the engine.

"Come on. Grab those pillows in the back and let's look at the stars."

He put a sleeping bag on the roof of the van, and we climbed on top. I placed the pillows down and he shook out a quilt that he said he'd bought at some roadside store. We lay down on top of the quilt and stared up at the scattered stars. I held my hands over my chest and inhaled the night.

"Jackson, where are you going?"

"Key West."

"Why?"

"It was as far from Michigan as I could find when I looked at the map."

"Why do you want to get away from Michigan?"

"I'm running away."

"From what?" I could feel the warmth of his body beside mine.

"A chick."

"A chick?"

"My girlfriend."

"Oh," I said.

"See those three stars in a line? That's Orion's belt. And those stars are his limbs. There's his dog, Sirius. The dog star."

"Dog star?" I asked.

"Yep, Orion is a hunter and all hunters have dogs."

It seemed very weird to be lying on top of a VW Van with a guy I had only met that day, an older guy, and I didn't know what I should be doing. Should I get up and insist that one of us sleep in the van. But his breathing was soft and slow like someone about to fall asleep.

"Jackson," I said. "Why are you running away from your

girlfriend?"

"She's pregnant," he said. Then he rolled over on his side and fell asleep.

39

I staggered sleepily into the dingy bathroom of the Gulf station. Man, what a grimy place—rust on the sink, muddy puddles on the floor. I peed very carefully, then washed my hands and searched my purse for my toothbrush and toothpaste. I thanked God I had finished my period the week before. I scrubbed my armpits with a soapy paper towel and wondered where my deodorant was. I would have to buy some. Not much I could do for the rest of my body, but I could take a shower at Miz Johnny's or Gretchen's when I got there.

When I came out of the bathroom, I found Jackson leaning against the van, holding a bag.

"Breakfast," he said with that smile so sweet it had managed to get a girl pregnant. I wondered what *she* was thinking right about now. Jackson handed me a moon pie and an RC cola, and I knew I was close to home. We got in the van and headed back toward the highway.

As we drove along the highway, we saw purple and orange and yellow wildflowers clustered in the median and on the roadside.

"Lady Bird Johnson did that," he said.

"Did what?"

"The wildflowers. That was her big project. At the time it seemed kind of stupid," Jackson said. "I mean, there was so much else going on in the world. The war on poverty. The war in Vietnam."

I gazed out at the vibrating purple and orange blooms.

"It's nice," I said.

"Yeah. Now it doesn't seem like such a bad idea," he admitted. "I mean we've still got poverty and we've still got Vietnam, but at least there's something pretty to look at when you're taking a road trip."

We were listening to Bob Dylan's raspy voice sing (if you could call it that) about Mr. Tambourine Man. Mattie had liked the Beatles, probably because they were British, but I think Dylan's warbling voice would have felt like acid on her ear drums. Not being much of a singer myself, I liked it.

"What are you studying?" I asked.

"English," he said. "I'm a poet."

"A poet?" I had never met a real poet. "Do you write songs?"

"No, just poetry."

I looked out the window at the billboard signs and we rode without talking.

Then Jackson said, "Hey, maybe you should drive for a while."

"I can't drive," I said. "I don't even have my learner's permit."

"Do you think that's important?"

You would think I had not recently witnessed my father in handcuffs for playing fast and loose with the law.

"Okay," I said. "You'll have to teach me."

We pulled off the highway and stopped at a gas station. I got behind the wheel and moved the seat up closer to the pedals.

"Okay, you gotta let up slowly on the clutch," he said. "Slowly."

We lurched forward about five feet, and the van sputtered and died. I felt like an idiot. Driving always looked so easy.

"Try again. Press the clutch all the way in. Turn the key. Yeah. No, you're all right. It's in neutral. Now, slip it into first gear, ease up on the clutch and give her a little gas."

I made it about ten feet this time before stalling out.

"Shit," I said.

"Once more," Jackson said.

Damn it, I thought, any moron could drive a car. Why couldn't I? This time I let the clutch out really slowly and amazingly we were going forward.

"Okay, you gotta change gears, Eli," Jackson said.

"Why? It's going," I said. The road unfurled in front of me. I was the captain of this ship and the only limit was the Atlantic Ocean.

"I love driving," I said.

"Just don't kill us," Jackson responded, shaking his head.

"I won't. Tell me a story. Or a poem. Let me hear one of your poems," I said.

"First, you gotta push in the clutch and change gears."

I finally figured out how to change gears. We tunneled along a country road, moving up and down hills. I never knew the world could be so green and glorious as it was at that moment. My heart was as open as that engine running beneath us. We had the windows open, and the air poured over us like holy water.

"This is a poem," Jackson said. "This moment right here."

40

*B*efore Chattanooga, we stopped at a Piggly Wiggly, bought a loaf of bread, some mayo, some cooked ham, and chips.

"Let's have a picnic," Jackson suggested.

We were getting into a really pretty part of the world with gorges and mountains, and I didn't mind taking a break from the traveling. Once we got through Chattanooga, Jackson told me to read the map and guide him to the National Forest, which I did. We ate our lunch at a picnic table in the shade. Then Jackson pulled out a book and started reading.

"What are you reading?" I asked.

He showed me the cover of the book: *On the Road.*

"What's it about?"

"It's about these beatniks traveling around the country."

"Like us?" I asked.

"Not exactly," he said. "See Jack Kerouac and his friend Neal Cassidy are crisscrossing the country, looking for their fathers, looking for women, looking for 'it.' They drink and get stoned and go to jazz dives, all in search of some divine ecstasy."

"Do they find it?"

"You'll have to read it yourself to find out," he said.

I went exploring while Jackson read his book. He'd said we'd leave in an hour. I told him there was no hurry.

*B*y the time we got to Atlanta, it was late afternoon, so I didn't complain when Jackson suggested we stop over at the house of a friend of his. I didn't want to get to Augusta at night. Miz Johnny liked to go to bed early. I watched TV while Jackson and his friend — a guy a little bit older than him — talked about poetry and other boring stuff. While I watched Columbo, they argued about something called "confessional poetry" and I couldn't imagine why anyone would argue about poetry.

We reached the outskirts of Augusta around noon the next day. I began to recognize the landmarks that we passed: the Krispy Kreme donut shop, an old factory, a smattering of stores, a post office. But the knowledge that Mattie was not in the city dribbled like liquid lead into my heart, and I suddenly felt so melancholy I could barely keep from sinking to the floor. I stuck my head out of the window, hoping the hot wind would revive me, but it only irritated my eyes, causing them to water. What had driven me to come back here? This wasn't home. Webster Groves was my home now. Or it would be if I still had a house to go to.

"Hey, you okay?" Jackson asked. I brought my head back in and wiped the water from my eyes. I guess the sharp drop in my mood was obvious. I nodded.

"I miss Mattie," I admitted. And I was worried about my dad, and I wondered when I'd ever see my half-brothers again. I touched my earlobes with the gold hoops Billy had given me a year ago.

Jackson was silent. We were closing in on the town now. I saw a few buildings in the distance. That was our little downtown. Augusta wasn't a big city like St. Louis, and it wasn't a suburban satellite like Webster Groves, but it wasn't a little country town either. For most of my life it had been the royal realm. I felt happy and miserable at the same time, and it was making me feel a little carsick.

"Where to?"

I swallowed. I wanted to go by the opera house. I wanted to go by the house where I had grown up. I wanted to go by the playground where Gretchen and I hung out and where Wolfgang had kissed me by the swing set. But I was afraid I would turn into a blubbering baby.

"I guess we should go to Miz Johnny's house." I scratched my knee through the hole in my jeans.

"Where does she live?" Jackson asked.

"In the colored part of town," I said. Then I remembered what Billy would have said if he heard me say colored. "I mean, Black part of town. Near the Baptist church."

I always had a good sense of direction. I had to develop one when I was a little kid because Mattie was all the time getting lost.

We rode through the streets of Miz Johnny's neighborhood, causing heads to turn as we passed. Not too many hippie vans came through here, I was pretty sure. A couple of Black guys called out to us, but I didn't hear what they said.

"They think we're here looking for drugs," Jackson said.

"Drugs?" I asked.

"Yeah, it's the same up north. The races have finally come together to get high. This is our revolution," he said. It made me feel sad when he said that.

I saw the towers of the Tabernacle Baptist Church looming against the blue sky.

"There's her street," I said. Jackson made a sharp right and there it was: fourth house on the right. I recognized the gray shutters against the red brick and the planters on the porch full of pansies and daisies and mums. Miz Johnny's house looked so tidy from the outside. She was probably enjoying not having to take care of that big old house where Mattie and I had lived.

"Is she home?" Jackson asked. "I don't see a car."

"She doesn't drive," I told him, and it suddenly occurred to me that maybe showing up on her doorstep with a long-haired guy ten years older than me wasn't such a great idea. Sometimes I didn't think things through. But Jackson had already pulled into her driveway and turned off the engine. It was too late to ask him to just drop me off.

I got out and went to the front door with Jackson behind me. When Miz Johnny opened the door, she peered at me for a moment with a confused and frightened look on her face as if we were the Manson family come to call.

"Hey, Miz Johnny. It's me," I said.

"Oh, Lordy. Eli, that you, child?" she cried. She swung the door open and said, "Come in. Come in. You, too, young man. Come let me see you, girl. Lord, you're all grown up. What a pretty thing. Your Mattie would be proud. And who is this?"

"He's a friend," I said. "He offered to bring me here." I wasn't about to tell Miz Johnny that I'd thumbed a ride from a total stranger. She could still swat me and I'd let her.

She led us into her living room, and I was happy to see one of Mattie's brass lamps on the table by the sofa and her settee in the corner. Dad had begged her to take as much as she could so the bank wouldn't get it, but Miz Johnny said her house was too small for all that stuff. I hugged Miz Johnny and she hugged me back hard. Jackson stood with his hands in his pockets till Miz Johnny made him sit down and offered us some ice water, which we both agreed would be nice.

When we were all settled down, she tilted her head and asked me, "What are you doing here, Eli? Where's your daddy?"

"He's in prison, Miz Johnny," I answered her, holding the cold glass of ice water between my hands.

"In prison? Lord, no." Her mouth hung open in shock.

"It wasn't his fault. He thought he was helping to stop the war."

Miz Johnny shook her head.

"My William. The only one of my boys to go bad."

"He wasn't bad, I swear."

"Well, foolish then," she said. "You're right. He was never bad. But he always had bad luck."

Miz Johnny's smooth dark brown face was placid as she stared out over my head at something only she could see.

"Miz Johnny, I've got something to show you. It's a letter from my mother," I said.

"Your mother?" Miz Johnny took the letter from my outstretched hand. "Get my reading glasses for me. They're over there."

I got her glasses and she slowly poured over the contents of the letter, muttering now and then. She read it twice and then took off her glasses and looked at me with her lips pursed.

"What does that mean about a baby, Miz Johnny? What did she do?" I scooted closer to the edge of the hard chair and set the glass of water on a coaster.

Miz Johnny dropped the letter on the coffee table.

"Let's go to the cemetery. I got something to show you," she said.

I looked over at Jackson, who was stroking his chin thoughtfully.

"Sure," he said. "Let's go."

*M*iz Johnny sat in the front seat of the van, and I'm sure that was a sight: her all proper looking in her blue flowered dress, holding her alligator purse on her lap next to this long-haired Jesus man driving a certifiable freak mobile. We pulled up to the cemetery, but Miz Johnny directed him around to the other side.

"They didn't used to let Black folks and white folks rest together," she said. "Which is fine by me. I always said I had enough of 'em in life. No offense to you, Eli. Or your friend."

"None taken," Jackson said.

The cemetery was beautiful and peaceful with mighty live oak trees strategically placed to spread wide swaths of shade. It covered several acres; a gorge with a little creek running through it dropped along one edge. A big fat blue jay flitted around branches above us and the thick grass shone a bright green color. It made me think of that psalm that Miz Johnny used to say to me: The Lord maketh me to lie down in green pastures.

We reached a section of the cemetery near the southwest corner. A black wrought-iron fence bordered the side.

"This is where my people are laid to rest," Miz Johnny said. "We bought this plot of land soon as we were freed. There's my grandpa and my mama. My husband Jacob who died in World War II. And this here is my grandbaby, Stephen."

I remembered that Mattie and I regularly brought Miz Johnny to the cemetery so she could tend to the graves of her family. Mattie and I would wander around, looking at headstones and giggling over the strange names of olden times. Our favorite was Oramel and his wife who didn't even rate her own name being on the gravestone. Mattie would make up stories about the people and give them strange secrets that she made me promise never to tell. But we never talked about Miz Johnny or why sometimes she was so sad and quiet on the way home. I knelt down in the grass by the headstone for Miz Johnny's grandbaby. It read:

Baby Stephen

Born Oct. 3, 1957

Died Jan. 1, 1958

I wondered why Miz Johnny had brought us here and what this baby had to do with my mother. I gazed up at her, waiting.

"Stephen was my grandchild," Miz Johnny said. "And he was your half brother."

I turned back to the headstone and stared at the sparkling granite. What did she mean? How could her grandchild be my brother? I stood up and tried to catch my breath but it was running away from me fast. The blue jay came screeching past me as shock reverberated through my body. Jackson was watching me curiously.

"I don't understand," I said. And yet I was remembering, remembering the tension between Billy and Miz Johnny's son at Mattie's funeral. Remembering how Mattie had once said my mother almost got three of them killed.

"Your mama, Carmella, fell in love with my son Randolph," Miz Johnny said.

I sank down on to the grass and stared at the baby's tombstone. I folded my arms close in to my body. In spite of the heat, I felt chilled.

Miz Johnny continued, "Carmella was a little wild. Everyone thought that marriage would settle her down some. Of course you were the reason she and William got married in the first place. When she got pregnant again, your grandpa and Miz Mathilda thought she'd gotten used to the idea of motherhood. But then Stephen came out with his milk chocolate skin and curly hair. Your granddaddy almost had a heart attack."

"The baby was Randolph's?" I asked.

"Yes," Miz Johnny said. "I raised him better than that. He shouldn't have been messing with a married woman, but she was beautiful and she swore she was in love with him. It's no excuse, I know."

I took a deep breath and gazed up at the clouds swimming over the blue sky.

"Is that when they went to the courts to get custody of me?"

Miz Johnny knelt down next to me.

"Not at first, child. Your daddy said he was going to stay with Carmella and raise Stephen like his own child, but Carmella didn't love Billy any more. She ran him off, say she was going to raise both y'all without him. I know she wanted Randolph to come live with her, but the KKK already came by the house, threatening to lynch my boy. I sent him away and told him don't come back. Randolph didn't love her. He felt sorry for her, but he didn't love her. I'm not saying he was blameless in all this, but Carmella hounded him something terrible."

I actually started to feel sorry for my mother..

"Your granddaddy sent your daddy off to college. That left your mama here with the two of you children. And her Jack Daniels. That's what she liked to drink. Miz Mattie goes over there one day and finds you just about naked and hungry. Carmella drunk on the couch. The baby was with a sitter."

That part I knew from what Mattie had told me.

"It wasn't no problem then for them to get the judge to

let them take you away. The baby, he was still nursing, and they weren't blood relatives to Stephen. I hoped Carmella would do right by him. I didn't have money to hire a lawyer and try to get him from her though Miz Mattie promised she'd help me soon as Stephen was weaned."

Miz Johnny sighed and her shoulders sagged.

"What happened to him?" I asked.

"She got drunk as hell on New Year's Eve. The next day when she was supposed to be giving him a bath, she fell asleep. No one knows what exactly happened. She liked to go crazy when she woke up and found him drowned."

Jackson put a hand around Miz Johnny's shoulders and she didn't seem to mind, which surprised me.

"So then she left town?" I asked.

Miz Johnny clutched her purse.

"Hmmph. They was gonna throw her in jail for letting that baby die, but your granddaddy couldn't stand the disgrace. Miz Mattie goes over there and gives her money, makes her swear she'll never come back and says they'll make sure the police don't come after her if she promises never to come back and never to try to see you. So she took the money and left town. No one ever heard from her again."

"Until now," I said.

"Until now."

Cinnamon Girl

41

*W*e drove back to Miz Johnny's house.

"Come on in and have some lunch," she said.

I had been hoping she would say that. Discovering our deep, dark family secret had done nothing to dull my appetite. To tell you the truth, I wasn't sure yet how I felt about this new information. I had never known what it was like to have a brother close to my age so how I could miss him? I did miss Jake and Turtle, but they were little kids and cute when they weren't terrorizing someone. I tried to imagine what Stephen would look like. He'd be 13 now, two years younger than me.

We sat at a scarred wooden table in the kitchen. Miz Johnny got out some pot roast, mayonnaise, lettuce and bread for sandwiches. She scooped macaroni salad onto plates for us and poured two large glasses of sweet iced tea.

Jackson leaned forward on his elbows, asking Miz Johnny about her sons. "Herb owns two barbershops now, and he's doing real well with that. He and Mary have three kids. Randolph started working for an insurance company in Atlanta when he left here. He's been one of their top salesmen for years now. Say they going to make him vice president. And he's married to a real nice girl."

I remember one time when Miz Johnny left us to go visit Randolph. Mattie and I took Miz Johnny to the train station. Miz Johnny always sat in the back seat when Mattie drove her anywhere. She said that it was the proper way to do things in Augusta and wouldn't sit in the front seat. When Mattie tried to insist, Miz

Johnny just gave her a look and Mattie always backed down.

When we got to the train station, Miz Johnny, who had rheumatism in her knees and generally moved at a slow, grand pace, practically hopped up and down in excitement when it was time to board the train.

"Have a good time, darling," Mattie called to her, completely forgetting the rules of protocol. It was 1968, after all, and we were in the heart of the South, and that heart had some rotten pathways in it. But Mattie insisted on hugging Miz Johnny goodbye. She brushed tears from her eyes as Miz Johnny waved before disappearing into the train car.

Miz Johnny was still talking about her sons. She spoke in the old Black dialect of the south. Miz Johnny could talk proper when she wanted to, but that meant she probably didn't like or trust whomever she was talking to. I was glad that she didn't do that to Jackson even though he was bonafide Yankee and might not perfectly understand her. Since he was a poet, I figured he could hear the beauty in her speech and appreciate it the way I did.

"Miz Johnny?" I asked after stuffing myself at her delectable table. "Would you mind if I took a shower?"

"Child, go on ahead. I was gonna say you was smelling a little ripe. Course you always did." Then she chuckled.

I wanted to sink under the table, but Miz Johnny kept right on, "Your friend can help me out here. I got a loose board on this back porch needs mending. Give him something to do to earn his lunch."

I got some clean clothes from my duffel bag and took a steaming shower, washing my hair with a bar of Ivory soap because I had no shampoo. As I dried off, I could hear Miz Johnny

Cinnamon Girl

outside, talking to Jackson.

"Do you know that the two most famous Augustans are both Negro?" she asked.

"No, who are they?" Jackson asked.

"James Brown and Jessye Norman, the opera singer."

I remembered once going to the Black church with Mattie to hear Miss Norman sing. Miz Johnny asked Mattie if she'd help Jessye become an opera singer. And Mattie had said, "Darling, she doesn't need any help from me. She's a world class talent already. A natural."

Jackson said, "I'm Black and I'm proud."

I looked out the window to see Miz Johnny's expression. She looked perplexed.

"James Brown's song. 'I'm Black and I'm proud.'"

Miz Johnny chuckled and said, "I never minded being colored. I guess I don't mind being 'Black' either."

I never remembered Miz Johnny chuckling the way she did now. Maybe working as a maid had been a kind of enslavement and we just hadn't realized it. That's what James had seemed to think.

Things were changing. I thought about Zen and the night the policeman had beaten him. That had been bad, but for four months before that happened we had been a couple. We could be a couple because people like Jeremiah, Billy, Cleo, Janet, Mike, Stump, Joanne, Sassy, Val, David and so many others sacrificed to make it that way. They marched, they shouted, they had sit ins. They stood together in defiance of society and its stupid rules. Now my dad was in jail. Not because he was a bad man, but because he wanted to make society better, to make it more just.

My mom, I decided as I slipped on my jeans and a fresh

t-shirt, was another matter. She had dumped my dad and nearly gotten Miz Johnny's son hung by the neck when she fell in love with him. She was a cheater and even worse, a baby killer. I looked at myself in the mirror and wondered how much I looked like her? Why did she have to be my mother? And where could I go, if not to her?

Miz Johnny insisted that Jackson take advantage of a free shower, too. Miz Johnny didn't like people to be unhygienic. Cleanliness *was* Godliness in her rule book, not just next to it. Jackson didn't take much persuading to get in there with a fresh towel. While he was in the shower, Miz Johnny said she had something to show me. She led me into her bedroom. On the blue wall next to her closet, I saw some framed black and white pictures of her family – sons and wives and grandchildren – and then I noticed among them a picture of Mattie from *La Boheme*, her eyes thick with eyeliner, her wig hanging seductively over one shoulder—that twinkling in her eyes that seemed to let you in on the joke. I felt like she was looking directly into me, prodding my heart with one of her long red fingernails.

"Look here," Miz Johnny said from behind me. She opened her hand. Lying across her palm was a strand of pearls. "I saved these for you. I knew she wouldn't want them to be sold. Most of her stuff was just paste, but these are real, Eli. She wanted you to have them. She told me."

I stared, dumbfounded.

"Thank you, Miz Johnny," I said and wiped a tear from my eye. "Let me give you something."

I went back into the living room, dug through my duffel bag, and found the reel of Mattie's songs still in its little box.

"If you can find a reel-to-reel player, you can hear her sing anytime you want," I said, handing her the reel.

"I tell you what. I'll listen to it, but then I'll hang on to it for you because someday you'll want this back." Miz Johnny's brown eyes looked into mine as she took the box.

"Okay," I said.

We didn't hug because that wasn't what Miz Johnny did.

"You try to stay out of trouble," she said, which had more love in it than any old hug.

42

"You okay?" Jackson asked as we drove away from Miz Johnny's.

I nodded and then said, "It's weird to find out you have a dead brother."

"Yeah, that's some pretty heavy news," he agreed. He pulled his hair into a ponytail at the stoplight and then asked, "Ready to go to Miami?"

I stared out at the traffic passing by. I felt uncomfortable asking for another favor. I figured he was going to get tired of dealing with me after a while, but I couldn't leave without seeing Gretchen. And I wasn't entirely convinced that going to my mother was such a good idea. She'd already killed one kid.

"Would you mind if we went by Gretchen's apartment first? I want to see her really bad."

"You sure you're not wanting to see her brother?" he asked with a smile.

"He's in Vietnam. I guess I didn't tell you that part," I said.

"Bummer. Look, how about I drop you off at her place while I go get an oil change and buy some parts for the van?"

"Okay."

I directed him to the apartment building where Gretchen lived. It was about fifteen minutes away. I realized I had gotten so caught up in my life with Jelly Bean, Todd, Dave and Zen that I had forgotten about my old friends. I had not written to Gretchen in months. We passed my old school with its yellow walls and the park and turned the corner by the Minit Market. Everything looked the same though somehow older and dingier. We pulled into the parking lot of the apartment building. I saw the balcony where Gretchen and I had sometimes slept on summer nights.

Then someone came out and stood on the balcony. I watched a cigarette tumble from her fingers to the ground. It looked like Lana, Gretchen's older sister. But there was something so odd, so languid about the way she moved I couldn't be sure.

Jackson drove away. I realized as soon as the van was out of sight that my duffel bag was inside. What if he didn't come back? He was probably sick of being a babysitter. Then I wondered why I acted like such a dipshit around him. I wondered how it was that I felt comfortable with him and totally weird at the same time?

Once inside I bypassed the treacherous elevator and climbed the stairs to Gretchen's floor. There were six apartments on each floor, and hers was near the stairs. I knocked on the door and waited. I had never stopped to think what I would do if she weren't there. I looked around and noticed the walls had been painted but the cheap landlord must have only used one coat of paint because I could still the word "Pussy" faded but still visible in the stairwell.

I knocked on the door again and waited some more. I heard a television going—sounded like soap opera music—but still no one answered the door, so I sat down on the steps and waited and thought. I didn't want to think, but the thoughts were like flies buzzing around me and one thought was worse than a fly, much worse. I kept imagining my baby brother, lying in the bathtub, bloated and tiny.

I sat on the steps, the leftover smell of someone's dinner from the night before lingering overhead. I imagined Carmella waking up from her drunken dreaming to find her baby boy. The boy in my imagination was Turtle. I knew what something like that would do to Cleo, the utter horror, the howl of pain that would come from some deep region in her soul. And I thought about what it would do to the rest of us: Jake, me and Billy.

We trip along innocently enough through our lives, not imagining what might be waiting for us in the next year, month, day or minute. Miz Johnny had often worried about me, saying I swam in deep waters. And here I was again.

The door at the bottom of the steps opened and footsteps came slowly up from the depths. Before she turned the corner into visibility, I knew it was Gretchen. When she got to the landing below me, she looked up.

"Holy shit," she said. "What are you doing here?"

I grinned and stood up.

"Came to see you, Kraut-girl. What do you think?"

Gretchen laughed a big, wide-open laugh. She had large lips and large teeth and a warm watery laugh. When she got to the top step of the landing, she looked appraisingly at me.

"Shit, Eli," she said, placing a hand on her hip. "You got boobs!"

"Yeah, I know," I said, embarrassed, and laughed.

"Why are you waiting out on the steps?"

"I knocked, but no one answered. I thought I saw Lana on the balcony earlier, and the TV is going. Maybe she's asleep."

"That bitch isn't sleeping. She's nodding off," Gretchen said angrily and went and banged on the door.

I had no idea what 'nodding off' meant or why Gretchen

was so pissed. Lana had always been a temperamental shrew, but we had learned never to expect anything less.

"Open the door, you junkie bitch!" Gretchen yelled and banged incessantly on the door until it finally swung open and Lana stood there, weighing in at maybe 90 pounds and staring at the two of us with eyes so glassy you could drink from them. Lana scratched her face and gazed at me.

"Hi, Lana," I said.

"Oh, it's you," she said in a voice like sawdust. "Again."

"She hasn't been around here in a year, stupid," Gretchen said, brushing past her older sister. I followed a little sheepishly. Lana had terrorized us in the past, but she didn't appear to be much of a terrorizer these days. She went back to the same plaid couch I remembered from before and sat down in front of a small black and white TV. Her eyelids lowered to half-mast and she seemed to forget we were there. I stared at her while Gretchen went to the bathroom.

A few minutes later, Gretchen came out and we drifted out to the balcony. The heat surrounded us like the belly of a whale, and we sank down to hang our legs between the bars like we did when we were kids, hoping for a shred of wind to come by.

"What happened to your color TV?" I asked, remembering how proud they had been of that thing. I liked coming over to watch with Gretchen considering the fact that Mattie would never buy a color TV after the black and white broke. She thought it was somehow a sign of the lower classes to own a color TV.

"That junkie bitch sold it for drugs," Gretchen said bitterly.

I glanced through the glass door at Lana. She had bent over so far that her head seemed to be resting just a few inches above her knees. I'd never seen a real junkie before. This was turning into an interesting day—interesting in a way I could have lived without.

"What did your parents say?" I asked.

"Nothing. They just went out and bought that cheap piece of shit, figuring she couldn't get any money for it. They're scared of losing her. They've already lost one kid." Gretchen leaned her face into the bars and sniffled. I felt a slowly creeping numbness move through my body. I didn't want to ask what she meant. I didn't want to know. Suddenly the bars that kept us from pitching to the ground didn't seem strong enough to hold me. I moved back and the words came out of my mouth of their own accord.

"What happened to Wolfgang?"

Gretchen shrugged. "MIA. Missing in action. So we don't know. Maybe he's dead. Maybe he's a prisoner. Maybe he's gone AWOL and is shacked up with some Vietnamese chick somewhere. That's what I keep hoping."

I squeezed my hands together tight. It was too much for one day. I felt like I was made of clay and someone was pouring water on me. I didn't tell Gretchen that I had met some veterans back in Webster Groves. I didn't tell her how angry they were, how Stump had said if he could have figured out any possible way to desert he would have been gone in the first week. But in Vietnam there was nowhere to run and definitely nowhere to hide.

"I'm sorry," I said. "Wolfgang means a lot to me."

"Yeah, me too," Gretchen said. "I wish he would have made it to Canada."

I looked down in the parking lot below. Some kids were chasing another kid down, probably to beat the crap out of him. It was the nature of the beast.

"Let's talk about something else," Gretchen said. "This

shit makes me sad."

"Okay. My mom wrote me a letter," I told her.

"Your mom? I thought your mom was dead."

"Apparently not," I answered.

Gretchen smiled. "You talk so funny, Eli. I miss you. Do you have a boyfriend?"

I pulled an errant toenail and said, "I had one, but we broke up."

"Too bad. I'm going with Marvin."

"No," I said, unable to hide my disgust.

"He's not so bad. Are you still a virgin?"

I hesitated. Gretchen was always ahead of me in these matters, and once again, I sensed she would already be there.

"Yeah," I said. "I mean, I don't want to get pregnant. And I'm not on the pill yet."

"I don't care if I get pregnant. Marvin and I fuck a lot," she said and giggled.

I was starting to wish that Jackson would hurry up and get back, at the same time praying he hadn't left me for good and wondering if Fallene or Carl or one of Mattie's other opera singing friends would take me in if he had.

"Remember when Marvin and I got in that fight and Wolfgang showed up and ran him off," I said.

"Yeah. Hey, I got a picture of Wolfgang he sent us from Vietnam."

She went inside and came out with the snapshot. Wolfgang's hair was all cut off and he wasn't smiling in the picture. He stood in front of a tent with his arms crossed and a look on his face that reminded me of Jake when he had a bad toothache and had to go to the dentist. We talked about Wolfgang and about Marvin, and I told her about Dave, Todd and Jelly Bean. Finally I heard a horn beeping. I looked down and saw Jackson get out of his van and wave up at me.

"Who is that?" Gretchen asked.

"Just a friend," I said.

"A friend?" she laughed. "You won't be a virgin too much longer."

43

*W*e crossed the border into Florida, and Jackson wanted a story so I told him about the one time I had been to Florida when I was about eight. Mattie had tickets to hear the London Philharmonic in Daytona Beach and didn't realize it was Spring Break, so all the motels were full. We drove around the city completely lost and wondering where we would sleep when we saw this big white house with a veranda and white rockers, and a sign out front said, "The Magnolia." We went inside and asked for a room for the night. The old guy behind the desk looked at us very strangely, but then with this mysterious smile he gave us a key to a room and told us the pool was available to use until eight p.m. I hadn't seen a pool from the street, but we went to our rooms and put on our bathing suits and followed his directions to the pool. When we found it, we were amazed. It was a huge blue rectangle and no one else was using it. The day was hot and bright and we couldn't believe we had this big pool all to ourselves. Mattie and I swam around. We played lifeguard and she let me save her from drowning several times. Occasionally some old person walked by and smiled at us. We knew lots of old people came to Florida and lots of teenagers for spring break. We were the odd ones—a middle aged lady and a kid. Some of them thought Mattie was my mother, which made her happy.

After a while we got dressed and went to the concert. The next day as we sat in a dining room full of white-haired women and bald old men we realized we had strayed into some sort of old folks home. The old people kept smiling at us and coming over to our table to visit with us as if we were celebrities or long-lost family.

"Life was like that with Mattie — an adventure," I said.

Jackson liked that story a lot. I asked him if he would put it in a poem and he said maybe.

We were traveling along highway 90 when we came to the Suwannee River.

"Let's stop," I begged. I didn't even know the Suwannee was a real river. I thought it was just some song we learned in school.

Jackson didn't mind stopping. We found a spot off the highway and I got in the back of the van and changed into my old one-piece bathing suit. Jackson put on a pair of cut-offs. It was summer so there was still plenty of light. All the strange sorrows of the day lifted off me, blown into the sky by the evening breezes.

Jackson and I waded into the water. It was a deep brown color and I could see a current in the middle. I loved rivers. Jackson splashed me and I splashed him back. For someone in his 20s he was more like a big kid. The laughter felt good. I wasn't thinking about Wolfgang or Miz Johnny or the impending meeting with my mother. Something inside me lurched up from the grave. Like the way a plant suddenly gets green and perky when you finally get around to watering it.

A mockingbird in a tree was chirping away, and Jackson suddenly started spouting poetry at it: "Hail to thee, blithe spirit! Bird thou never wert, that from heaven or near it, pourest thy full heart in profuse strains of unpremeditated art."

"Did you write that?" I asked.

"No, a poet named Percy Shelley wrote it in the 1800s."

"Oh, I like it."

"He was a romantic." Jackson grinned at me. I dug my feet into the wet sand.

"Aren't all poets?" I asked. "I thought that was what romance was all about—poetry and flowers and stuff."

"No," he said. "Allen Ginsburg writes about how screwed up America is. He's one of the beat poets."

"My dad would like him, I'm sure."

"Are you happy to finally be meeting your mother?" Jackson asked, as we sat on the sand. I scooted closer to him, trying to capture his body warmth. I liked being close to him. He was strong and nice and looked like Jesus. I had discovered that bodies want to be close to other bodies. The water gently lapped the banks of the river, the sand scratched the back of my legs, and the sunlight bled from the sky. Jackson put an arm around me.

"Jackson," I said. "I don't want to go to my mother's."

"What do you want to do?"

"Why can't I just travel around with you?"

"Aw, man," he said, his arm slipping off my shoulder as he leaned back. "No way, Eli."

"Why not?" I pleaded.

"Because you're underage. It's bad enough I'm even driving you down to Miami. If I kept you, I'd be like a kidnapper or something. They'd put me in the cell next to your old man."

I didn't like that he used the information I had told him about my father that way, but I wasn't ready to give up either.

"But I wouldn't tell anyone. Please? Come on, we have fun together," I said.

"No. It's not possible. I don't even know what I'm going to do next. I mean, I've been thinking a lot about Chris."

"Chris?" I asked. Who was Chris?

"And the baby."

"Oh."

"I just – I don't know what to do, but I think . . ." he didn't finish the statement. He didn't have to. He was going to go back to his pregnant girlfriend. He tried to act like some kind of free spirit, but he wasn't. He was just another working man in hippie disguise. For a moment, I hated him.

He pushed a strand of hair from my face and said, "Are you hungry?"

I was starving, but I shook my head and stared at the passing clouds.

"Well, I am. Come on. Let's go get some dinner. My treat. We can spend the night in that campground we passed by the highway."

After we ate, I went to the bathroom. When I came out of the restaurant, I headed toward the van. Jackson wasn't inside. I glanced around the parking lot and saw a tall figure leaning into a pay phone intently as if he were trying to reach through the phone. Jackson was talking to *her*. He was definitely going back to her. He probably wouldn't even want to drive all the way to Miami now. Well, good for him, I thought. It's bad when a guy abandons his pregnant girlfriend, free spirit or no free spirit. And yet I didn't know why she couldn't just go somewhere and have an abortion. They were legal in New York, weren't they? Or Puerto Rico? But who was I to stand in the way of true love? What was he to me anyway? He was just some stranger who picked me up and gave me a ride. There were plenty of cars and plenty of drivers. I could travel all over the country if I wanted to, never staying in one place very long. I had my thumb. What else did I need besides my duffel bag? I opened the sliding side door on the VW bus and pulled my bag out. I felt strong and determined. I was getting away from this phony Jesus right now.

I glanced over at the pay phone. His back was to me. Maybe the conversation wasn't going his way. Too bad, so sad. I hitched the duffel bag handles over my shoulder and strode purposefully toward the road. Before I even got to the pavement, a car slowed down. It was a big yellow Cadillac, looked like a Fleetwood and since I liked Fleetwood Mac, I figured this was a good sign. The passenger window opened automatically which was pretty cool, and a man in his 30s or maybe 40s with short sandy brown hair and round eyes leaned over and asked if I needed a ride.

I hesitated. I was pretty sure this straight-arrow dude wouldn't have much to offer in the way of scintillating conversations. He wasn't going to have a lot of information on Jack Kerouac or any of those other dudes that Jackson had expounded upon. He looked like a salesman with a wife and 2.5 kids at home, waiting for him. He looked as interesting as a Twinkie.

Then I heard Jackson call out my name, "Eli!"

I opened the door to the Caddy and got in.

"So where you headed?" old round eyes asked.

"South," I answered, thinking that seemed a reasonable answer.

"Well, I'm going as far as Orlando. Will that work for you?"

"That's fine," I said. I wasn't all that hip on geography but I knew it was somewhere in Florida.

The man asked me my name. I lied and said, "Tina." I didn't owe anyone the truth. Maybe I'd never be Eli Burnes again.

I could have a different name for every ride I got, a different history for every driver.

"Hello, Tina. I'm Rick," he said.

We were on the interstate, flying south. Maybe because I had just lied, it seemed as if he did too, as if his name couldn't possibly be Rick. He looked like a Simon or a Howard. But in this brave new world, all lies were the truth.

"Why are you hitch-hiking? Don't you know it's dangerous?" he asked.

"It's been okay, so far," I said.

He seemed to get the message that I didn't feel like telling him my whole life story. So he started rambling on about his work selling automobile parts. He was the distributor for some national manufacturer and blah, blah, blah. Eventually he found a radio station playing easy listening music.

"Do you like this music?" he asked.

"It's egregious," I answered, echoing Mattie's sentiments about anything she didn't like.

"Yeah," he smiled. "I like it, too."

I desperately missed Jackson's 8-track tape player with its funny clicking noises as it changed tracks, even the way songs were interrupted from one track to another. I thought that I could be listening to the Doors right about now—"when you're stra-ange." But Jackson was probably already headed north back to Chris and her belly full of baby. She would probably be a good mother, probably wouldn't get drunk and fall asleep while the baby was in the bathtub.

I couldn't say why I was feeling so huffy. It's not like Jackson treated me as anything other than a friend. That's when I started feeling sick to my stomach. He had treated me like a friend, a good friend. He had driven me from one place to another without complaining and I had snuck off without even saying good-bye.

Tears began to trickle from my eyes. They were tears for baby Stephen, tears for Wolfgang and even tears for Lana. I looked through my bag so "Rick" wouldn't see me crying.

"Looking for something?" Rick asked.

"I thought I had some gum," I said. "Guess not."

I leaned my head back. How could this day get any worse? I had found out I had a dead brother; Wolfgang, my first love, was lost and maybe dead in the jungles of Vietnam and my best friend was probably going to wind up pregnant while her sister committed a slow suicide with drugs. I couldn't bring myself to care what happened next. We rode silently through the blackening night. Rain began to fall, drumming the roof of the car and sliding like glassy snakes along the windows. Mercifully, we'd driven out of range of the easy listening station. I shut my eyes and listened to the metronome beat of the windshield wipers and for a brief moment I was a little girl again, falling asleep under the grand piano while Carl played and Mattie and Fallene sang.

I startled awake. Sitting up quickly, I tried to get my bearings.

"You fell asleep," he said. What was his name?

I rubbed my eyes. The car was stopped at a stop sign at the end of an exit ramp.

"Where are we?"

"Near Orlando. I can't drive any farther in this rain. I was hoping you'd keep me company but you went and fell asleep."

"It's been a long day," I said.

I saw a gas station up head and a sign for a Budget Motel just beyond the gas station. The rain was falling hard, slapping the ground, drops bouncing off the hood of the car.

"Tina, I can't drive any more tonight. I'm going to get a motel room. If I keep driving, I'm likely to fall asleep, drive off the road and kill us both. Do you want me to let you out at this gas station and maybe you can find another ride?"

I looked out at the pouring rain and at the dark gas station.

"It's closed," I said.

"Oh, you're right. Well, if you want to, you can stay with me and I'll take you as far as Orlando, bright and early in the morning. We can get a room with two beds. I need to call my wife and let her know where I am. Boy, I'm tired."

I was tired, too, more tired than I could ever remember feeling. I did not want to stay in a motel room with this man. What an awful idea, but it was raining so hard, like the rain pellets were stabbing the earth. And it was so dark and I had no idea where I was.

"I'm not used to staying in a motel room with a total stranger," he said. "You're not carrying a knife or a gun or anything, are you?"

"Of course not," I said. Wasn't it obvious? I was a hippie. We didn't believe in guns and violence. I was wearing the peace sign necklace Zen had given me for crying out loud.

"Well, how about we get a few hours of shut eye and then get back on the road?"

"Okay," I said. If you're going to live on the road, I realized, you have to be willing to accept what the road brings you. Besides, what choice did I have?

Rick went into the office of the motel and came back a few minutes later. If I'd had my money I could have gotten my own room. What an idiot I had been. He drove the car down to the end of the row of motel rooms.

"I got us the room on the end. It'll be nice and quiet that way," he said.

He went in ahead of me while I got out my duffel bag. The rain had let up some and I thought about offering to drive us the rest of the way while he slept. If I could drive Jackson's van, surely I could drive that Cadillac. When I came in the room, he was on the telephone. On the table was a big ugly ceramic lamp.

"Yes, honey, I love you, too. Give a big hug to Ronnie for me," he said. The room was awful. It smelled like mold and I wondered why a man who drove a Cadillac couldn't afford better than this. I set down my duffel bag and went in to use the bathroom.

This, I realized, as I sat down to pee, was a huge mistake. Something didn't feel right. Maybe I should just walk back to the highway. Or I could ask him if I could sleep in the car. Maybe there was some shelter behind the gas station? He might be insulted but so what? I washed my hands and splashed water on my face and then dried off using a measly threadbare towel. They weren't kidding when they called this the budget motel.

When I came out of the bathroom, a blow to the side of my head sent me sprawling to the floor. He rolled me over on my back and sat down on my hips. I tried to shove him off me, but he grasped my throat with one hand and started pawing at my t-shirt with the other. I grabbed his hand, and then he hit me. Hard.

"Don't move and I won't hurt you, Tina," he said in a breathless voice. "Tina. I won't hurt you, Tina. I promise."

Sweat dribbled down his face, and his clammy fingers had pulled up my shirt. He was pulling at my bra, pulling and tugging and then touching me, grabbing me, squeezing. I didn't care if he hit me again, I hauled off and punched his nose.

"Damn it," he screamed and he started choking me. He slid off me but kept his hand on my throat as he tried pulling my pants down. "I said I won't hurt you. I'm not going to hurt you," he whispered, blood trickling down his chin. And all along I knew without the tiniest dust mote of doubt that he was going to hurt me a lot. Maybe even kill me.

44

His face had transformed from the bland salesman into something alien, eyes with no more depth than a dime, skin like jelly and lips that alternated between grinning and grimacing. Some part of me seemed to have left the building and was merely watching events unfold on a movie screen far away. But another part of me was sick with grief and guilt that I had been so stupid, so gullible, such a fool. He was trying to yank my jeans off my hips but it's not so easy to strip someone with one hand. I resisted as much as possible, all the while waiting for his hand to ease up on my throat.

As soon as he let loose of my neck, I started screaming, but at the same time he was shoving a washcloth in my mouth. The scream became stifled, stuck in my hollow throat. I grunted and bucked. Don't give up, I thought. Don't give up.

But he was stronger than I was, and soon he had hold of both of my hands. He slipped his belt over them and bound them together as if in prayer.

He smiled briefly.

"Gotcha now," he said. "Hog-tied."

He stood up and pulled me up by the belt and by the hair. Tears sprang to my eyes from the pain. He threw me on to the bed and rolled me on my back. I tried to yank the washcloth from my mouth and he slapped me hard. Bastard, I thought. I would kill him before this was over.

He pulled my jeans and my underwear off, exposing my

body. For a moment he just stared. Then I kicked at him. He shoved me back down on the bed and held his fist above my face.

"Tommy, get over here right now!" a voice called from the walkway outside.

There was a thud against the door. The monster's eyes grew wide as he looked at the door. Then he said to me, "Move, and I'll beat the living shit out of you." He bounded over to the TV set and turned it on loud. Then he sidled over to the door and looked out the peephole.

I glanced up at the curtains. Just beyond the window there were people! I flung myself toward the window and grasped the cheap cloth curtains, pulling with all my body weight. The salesman turned to me in shock as I fell, ripping the curtains from the rod above.

There was no one on the walkway. What happened to the people? I pushed the cloth from my mouth with my tongue and screamed. Then he was on me again, his hand pressed hard over my mouth. As I fell backward, a boy about ten years old rose up from the ground and stared into the window. A moment later a man and a woman were next to him. The salesman looked up and saw them. We all stared at each other.

Then the man outside banged on the window while the woman tried to cover the boy's eyes. The salesman shoved himself off my body and threw open the door.

"Mind your own business," he said. "This is my girlfriend."

I screamed. Piercingly. My scream was a living thing that clawed at the walls and stung the air.

The next thing I knew Cadillac man was grabbing his keys. The man outside yelled at him, something about the police and telling him to get the hell away from "that girl."

I lay there, nearly naked, whispering, "Thank you, thank you, thank you."

The woman came in and undid the belt knotted around my wrists and helped me get dressed while the man tried to get through to someone on the motel phone. They were a couple on their way home from visiting a grandmother. The boy, Tommy, had been bent over tying his shoe when I pulled the curtain down.

"The office is closed," he said. "This phone doesn't even work. We'll have to find a payphone."

"Please don't call the police," I said.

"You're just going to let that guy go?" the woman asked.

"If the police come, they'll take me away. I need to get to Miami. I need to find my mother."

"Honey, we're heading north," the woman said. "We're not going to Miami."

"Could you take me north then?" I asked. "My friend was going to spend the night in a campground a couple of hours north of here. He can take me. I was stupid and got mad at him."

"We were planning on spending the night here," the man said.

"The office is closed anyway, John," his wife said. "Why not take her and we'll stay at another motel after we drop her off."

His long face had a confused and annoyed expression. Tommy stared at me, and I finally looked at him. A good-looking boy with dark hair and a baby face. He looked like an angel to me.

"Thank you for saving me," I said.

He didn't answer but looked at the ground and said, "She can ride in the back seat with me."

We pulled into the campground near the highway that

Jackson had mentioned earlier. I held my breath, praying he hadn't decided to turn around and drive home already. I thanked my good Samaritans, and promised them I would be all right. They looked doubtful, but they had done enough for me.

"Bye, girl," Tommy said.

"Bye, Tommy."

I shut the door. They pulled down the gravel roadway and out of the campground. I walked through the entire campground before finding Jackson's van in a corner lot.

I knocked on the door.

He sighed when he saw me.

"I was hoping you'd come back."

"*I*'m gonna take you to a hospital," Jackson said as we drove south. He'd said he couldn't sleep now, anyway, and I didn't want to sleep either.

"No," I croaked. "I'll be okay." If the two of us showed up at a hospital in the middle of the night, we would probably wind up in jail. I was an under-aged girl, he was a hippie man, and who would believe that a nice salesman in a Cadillac had tried to rape me.

"Why did you leave me?" he asked.

"I don't know," I said. "I guess I figured you'd want to get back to your girlfriend right away."

"That can wait," he said.

We rode in silence for a long time. I didn't even ask where we were going. I was like someone made of rubber. I felt thick with fear and something I couldn't name, some sense of deserving the worst, some awareness of loss. I leaned my head against the window and let the steady hum of the wheels against the road lull me to sleep.

"Where are we?" I asked, waking as the van came to a stop and the engine shut off.

"A parking lot at the beach," Jackson answered. "Come on."

We got out of the van. I had no idea what time it was. It was still dark. Jackson brought the sleeping bag and we walked down the sandy beach, the ocean mumbling beside us. I'd never heard the ocean before. I had only seen it through Mattie's car window that time when we came to see the London Philharmonic.

"Want to go for a swim?" Jackson asked.

The idea came as a complete surprise, but just as swiftly it seemed like the most right and perfect thing to do. We went back to the van where Jackson stripped down to his underwear and put on his cut-off shorts. I dug through my duffel bag, found my old one-piece bathing suit, and changed awkwardly under my t-shirt while he turned his back to me.

We hurried back down to the beach. The water was surprisingly warm, not quite like bath water but almost irresistible. The waves were mild and white foam spilled out of the inky black water. All around us tiny neon green flecks swirled.

"What is this?" I asked.

"I think it's called phosphorescence," he said. "I've never seen it before."

He splashed me, and I splashed him back. And incredibly, I was laughing. I dove under the water and felt it scrubbing the salesman's fingerprints off me. I was thrilled to be alive. He hadn't killed me. He wanted to, I was sure of it, but I had prevailed like a comic book hero. He couldn't touch me. He couldn't touch me. I had found myself worth fighting for.

Jackson and I laughed and swam around for a while. I remembered how I had thought he was Jesus at first, and now I was seeing Jesus in cut offs in the Atlantic Ocean and I laughed even harder.

After we got out, we huddled together on the sleeping bag. Jackson kept his arms around me and asked more than once, "You okay now?"

"Yes," I told him.

We lay down together in the sleeping bag facing the ocean, him holding onto me, his chest warm on my back.

"Thank you," I said.

"Shh. You don't have anything to thank me for."

So I didn't say anything else, and I dozed off, feeling his arms holding me.

When Jackson nudged me awake, a pink glow glistened on the horizon.

"Sunrise," Jackson whispered as if talking loud might make the sun change its mind. Orange ribbons streamed across the sky while lavender strips of clouds mottled the far edge. Then the tiniest red crescent appeared directly in front of us.

"Hey, what's the date today?" I asked.

He shrugged. "June Fourth," he said.

"Wow. Yesterday was my birthday. I'm sixteen," I said. I rolled over and faced him. "I promised a friend I would stay a virgin until I turned sixteen."

Neither of us mentioned the fact I had almost lost it on my birthday to a creep.

I looked into Jackson's turquoise eyes. His lips were parted. It would be so easy. I could give to him what that sick-o in the Cadillac had wanted to take from me. I thought of the lyrics from that Gary Puckett and the Union Gap song, Girl, "Girl, you'll be a woman soon," and it felt right. This was the moment. This would be the story I would have for the rest of my life, the loss of my virginity at sunrise to a man who looked like Jesus. I thought by the expression of yearning on his face that he would succumb if I wanted him to.

My fingers stroked his chest.

"Do you want to go to the van?" I asked.

He looked deep into my eyes.

"Eli, I would love nothing more than to take you to that van and make love to every inch of you, but I'm not going to," he said, his voice like sandpaper.

"Why not?" I asked. I was hurt and surprised and maybe a little relieved.

"Because when you make love for the first time it should be with someone you really know and really love, not some fool who's on the run from his pregnant girlfriend," he said. "Do you understand?"

"Not really," I said.

"Just take my word for it."

I felt disappointed and also somewhat relieved. Later, I would understand what he meant, but at the time, I decided that it was probably for the best because my mother had missed out on my childhood, and it wasn't fair for me to become a woman — if Gary Puckett was right about that — just hours before I met her.

We unlocked our bodies, sat up, and stared out at the horizon. The sun crept up its morning ladder. We watched its ascent. I wanted to hang on to every moment, reveling in the psychedelic colors. But in a short while the sun pulled back its orange and pink tentacles; it was a red ball rapidly on its way to becoming the familiar yellow-white orb it always was.

"Ready to go find your mother?" Jackson asked.

"Yes," I said.

We stood up, shook the sand off the sleeping bag, and turned to go back to the van.

"How far is it to Miami?" I asked.

"About two or three hours, I guess."

We trudged through the soft sand to the parking lot, and then both of us stopped short. A cop car was pulled next to the van, and an officer was peering into the front window. The words on the cop car were: "Melbourne City Police." So that's where we were. Some little beach town in Florida I had never heard of. I was awfully glad we weren't inside, naked, having sex, and I was sure Jackson was thanking his stars, too.

"What do we do?" I asked.

"Play it cool," Jackson said in a low voice.

He walked toward the van with me following. So close, and now I was going to wind up in some Florida juvenile facility. I thought about turning and running. I knew I should trust Jackson knew what he was doing, but I didn't. The only thing that would save me now was luck, and I figured I had used up all my luck when little Tommy and his family decided to stop at that motel.

"Morning, Officer," Jackson said.

The cop looked at him and then turned to look me up and down.

"This your van?" the cop asked.

"Yes, sir," Jackson said.

"Got a registration for it?"

Jackson opened the van and started digging through the glove box for the registration. The cop stared at me.

"How old are you?" he asked.

"Eighteen," I said.

He looked at Jackson's registration and looked at me again. Suspicion oozed from every pore in his body.

"You don't look eighteen," he said.

"Yesterday was my birthday," I said, gazing at my reflection in his sunglasses.

He handed Jackson the registration, taking a few extra moments to peer into the van. Then he checked his watch and said, "My shift ends in ten minutes and I want to go home. But I'm gonna tell the fellas back at the station to come by, and if you're still here they're gonna haul your asses back to the station and find out a little bit more about the both of you."

Then the cop got in his cruiser and drove away.

Jackson wasted no time finding the highway and leaving Melbourne behind.

45

*W*e stopped at a gas station in Miami and bought a map. Jackson studied the map while I went into the bathroom and tried to make myself presentable. There were two purple bruises on my neck, but Jackson had given me a bandana and said I could have it. I tied it around my neck and you couldn't see the bruises anymore. I ran cold water through my hair and brushed the salt and sand out of it as well as I could. Would she know me, I wondered.

"I think I found it," Jackson said when I got back in the van. He pointed to a tiny line between the highway and the ocean. Then he started up the van, and we drove into the bright day.

Miami was a revelation to me. I'd never seen such trees or flowers. I marveled at the thick jungly plants in people's yards. There was a scent in the air like some kind of ambrosia.

"This is a weird place," I said.

"Yeah."

We found the street, and Jackson turned down it, slowly looking at addresses. The houses were small and neat. I stared, stunned at the sight of a strange tree that looked like it was several hundred trees all bound up together. In another yard enormous red flowers bobbed in the breeze. The rest of Florida had seemed so grubby compared to this. The houses, which were white or tan plaster houses—not brick or wood, were spruced up with bright green lawns that gleamed under a thick layer of sunlight like new varnish.

Jackson slowed down, peering at the addresses. Then he

pulled into the driveway of one of the houses and said, "This is it."

I looked at the house and noticed bright blue shutters on either side of the windows; a ceramic pink flamingo stood on the stoop beside the front door. White stepping stones led to the door. I got out of the van. Jackson followed me, carrying my duffel bag. I climbed up the steps, holding onto a black wrought-iron rail. Jackson was right behind me. Jackson set the duffel bag down beside me. Then he opened the bag and shoved a book inside. I recognized the cover.

A green lizard scooted past my foot. A tiny brown sparrow pecked in the dirt by the steps.

"This is it," Jackson said. "End of the road for you."

He kissed me on the cheek and turned to leave.

I rang the doorbell. I couldn't exactly breathe. I looked back at Jackson; he was walking toward the van. A sound came from inside, someone coming toward the door.

Jackson got in his van, and the engine whined as it came to life. The dark asphalt of the road lay like a strip of night sky in front of the house. I waved at him as he backed the van out of the driveway, but he didn't drive off yet.

I heard the door unlock. In my head I had practiced introducing myself. It had not occurred to me that I would not need to, that Cleo would have called up to find out if I'd made it all right and that Miz Johnny would have followed suit, assuring my mother that I was on my way. I had not known that if I hadn't shown up when I did, my description would be going to out to every police station in the southeast.

I only knew that when the door opened, a dark-haired woman with eyes like my own seemed to be expecting me.

"Hi," I said.

Before I could say anything else, she pushed open the screen door, and peered at me as if she weren't sure I was real.

"It's you," she whispered. She held a hand over her heart.

"It's me," I answered. "Elisa."

The van's engine shifted gears as Jackson drove away. I gripped the handle of my duffel bag and stepped inside.

Acknowledgements

Much gratitude my brother John, a father-figure, a spiritual teacher, a political warrior and friend, and also my brother David for his stories about growing up in the south. Thanks to Camille, John the fourth and Sharen for a wonderful year growing up together in Webster Groves. Thanks to my mother for guidance about singing and operas and for giving me a childhood in the theatre; to my daughter Celina for reminding me of the joy of adolescence. Deep gratitude once again to my friend Pamela Ball, whose balance of comments and encouragement made this a much better book. Thanks as well to my friends and readers, Vicki Moreland and Tamara Titus. I would also like to acknowledge Cathy Wilkerson for helping me understand the dynamics of the anti-war Movement in a personal interview as well as in her fantastic memoir on the Weather Underground, *Flying Close to the Sun*. Many thanks to Mary Jennings Sluder for sharing her opera stories with me. Much gratitude to Joe Taylor for giving this book the perfect home. Thanks to everyone involved in the Kaleidoscope Arts Camp at Winthrop University and to the students there (and Annamarie!) who asked every year: "When are you going to finish the book?" Here it is finally — thank you for your enthusiasm, your applause and your inspiration.

Trish MacEnulty is the author of the historical novels, *Delafield & Malloy Investigations*, as well as two memoirs, a novel, and a collection of short stories. A former professor of English and film, she currently lives in Tallahassee, Florida. Visit her website at trishmacenulty.com and subscribe to her newsletter for freebies and info about new releases